MISHA'S PROMISE
KARST SERIES
BOOK THREE

RENEE MACKENZIE

MISHA'S PROMISE
KARST SERIES
BOOK THREE

RENEE MACKENZIE

Affinity
Rainbow Publications

2020

Misha's Promise
© 2020 by Renee MacKenzie

Affinity E-Book Press NZ LTD
Canterbury, New Zealand

1st Edition

ISBN: 978-1-98-858864-3

Editor: Angela Koenig
Proof Editor: Alexis Smith
Cover Design: Irish Dragon Design
Production Design: Affinity Publication Services

ACKNOWLEDGMENTS

I want to thank my Affinity family for all their support over the years. Y'all rock! Thanks to Angela Koenig for a wonderful edit, Alexis Smith for the great proofreading, and Irish Dragon Designs for the incredible cover.

Thanks to Sandi Baum and Teresa McKnight for their early read-throughs. Your insights were phenomenal.

Thanks to Pam for always being there. Love you!

And big thanks to the readers—without you there wouldn't be nearly the amount of joy in writing as there is.

DEDICATION

TO PAM, ALWAYS.

TABLE OF CONTENTS

PROLOGUE

From the plane I can just make out small structures and what must be people moving around off in the distance. They will hear us; they will be readying for us.

She reaches to me and squeezes my knee. "Are you ready for this, Misha?"

I lift the small gun out of my lap and stare at it for several beats before saying, "Yes, I am ready."

She gives me a nod and moves her right hand from my knee to the steering apparatus.

Within minutes, she fires upon the scurrying people. We are nearing the only plane I can make out on the ground. We get closer and closer, bringing the faces of the people into focus.

"Oh," she says with a hitch in her breathing.

I see recognition flash across her face. I wait for her response. Am I relieved or disturbed when she stays the course and annihilates everyone in our strike zone? I wonder if I will ever ask her about the person who elicited that bewildered "oh" from her lips.

The plane I saw upon our approach has taken off now and is joined by another.

She reaches down to her left side, not taking her eyes off the direction she flies, and I know what she's done when I hear the staccato sounds of the large gun firing round after round.

She banks the plane hard to the right to outmaneuver one of the enemy planes and her arm shoots out across my chest as she tries to anchor me in place.

"I will hold on," I tell her. "You concentrate on flying this thing."

Ammunition from the long gun hits the wing of the closest plane, causing it to tilt awkwardly to its side. When it falls from the sky it clips the back of the other plane and sends it, too, somersaulting out of the sky.

I gasp, surprise overwhelming me.

"Hold this," she yells, her nod indicating the steering apparatus.

"I cannot—"

"Yes, you can. Please."

I grab where she indicates, and she reaches out, leaning so far to her left that I fear she will topple out. She grunts as she yanks upward, then she straightens up for a moment to fly the plane toward what I assume to be the bunker.

The plane lurches when she reaches down again, and I am startled by the loud explosion beneath us. We ascend higher, then she drops another bomb, then yet another.

People on the ground are firing large guns at us, so I take aim with the small gun. I know that once I pull the trigger, I will not be able to undo what I will have done.

I concentrate, and return the fire. I hit two people, miss a few others.

Then the gun jams. "Oh, no."

She looks at me, then at the gun. "I guess now I'm not allowed to crash in Perry," she says, a teasing lilt to her voice.

"I guess not," I agree.

When I look down now all I see are a few immobile people and a lot of destruction. She banks hard to the right and aims the plane away from Perry.

My heart jumps around in my chest as a series of other explosions rock the ground below us. I glance at her and her face is awash in orange light, a reflection from the massive fire growing below us.

"There must have been a chain reaction, probably their arsenal exploded when it caught fire," she says.

I look behind us and see nothing but flames. I am about to whisper a prayer to the Goddess to bless the dead, when I feel her hand on my leg. I turn to face her.

"Are you okay?" she asks.

"Not a scratch on me," I say, half teasing.

She taps a finger against my temple. "In here. Are you okay with what we just did?"

I do not know if I am truly all right, beyond the relief that we don't need to use the jammed gun to keep from being taken alive. I take several deep breaths, center myself, and realize that yes, I am all right with ensuring the survival of myself, my lover, and my fellow New Americans.

"Yes, I am fine." I give her a smile. "Now, what is next?"

3

"We should have enough power to make it to the top of that ridge," she says as she points to the mountain to the west of us. "Then we will need to make use of every bit of wind we can to help us glide over the next, smaller range and eventually to the easternmost part of New America. From there we should be able to hike to Karst—or to Kai's village?"

"Kai lives much farther west, if she has gone home yet by the time we get there. Naomi's village, Liberté, is much closer. Or we could go to Las Estrellas. I know the leaders and healer there, who might be willing to help us." My words come out in a rush.

She nods. "I adore you."

"I love you," I counter. I place my hand on her leg and give a gentle squeeze. She takes my hand in hers and kisses the palm.

"Hang on, my love."

I settle back into the seat and take a deep breath.

"Here we go," she says.

She forces the plane up, at an angle that feels totally unnatural, even more so than the actual act of flying has felt. I am forced back against the seat and feel my head growing heavy, the pressure in my ears building again.

Up, up, up we climb!

The plane jerks, sputters.

"No, no, no," she chants in a low voice.

"Are we—" I don't finish asking, just watch as the mountain we were originally paralleling ourselves with comes closer and closer.

"I know this sounds counterintuitive, but try to relax."

"*Counterintuitive*?" I laugh. "Really?"

"That was a Suzanna word, wasn't it?" she asks as she struggles to hold the plane steady.

I smile, bittersweet. "Suzanna, if you are listening, we could use some wisdom right now."

"Hold on with every—ounce—of—your—strength," she says through gritted teeth.

She jerks the steering apparatus sharply to her left, away from me, and the plane lurches violently away from the side of the mountain.

The sputtering of the engine ceases and all I hear is the wind rushing past us in our rapid descent, and the sounds of our breathing.

She struggles with the steering, her knuckles turning white in her grip of it.

"Hold on tight," she tells me. "We can't have you falling out of this beast, can we?"

I increase the strength of my grip on the edges of the box I sit upon.

"No," I agree, "no we cannot."

The ground is coming at us faster and faster. She grunts and sits back hard against the seat just as the front end pulls up slightly.

I am gasping for air around my constricted throat. I do not want to die in this strange land. I do not want to lose my love now that I have finally found her.

PART ONE—KARST

THREE WEEKS EARLIER

CHAPTER ONE

The meadow stretches out before me, a blanket of colors that takes my breath away this time of year. The sun is warm on my face, but not so bright and hot yet as to require eye shades. It is my favorite time of year.

I close my eyes to focus on the buzzing of insects. When I open them, I see the bees as they zip and zigzag around the blossoms.

I am drawn to a pale-yellow flower and bend to pick it. Within seconds of standing back up, a bee hovers just over it, mesmerizing me. She alights on the flower and I can see, quite clearly, the dusting of pollen on her.

Another bee joins her.

"Hello," I whisper.

I love my time helping others in Karst, the cave city I have called home for five years now, but there is a freedom of spirit I only know when I stand in the meadow, contemplating flowers and bees during the day, and recharging with the stars at night.

A third bee joins the others on the blossom and they jockey for position. When the fourth bee lands on my hand instead of the flower, I force my hand to stay steady.

The energy around me intensifies and I let my mind clear, welcoming the message the bees bring to me.

I do not hear words, but I know from the flutter in my belly that change is coming. This message I get loud and clear.

"What is coming my way?" I ask the now dozen or so bees covering my hand.

I feel the vibration of the bees all through my body. They continue to cover my fingers and hand, and then move down my arm until every inch of skin from my elbow to my fingertips is covered with the insects.

They feel light and tickle the skin they cover.

The swarm grows thicker and thicker as the bees alight on one another. I am spellbound by their sound and their energy.

A shadow moves over us as a cloud drifts in. I glance up just as a bolt of lightning streaks through the sky and the thunder crashes. I jump at the sound and the bees scatter. Before they are all in flight, a stinging sensation pierces the palm of my hand.

I do not see the bee that has stung me, but I find the stinger. I gently scrape it from my flesh and study the little red dot as it grows larger and angrier against the pale flesh of my palm.

Then just like that, my fingers tingle and the sting site lightens and shrinks.

I turn back towards Karst as the first heavy raindrops fall upon my hair.

†

I am in the corridor when I catch up to Suzanna. Her long, gray-white hair flows off her shoulders and down her back. When her eyes meet mine, I cannot help but smile.

"I believe the night will clear soon," I say.

"That is good," Suzanna responds. "How are you today, Misha?"

I smile. "I am well. Shall I come to you after I spend time under the stars?"

Now she smiles at me. "That would be lovely, dear."

"Will you go testify with the others now?" I ask as I offer her my arm.

She grasps my elbow and I walk with her to the lounge.

"I'm not so old that I cannot still get around, you know," Suzanna says.

"I know." I give her a big smile. "Maybe it is I who needs an arm."

She rolls her eyes at me.

"At least I will never be older than Frida or Stella," she jokes as we enter the lounge area.

"What?" Stella asks. "What did you say about me?"

"Nothing dear," Suzanna says as she winks at me.

Suzanna gives everyone a bright smile, nodding at a few people, taking the hands of others. I always wonder how it must feel to be so beloved by a community. I have never had that, nor do I begrudge it of Suzanna. She is the warmest, most loving person I have ever known, and worthy of all the love shown her at Karst—and more.

9

I take my leave of her and wander back through the corridors to the small, high opening on the north side of the mountain into which Karst is built.

A young man I do not recognize stands guard at the eight-foot-by-eight-foot opening.

"Good evening," I say.

He locks his gaze onto mine, begins to speak, but then remains silent.

"I am Misha," I say. "And I will be stepping out into the night for an hour or so."

"You're the healer," he whispers, taking a step back.

I glance down at his feet and arch my brows.

His eyes go wide as he seems to notice then that, in backing away from me, he has come precariously close to the edge where the narrow steps meet the mouth of the cave.

I am saddened that after five years there are still people in Karst who fear me. *Witch hands.*

"I just need to get past you," I say, keeping my voice gentle. "I will not touch you."

"Oh," he says, blushing. He shakes his head. "It is not that. I've just heard about you but haven't actually seen you. The talk is accurate."

"The talk?"

"About your eyes." He finally holds my gaze.

"My eyes?" I ask, confused.

"They are as beautiful as I have always heard they are." He looks away.

I am stunned into silence. Fear about my healing abilities, chants of *witch hands*, the backing away from me unless someone is in dire need of my energy work, these are the things I expect. But a compliment?

"So," I say in a soft voice. "I may pass?"

"Oh, yes, sorry, absolutely." He steps to the side and I edge past him.

Foregoing the stone steps, I take care to watch my footing on the narrow rim as I edge along until I am several yards away. Where the shelf widens there is a concave area where I sit while regenerating under the stars on the nights I choose to do so up here. Some nights the meadow beckons to me, other nights it is here, along the side of this mountain.

There are no longer clouds in the darkening sky. I release my hair from the band holding it behind my head and close my eyes as the last of the light fades. After a few moments, I take a deep breath and open my eyes.

I stare into the vast number of stars alighting the sky and listen carefully. There is a slight murmur and I am not sure if it is wishful thinking or if I am indeed connecting to the collective consciousness my grandmother was so keen to introduce to me.

"Help me to heal the hurting, the sick, the injured," I say in a low voice.

The glittering sky before me is glorious in its wealth of sparkling stars. I feel my body tingle, grow warm, then surge with energy. The hum that begins deep in my chest is not anything I can control, nor would I want to. The vibration radiates outward, sparking down my arms as I spread them out to my side.

My mouth opens in a silent scream of wonder at the regeneration every cell in my body undergoes.

Once the surge of energy through me levels off, I close my eyes again and listen. Will the universe speak to me tonight? Will I understand if she does?

I hear not a spoken word, but understand it nevertheless. *Change.* This is the second time I've sensed this, the second time I know this without explanation or elaboration. There is no denying that something is stirring, that change is indeed coming.

†

After an hour under the stars, I go to Suzanna's room. Over the last several months I've taken to going to her quarters instead of doing our energy work in the meditation room as we once did.

"May I place my hands on you?" I ask. I *always* ask.

Her smile is sweet. "Yes, please do, dear."

I kneel behind her and place gentle hands on her shoulders. She relaxes into my touch.

I smile when she lets out a long sigh.

I envision the energy leaving my hands and settling in the aching joints of her shoulders. *Heal*, I think. *Heal now*.

My hands grow warm as I move them in small circles, barely touching her.

"Thank you for this," she whispers.

"Of course."

My hands travel to her neck, then become still. I feel the hum building in my chest as the energy travels from my abdomen and chest to my arms and out of my hands. She grows rigid under my fingers for a brief moment, then relaxes.

Next my hands travel down her arms to her wrists. I can feel the heat transfer, and close my eyes to assist its movement. The humming is louder and my body grows cold. Her hands feel thin in mine and I know she is finding relief from her aching joints, probably for the first time today.

"Thank you," she says.

I release her hands and she turns to face me without getting off her bedding.

"It is my pleasure," I say, meaning it.

"You have heard that Kai is coming for a few days?"

"No, I had not heard. And Rachel?"

"Rachel will stay behind this time to keep things running smoothly at the Rehab Center."

I nod. Working with Kai and Rachel at the Center had been one of my options when I'd settled at Karst. I'd chosen to stay at Karst and help Dr. Bradshaw instead of traveling to the Center in McNally with Kai and Rachel, or Liberté with Naomi and Camryn. At first, I'd thought of staying with Naomi and Camryn, as they were the first people to be kind to me since the death of my family and village. But something drew me to Karst, told me to stay.

"It will be lovely to see Kai," I say with a smile. "When is she to arrive?"

"She is still a few days out." Suzanna takes my hands in hers. "You are shivering."

"Oh," I say, surprised that I have expended so much of my own energy working on Suzanna.

"Shall we call it an evening then?" Suzanna's voice is so melodic that just hearing her speak brings on a sense of peace I cannot describe.

"As you wish," I say as I stand.

When she moves to also get up, I hold up a hand to halt her.

"Stay, you look comfortable. I will see myself out."

She pulls my hand to her and kisses the back of it. "I wish you a night of peace."

"The same to you," I respond, then take my leave.

As I settle back into my quarters, I think about Suzanna. Energy work on her has become more difficult. The change has been in miniscule increments, but I feel it nonetheless. Suzanna only asks from me the soothing of the aches that come with age. I know it will become more and more difficult over the coming years, but I will do whatever I need to make Suzanna comfortable and keep her mobile.

The thought reminds me of caring for Ewan Merrick's grandmother just over five years earlier. Nain, as she was called, had whispered to me not to prolong her life. Unfortunately, keeping her alive was the only way I had of keeping myself alive.

I was a slave of the Merrick clan, kept for the healing property of my hands, even as the less civilized members whispered about my "witch hands" and cast suspicious glances at me. I did all that I could to keep Nain comfortable, but in the end, it wasn't anything I did or did not do that caused her death. Mercifully, when an enemy clan attacked, her death was fast and the pain minimal.

I wonder how Naomi is doing, living with her family at Liberté. The Peace Warrior saved my life when she procured my release from the Merrick clan. I know I am past due a visit—her and Camryn's child, Radha, is probably growing so fast.

Yes, I will see that Dr. Bradshaw is not so busy with patients that she cannot afford me to take a few days to visit Liberté.

†

The next morning, I am in the corridor, almost to the southwest cave entrance, when I hear Suzanna's voice behind me.

"Misha, you are going to the meadow." It is not a question.

I smile. She truly is a gifted dreamer. She must have come to me in the night to know that I awoke with an intense urge to go to the meadow. Maybe it is the call of the bees, maybe it is just a need to escape the confines of the cave city momentarily, but I awoke knowing I must go this morning.

"Yes," I say. "I am going to the meadow. Care to tell me why?" I tease.

"And ruin the surprise?" she responds. She places one hand on the wall to help balance herself. "All I know is that I dreamed of you going to the meadow and having ash rain down onto you, gathering in your eyelashes, your hair."

"Will there be a fire?" I ask.

"I do not know the specifics, dear Misha." She hands me my medical bag. "Just in case."

I think of the swaths of charred earth that crisscross New America and hope that no further fires are on the horizon for us. The fires may have been before my time, but the effects are still quite visible.

"Be safe," Suzanna says as she leaves me alone in the corridor.

I strap the medical bag to my back and exit Karst, nodding at Andre at his post. The air feels charged as I run into the meadow where the blanket of wildflowers stretches out in all directions—to the farmland northeast of Karst, the foot of the mountain housing the cave city, the tree line to the west, and the scorched land to the north and east.

Yellow, orange, blue, purple, and red dot the ground I stand upon.

I bend to pick a blue blossom and raise it to my nose to breathe in its calming scent. I hold it then, just away from my face, where I can study the delicate folds of the flower.

A bee lands on the flower and I smile. "Hello, little one," I whisper.

I focus on the buzz and study the tiny flecks of pollen that have collected on her fuzzy body.

The buzzing grows louder and louder, becoming a roar, even though only one bee has landed on the flower I hold up in front of me.

The roar fills the sky and just as I realize it isn't the bee at all, an airplane comes careening over the mountain, coming right for the meadow.

My arms instinctively move to cover my head and I drop the flower I have been holding.

The plane disappears and I hear shouting coming from the gardens to the northeast of where I stand in the meadow.

"Run," someone yells. "Run for cover!"

My mind makes to start moving toward the entrance to Karst but my legs do not follow its orders. *People will also come from the east. Like the bees, they will fly.* I shake as I remember the words I spoke to Naomi, years earlier while we prepared to leave Karst to warn Breanne Brodie about impending danger. The vision had shaken me at the time, but I have not thought of it for years now.

The noise vibrates in my chest as the machine becomes visible once again above the mountain range. I stare up at this metal beast as it begins to rock furiously from side to side. Its sounds grow in intensity, and then abruptly end as the plane drops from the sky, skidding across the meadow, throwing up dirt and flowers and billows of thick, black smoke.

I pivot around on my feet, and then decide to run toward the wreckage instead of away from it. I know this is the ash of which Suzanna has spoken.

Thinking stops and I move with pure adrenaline as I jump onto, and walk along, the wing of the plane until I can look inside. The sight of the pilot wearing a metal face shield over his face shocks me. In addition to holes for his eyes, nose, and mouth, there are several smaller openings that create a pattern that resembles a sunburst extending from the nose outward.

I climb into the cockpit, through the shattered windshield, and straddle the pilot. I reach into my medical bag, ignoring the herbs and poultices, and grab gauze, using it to apply direct pressure to the pilot's abdomen where a shard of metal impales him.

A small groan escapes the pilot and I realize how very feminine the sound is. She opens her eyes and stares into mine.

"It's you," she whispers.

I stare into her eyes and feel a jolt. Then my gaze drifts lower and I am alarmed by the amount of blood oozing between my fingers.

"Hi," I say, keeping my voice steady in an attempt to keep her calm. "I am Misha." I gesture to how I sit atop her. "I'm sorry about this."

"Did you make me crash?"

I am confused. "No—"

"Then you've nothing to be sorry for." The area around her eyes crinkles as if she is smiling beneath the metal face shield.

17

I cannot help but smile in response. "What is your name?"

"Call me Yaz."

"Okay, Yaz, you have quite a nasty wound to your abdomen. I need to pack gauze around it for stabilization before we can attempt to remove you from this—" I gesture to the plane.

"The plane," Yaz says. "Is it totaled?"

I stare at her. I don't understand what she asks.

"Is the plane damaged badly?"

"Oh. I don't know how the machine is."

What I do not say is that I really do not care. I can hear Andre and Jackson arguing over our next move. I know what mine is—it is to keep Yaz safe while the others worry about what to do about the situation.

I turn my attention back to Yaz. She gasps as I surround the shard of metal protruding from her with strips of cloth and layers of gauze.

"Get it out of me," she whispers.

"No, I cannot do that yet. It is too dangerous." What I do not say is that she will surely bleed to death if I remove it here, now.

Her lips, visible around the opening at the mouth area, grow paler now than even just moments ago.

She moans and her hands go to my hips. Her fingers dig into my flesh and my breath catches in my chest.

I place my hands on the pilot's and remove them from my hips.

I am pretty sure my cheeks are red when I lift off her and crane my neck to look out the top of the machine.

"What do you think?" Jackson calls to me.

"We must get her to the medical center immediately."

"Is she conscious?" he asks.

I glance down at her and she holds my gaze for a moment before her eyes drift shut.

"In and out," I reply. Her face contorts into a grimace. "We need to get her free of this wreckage right away," I add.

There is loud clanking, and then Jackson appears beside me. He's tall and lean and has to bend down to see once he's climbed up. His slight smile disappears within moments of arriving next to me.

"This does not look good." His gaze skitters across the pilot and plane.

"Shh." I narrow my eyes at him. "Let us wait until we get her out of this thing before we make judgements, okay?"

He nods his head.

"Help me unstrap her," I say as I struggle with the thick material forming an X against her chest, holding her in place.

He pulls at it. "There should be a release."

We search around for a release button or lever but do not find one.

"It has got to be here somewhere," Jackson says as he continues searching.

"I'm not meant to be removed," a small voice says.

"You speak English," Jackson says.

"Perry. I speak Perry," she whispers before closing her eyes again.

"What do you think she means, that she is not meant to get out?" I ask.

Jackson shrugs. "Let's see about this face thing."

A long cord dangles from one side of the metal face shield. The other end rests against the pilot's chest. I examine the straps holding the mask-like contraption in place. They are the same heavy mesh strapping as that holding the pilot into the plane.

I slip the fingers of one hand between the strap and her shirt. My fingers tingle with the need to help this woman.

"Do you have a knife to cut through these?" I ask.

"Be right back." Jackson jumps down off the plane.

It is only moments later when Jackson returns with his knife and struggles to cut through the straps of the harness holding her in place. He is forced to put so much effort into it that I fear he will slip with the blade and hurt either himself or the helpless woman.

Finally, the blade slices through the material. Jackson's hand knocks into the control panel and he grunts.

"Are you all right?" I ask.

He nods. He looks over the top of the plane and says, "Andre—some help over here?"

"I cannot leave my station. You know that."

"Jackson, we can do this ourselves. We can get her out," I say.

Jackson and I work together to pull her free of the wreckage. Other than an occasional groan, she is unresponsive.

Her clothing is ripped and bloodied, practically shredded, as expected with such a crash. But it is also worn thin in some areas—a wearing down that happens over time, not in one traumatic moment.

After a few moments of being prone on the ground her eyes flutter open.

"You," she says.

Quick flashes of a vision of us together crashes through my mind. I am confused by the ache in my chest and belly.

"It is you," she says.

20

Jackson kneels beside us and she closes her eyes again. He cuts the straps to the face shield. It is removed and she opens her eyes. A smile, or something almost resembling one, plays on her lips before she loses consciousness again.

I stare at her, amazed by how utterly beautiful she is.

"Wow," Jackson whispers. "She's gorgeous."

I can only nod in agreement.

Jackson holds up the metal face shield and examines it. He fingers the long cord dangling from it. "I wonder what this is."

I do not have time to be worrying about the gadgets. My patient is bleeding profusely and needs to get inside and probably into surgery.

"Can we play with the new toys later?" I ask, letting a little playfulness into my tone so as not to be too harsh toward one of my closest friends. "We need to get her to Dr. Bradshaw."

"First name Doctor, last name Bradshaw?" he teases.

"The very one," I say in response to his joke that, for all we know, Doctor is her first name since no one has ever spoken of any other name that we know of.

Jackson scoops the pilot up in his arms and begins to carry her toward the cave entrance. I grab my medical bag and run ahead of them, leading the way.

Suzanna meets us in the medical center as Jackson is placing Yaz on an examination bed. She places a hand on the pilot's forehead.

"How is she?"

"Many injuries," I say.

Dr. Bradshaw comes in now. She is covered from head to toe in protective clothing, as is the norm when dealing with unknown risk factors. She gives her head a slight shake of disapproval as she looks us over.

"There was not time," I say, holding her gaze with as much confidence as I can. I know better than to expose myself this way, but there truly was not time.

She hands me a medical facemask and gloves. "At least put these on."

"I'll just go back to work," Jackson says as he begins to back out of the room.

"No, you will go to Exam 1, take your clothes off, and wait for me there."

"Come on, I barely—"

"*Now*, Jackson."

"Yes, ma'am."

"And you," Dr. Bradshaw says as she turns to Suzanna, "you were not out in the meadow when this happened. You did not need to be exposed like this."

"It will be fine," Suzanna says. "I just needed to make sure."

"Make sure?" Dr. Bradshaw asks.

"That it was who I thought."

"And who did you think it would be?" Dr. Bradshaw gives another shake of her head. "Never mind. Go to Exam 2. You know the routine."

"Who?" I ask Suzanna as she heads to the door.

"She is Ash," comes the answer.

"Her name is Yaz," I correct her.

"Of course," a smile plays at the corners of her mouth as she turns to leave us.

When Dr. Bradshaw looks at me now, I say, "We are running out of exam rooms. I will stay with Yaz while you treat her, and after, while you go to examine the others."

"Okay, let me look at the abdominal wound first," she says, sighing heavily in exasperation. "Then we will address the other, lesser wounds."

I step back a few paces to give the doctor room to work.

"Has she been unconscious all along?" Dr. Bradshaw asks.

"No, she's been in and out."

"I will try to work on her while she's out, if she comes around, we may need to give her a sedative."

"And something for pain?" I ask.

"Yes, if she awakes."

"When she awakes," I counter in a whisper.

"We will need to remove this shrapnel impaling her. Grab a surgical tray, please."

I do as I am told and the doctor sets about removing the object, cleaning the area, and exploring the wound for further damage.

"She is lucky this thing missed all her vital organs," Dr. Bradshaw says.

I nod, watching the pilot closely for any signs of waking up. Her face is still, the fine features showing no signs of consciousness or pain.

"Okay, let's get her sutured. Would you like to?"

"Yes, please." I appreciate that the doctor is letting me work on improving my traditional medical skills. It has greatly helped my healing abilities to add them to the energy work I perform. "Thank you," I add.

I suture the wound and we assess the rest of the patient by taking off all of her clothing and examining her closely. We wash her, not thoroughly, but enough to see to a few scrapes and bruises, then we cover her with a light sheet.

"I will go see to Suzanna and Jackson now if you would like to stay with the pilot," the doctor says.

"Yes, thank you."

"Then we will need to get you cleaned up as well."

I nod. I do not want to leave Yaz's side, but know it is for the best and will do so when instructed to.

I watch Yaz sleep. Her face twitches occasionally at first, but then she rests peacefully. I study her features. She is the most beautiful woman I have ever seen and looking at her stirs heat low in my belly, catching me by surprise.

CHAPTER TWO

The patient is still under the light sheet when I return to her treatment room after taking an hour to get cleaned up and letting Dr. Bradshaw draw a blood sample from me. Yaz's eyes are closed, her full lips slightly parted.

I inch the sheet down from where it rests against her clavicles to just above her navel. I try not to stare at the perfect brown nipples topping the full breasts.

The shadow of a bruise is making its way up to her skin. It matches the pattern of the straps of the harness Jackson had to cut off her before we could remove her from the plane's wreckage. I know soon it will be deep purple.

I am hesitant at first, but when my fingers begin to tingle, I know my decision has already been made.

I pull off my gloves and place my hands on the discolored flesh and close my eyes.

"Heal," I whisper. Guilt over not acquiring her permission to touch her like this is fleeting. "Heal now."

The humming comes from deep in my chest—an action I have never had control over—and I feel the energy rush down my arms and into my fingers. All the heat rushes from my body to my hands, leaving me cold.

When she moves under my touch, I refocus my gaze. She stares at me with dark, questioning eyes.

She jerks against the restraints on her wrists and ankles before looking down to where my hands linger on her chest.

Self-consciously, I remove my hands from her body.

"I am sorry," I whisper. "I only meant to—"

"Ah, I see our prisoner is awake," Naomi says from behind me as she enters the room.

I turn and remove my mask so she can read my lips. "You mean you see *my patient* is awake." I sign the word for patient so there is no mistaking my intent.

She struggles not to smile. When she loses that fight, I too smile. She takes one step toward me and I put up my hand. "Not without a mask, gloves, and gown."

"It's good to see you my friend," she says as she takes several steps backwards.

"You as well," I sign. I slip the medical mask back into place over my nose and mouth, then pull on a pair of fresh gloves.

Of everyone in my life of freedom in New America, Naomi is the one who first saw the potential in me. Had it not been for her getting me away from the Merrick clan, I am pretty sure I would not have lived to see the culmination of my eighteenth year.

"Have you just now arrived?" I sign.

"Yes. I saw the plane begin its descent and knew it was going to crash. I left Liberté immediately."

"I imagine Karst will be ablaze with warriors in no time."

"I'm sure it will be," she agrees.

Naomi uses her head to gesture toward the door to the corridor. I take one last look at the now unconscious pilot and turn to the door. I stop just shy of leaving the pilot's room.

Once in the corridor, Naomi stops. "Tell me what happened."

Since losing most of her hearing after falling into toxic water shortly after I met her, Naomi relies on reading lips and sign language. I use sign language to tell her about the plane crash and the extent of the injuries the pilot suffered.

Naomi's brow furrows.

"She made reference while still trapped that she was not meant to get free of the wreckage," I tell her.

"Suicide mission? Where the hell did she come from?"

"She doesn't stay lucid long enough for me to ask any of those questions."

Naomi nods, absently, seeming to ponder the situation for several long moments.

"Will you take your meal with me?" Naomi asks.

"I should stay with the patient."

"As you wish," she says with a slight bow.

"Camryn and Radha are not with you?"

She shakes her head.

It is probably for the best, I think, as five-year-old Radha should not be exposed to any potential infectious illnesses at her young age.

Suzanna approaches Naomi in the corridor. I feel her energy before I hear her address the warrior. "Naomi, it is most wonderful to see you."

Naomi bows. "You as well."

"I have been decontaminated," Suzanna says both verbally and with her hands, making a face at the last word. "But I will still keep some distance from you since you have a young one at home."

"Thank you," Naomi says.

I take my leave of them, stepping more fully into Yaz's room and closing the door behind me.

I watch the steady rise and fall of the pilot's chest as she sleeps. There are so many things to learn about this woman, so many things I want to know.

But first, I must try to speed her healing. After removing my gloves, I place both hands over the bandage covering the worst of her injuries. This time, I barely give any consideration to the fact that I am putting my hands on her without her consent.

Heal, I think. *Heal now.*

I close my eyes, feeling the hum deep inside me and the movement of energy from my chest and back, down my arms, and out of my fingertips. The area I work grows warmer and warmer, even as my own body cools, then chills.

†

The pilot's body has been cleansed to help control infection at the severest of her wounds, but her face is still quite dirty. I dampen a cloth and gently press it to her forehead. I do not even bother with gloves now. The dirt and dried blood do not come off easily and I hold my breath, hoping that I do not cause her too much pain.

I study her fine features. Her nose and chin are somewhat pointed, her lips full, her skin a dark tan.

Her eyes open and I jump, pulling my hand and the cloth away.

"Oh," the word escapes me.

"Oh," she repeats. She stares at me, her lips parted slightly. "It's you," she whispers.

"I was cleaning your face," I say.

Suddenly she lurches upright, but only her head and torso come off the bed. She looks wildly at one restrained arm, then the other.

"It is okay," I whisper. "Stay calm."

Her legs struggle against their restraints and her breathing becomes labored.

She grits her teeth and her lips curl back slightly. The teeth exposed by the grimace are white and big. Their color stands in stark contrast to her dark skin.

My eyes go to her lips and I cannot stop staring at their fullness.

"Let me go," she says, breaking my concentration.

I wince at the desperation in her voice.

I have been held against my will too many times to count, so I understand what she is feeling, but I also know that it is indeed for her own good.

"Stay still, please," I say. "You are injured and must stay calm and rest."

The sheet has fallen from her torso and the now exposed bandage shows signs of new bleeding from her abdominal wound.

"Take care not to disturb your sutures," I say.

"As if you care," she mutters.

"Oh, but I do." I feign deep concentration. "What good would I be as a healer if I did not care to heal you?"

She stares at me for a long time before she speaks again.

"What will your people do to me now?" she asks.

Heat sears my face as I must admit to myself that I have not even considered the options. I have been focused on making her better. The fact that I do not immediately think that the people of Karst and New America will fully embrace her as a guest causes me pause.

My hair has come loose somewhat and I gather it up to retie it away from my face. I keep my hair tied back, away from my face, during the day but loosen it when I am under the stars or sleeping.

The pilot's hair is not quite long enough to fasten behind her head. It is wavy in a reckless way, dark but highlighted in a manner that shows she spends a lot of time under the sun. The front falls into her face, causing her to jerk her head in an effort to get it out of her eyes, the sides are just long enough to tuck behind her ears, and the back rests in waves against the back of her neck. I am constantly fighting the urge to touch the rebellious locks, and not because her hair is in need of healing.

She jerks her head but the hair remains in her eyes.

"Please untie me," she says.

I glance at her hands, and then to the door. The temptation to grant her request is but fleeting. I reach to her and, with gentle fingertips, brush the errant strand of hair away from her eyes. Oh, those eyes.

I am lost in her dark gaze, only mildly aware at first that my fingertips still linger on her forehead.

It is a curious sensation, where I touch her flesh, not unpleasant but disconcerting in its differentness. I imagine the nerve endings in my fingers, and my arm vibrates with an unknown energy. This is not the energy of healing. This is something else and I cannot seem to break its hold on me.

She blinks rapidly—once, twice, three times—and I pull my fingers away from her soft flesh. I flex my fingers down at my side, not breaking our gaze.

"Who are you?" she asks.

"I am Misha Wyatt."

"Yes, but *who* are you?"

I look away, not prepared to reveal anything further about myself. "I must go now, but I will be back."

"Please don't leave—"

"I won't be gone long," I say. "I promise."

†

A few moments later, as I linger in the corridor outside the pilot's room, Jackson approaches me.

"The council wants some answers," he says. "I've assured them that you are doing your best to get them for us."

I stare at him.

"What has she told you about her people and her mission?" Jackson asks.

"She has only been settled in for three hours. We have not yet discussed that."

"Surely, you've asked?" he asks, incredulously. "What have you asked of her?"

"I have asked of her comfort, her pain level."

31

"Misha! Do your duty!" Jackson says, his voice rising further on each word.

"I am. My duty is as a healer."

"Your first duty is always as a protector of Karst."

"Healing Yaz and protecting Karst are not mutually exclusive."

"Aren't they?"

"Why are you being like this?" I ask.

"Why *aren't* you being like this?"

"Stop answering my questions with a question," I say.

"Why?"

I hold his gaze, and can feel my eyes narrowing.

He smiles. I am accustomed to his teasing. But I am not accustomed to it having an edge of desperation. He looks very tired.

"Misha, my friend, please just ask her for the key information—how many others like her there are? From where did she come? What is their intent?" He takes a deep breath. "Please do it so I do not have to. Or worse, so Shelton does not have to come to interrogate her himself any sooner than necessary."

"Okay. I will ask her the questions."

I have no ill feelings toward Shelton, but neither do I harbor any warm feelings for him. He may be an effective leader, but he lacks the heart of warriors such as Naomi and Kai, and also lacks the soul of Suzanna, Karst's spiritual leader.

I reenter Yaz's room and she stares up at me with those big, brown eyes.

"Hi," I say.

"Hi." She swallows hard. "I was afraid you'd left me."

"I am not going to leave you," I say, hoping it is true. "May I ask you a few questions?"

She nods her head slightly.

"Where are you from?"

"Perry."

I tug at the medical mask covering my nose and mouth, wanting to remove it, but leaving it in place. "Where is this Perry?"

"Northeast of here." She adjusts herself in the bed to almost face me, and the movement causes her to wince.

"You are okay?"

"Yes," she whispers.

"How many more of you are there?"

"I don't understand."

"Will others like you be coming to New America?"

"Most likely. But not until they ready the other planes."

"How many other planes?"

"Two." Her voice is getting lower with each response. "I don't know when."

I can tell she is drifting off, so I squeeze her hand slightly and say, "Rest now."

I become inordinately happy when she returns the squeeze gently to my fingers.

†

I send Laura for Jackson, trying to be proactive, trying to keep Shelton away for as long as I can. Disappointment jabs at me when Jackson's presence is immediately followed by Shelton's.

I give the two men a brief summary of what Yaz has told me about where she is from.

33

"That's impossible," Shelton says. "The northeast of the United States was annihilated during the war. They suffered the worst of the bombing—"

"I believe her," I say defensively.

"Of course you do," Shelton says.

My stomach drops at the tone of his voice.

"What if everything we ever thought about the east coast is wrong?" Jackson asks.

"We need more information from the prisoner about those living in the east," Shelton says.

"I will let my patient rest a bit longer, and then ask her for more information." I cross my arms over my chest.

"Get on with it then," Shelton says, his voice cold.

I take my leave of them and return to Yaz's room, where I find her awake.

I have brought tooth supplies with me, sure that she will appreciate the gesture. Eyes locked on hers, I gently part her lips with my fingers and bring the toothbrush to her mouth. She turns her head away from me, making me miss her mouth and streak some gel across her cheek.

"Why did you do that?" I ask her, my voice low. "Let me do this for you."

She turns back toward me and opens her mouth. I take a quick, visual inventory. Her teeth are clear of hard buildup. She misses a molar in the back, but the others all appear healthy.

I wash her teeth gently, brushing the minty gel over each tooth, one by one, until I have touched every one of them, only pausing periodically to let her relax her jaw and spit out the excess gel.

Upon finishing, I lock my eyes onto her and pull the toothbrush from her mouth.

"You have tooth gel where you come from?"

She shakes her head. "Not me. Only the elite get tooth gel."

The tone she uses when she says the word "elite" is harsh. I want to know more about these people and her reaction to them, but I don't want to prompt any more of the malice she seems to feel upon speaking of them.

I hold a small cup of water up to her mouth. She sips it, swirls it around, and awaits the return of the cup before spitting the now frothy water back into it.

"If you don't use gel, then how do you clean your teeth?" I ask.

"Bark," she says.

"Bark?" I cock my head but hold her gaze. "What is this bark?"

"Pallu bush. It grows just outside of Perry. Chew the bark to keep your teeth healthy, suck on the leaves to make your mouth taste good."

"I do not know pallu. It is good for you?"

"You don't swallow it. That will make you sick. Chew it and then spit it out."

I know I am meant to ask her more of the questions Shelton wants answers to, but I do not want to ruin this time with her. Her eyes hold such tenderness at this moment, I do not want to change the way she looks at me. What is a little more time without the answers the others seek?

†

I have left Yaz for a few minutes so I can scrub up when I once again see Jackson in the corridor. He does not look very well.

35

"Jackson, are you all right?" I ask.

"I am just tired. Really tired." He shakes his head vigorously, and then groans. "I probably should not have done that."

Jackson places his hand over his mouth and quickly leaves me standing alone.

I belatedly register seeing sores on his hands as he had brought them to his mouth. Had he burned himself on the wreckage of the plane?

I go to the doctor's office and knock on the door.

"Come in," she calls out from inside.

I do as she instructs.

"How is the pilot?"

"She still gets tired easily, but I think she is coming along from her wounds quite well."

"Good."

"I just wanted to give you an update on the patient." I use the word "patient" every chance I get, trying to ingrain it into everyone's mind that she is indeed a patient and not a prisoner.

"Thank you. I appreciate that."

I nod. "I need to speak with Suzanna. I will return to Yaz's room shortly thereafter."

"I'm sorry, seeing Suzanna is not possible. She has taken ill. She is just now finally sleeping after suffering from severe vomiting."

"Oh," I say, my thoughts going to Jackson and how he was feeling ill as well. "Perhaps something in the food did not sit right with her."

As my gaze bounces around the room everywhere but on her, I can feel her eyes on me, studying me.

"Are you feeling poorly, Misha?"

"No, not at all. I am tired, but that is to be expected." I still do not look at her as I speak.

"What is on your mind?"

"It is probably nothing," I say.

"Tell me."

"It is just that Jackson is feeling ill as well."

"I will look in on him then."

"Thank you," I say. "Can I please go to Suzanna for just a few minutes? If I find her sleeping, I will not disturb her."

"Just a few minutes," she concedes. "She is not in her quarters. I have her resting here in the medical center."

When I get to Suzanna's med center room she is sipping on some honey-sweetened water. A plate of toast sits untouched on the small table beside her bed.

"Suzanna. Can I bring you anything?"

She shakes her head, and then winces. "No, thank you."

I take the plate in my hands. "Shall I help you with this?"

"No, please. I am quite nauseated."

"I am so sorry you are not well," I say.

She puts up a hand to stop me saying anything further. I notice sores on the palm of her right hand. It sends a shiver through me.

"It will pass," she says, smiling. "It all will pass."

Her voice is so weak that my heart hurts.

"May I place my hands on you?" I ask.

"Not at this time. I'm sorry, dear."

"Do not be sorry. I understand," I say, even though I am quite sure I do not really. She has never before declined my energy work. "I should let you rest?"

"Yes. That is good, but do come back?"

"Of course, I will."

A boulder is building in my belly as I leave her room. This feels very wrong.

Naomi waits for me in the corridor when I leave Suzanna's med center room. I do not get too close to her.

"How is she?" Naomi asks.

"She is very sick," I sign.

"As is Jackson."

I nod, but do not speak.

"You are not showing any signs of sickness?"

"No. Nothing."

"The prisoner could have brought a virus into Karst."

"You mean I could have done so when I brought my patient inside?" I ask. I don't look at Naomi when I say this, because I cannot bear confirmation that she thinks such.

"Has your work helped Suzanna any?" Naomi inquires.

I shake my head. "She will not let me help her."

"I see."

I was not able to heal Naomi's hearing loss. This bothered me. Naomi knew it did, and made a point on several occasions to remind me that, without my energy work when she'd fallen into the toxic water, her prognosis would have been much worse. On a good day, I believe this. On a bad day, I am not sure I do. I will call today a bad day.

The energy work that took the most out of me was caring for Camryn. I used so much of my remaining energy trying to save her that I was unsure, at one point, if I could go on with our journey to Karst. Naomi was so consumed with Camryn that she did not notice. And if she had? Had I been unable to continue the journey, would she have left me out there to fend for myself in her quest to save her lover? I do not care to know the answer to that.

The look now on Naomi's face is so tender that I know she knows where my mind has gone.

I smile, trying to tell her that I am all right without verbally lying.

Dr. Bradshaw joins us.

"You have gotten some results from the blood tests?" I ask.

"Yes." She looks from me to Naomi and back to me again. "Suzanna and Jackson both show a severe drop in white blood cells."

"So, it's likely not an infection?" Naomi asks.

"They've also become anemic." Dr. Bradshaw looks pointedly at me now. "I need to take more blood samples from you."

"Of course."

"Have you eaten lately?"

"No." I had forgotten that I was hungry.

"Why don't you go eat something before I draw your next blood sample?"

I glance down the corridor but do not make the effort to move in that direction.

"You do not want to eat in the dining facility," Naomi says, reading me expertly.

"I would rather not." I find the idea of being around people right now quite distasteful.

"Very well," Dr. Bradshaw says. "I will have Laura bring you a tray of food."

"Thank you."

Less than an hour later, when Laura delivers the food to me, it is quite similar to the food Yaz has refused to eat today.

I sit in a chair near Yaz's bed and balance the tray on my lap. I glance up as I eat a blueberry. She watches me intently. I eat another berry and she licks her lips.

"Would you like some?" I ask.

She nods slowly.

I pull the chair closer to her and place the tray on the bed between us. I hold a blueberry to her lips and she gently takes it into her mouth. It is like this that we share the tray of food.

I want to ask her why she only now eats, but do not.

"You have blueberries where you come from?" I finally ask.

She hesitates before nodding her head.

I poke at the honey-slathered toast. "You have honey?"

She shakes her head.

"Try some. You will love it." I glance at her still bound wrist. "I will untie your right hand for you."

She flexes her fingers as I hold the plate of toast closer to her. She takes the smallest piece and sniffs it before nibbling the edge. Her smile is instantaneous.

Warmth grows inside me and I want nothing more than to keep making that smile occur on her beautiful face.

We have finished eating when she asks, "Are we in a mountain cave?"

I nod.

"It has a name?" she asks.

"Karst."

"How was it growing up at Karst?"

"I did not grow up here," I say, looking away.

"Oh. How long have you been here?"

"Five years."

"Where were you before you came here?"

I want to tell her that it is I who should be asking the questions, but do not.

I want to tell her about my past, about being an outcast, a captive, a slave, and finally a free woman at Karst, but I do not do this either.

†

Dr. Bradshaw calls me out into the corridor from Yaz's room. "Yaz's blood tests show her red and white blood cells are abnormal."

"And mine?" I ask.

"Yours show similar changes." She stares at me for several moments.

"I feel fine. Really."

She nods.

Witch hands. Misha's a witch. I shake off the memory of the many taunts.

"How is she?" the doctor asks.

I realize then that she has not checked on the patient herself since immediately after the surgery. I appreciate the show of confidence in me, but also know that it might not be that at all.

"She shows no signs of illness. She is healing quite well from her injuries also."

"Are you helping her with the healing?"

"Some," I say, knowing my voice carries a challenge.

"That is fine, just do not overdo it."

I hear the words as they are spoken but cannot help but feel like she means for me to save my energy for Suzanna and Jackson, or others at Karst worthy of it.

"I offered assistance to Suzanna and she declined. Jackson claims he feels much better and doesn't require energy work."

"I was not insinuating anything," Dr. Bradshaw says.

A growl of frustration calls my attention back to Yaz.

"Go," the doctor says. "Let me know if you need me."

I nod and take my leave of her.

"I need—I have to—" Her gaze looks everywhere but at me.

I cock my head then realization hits me. She's been in the medical center for at least seven hours and has not relieved her bladder or bowels yet.

"You need the toilets?" I ask, as delicately as I can.

She stares at me, and then her eyes flit toward the door at the rear of the room.

"I need to pee."

"Yes, of course." I hesitate for a moment before walking toward the counter where the portable pan lies. I am walking toward her with it when I hear her growl again.

"I will not pee in that thing. Please, allow me to go in private."

"I don't know," I say. I know she is meant to use the pan but cannot bring myself to make her if she feels strongly against it. "You are really too weak to get up."

"May I be the judge of that?" she asks, her voice icy. "Surely you aren't afraid I will escape if you untie me? It's not like I'm in any shape to harm you. It's not as if I would even know my way out of here if I did get free."

My nod is slow. I walk back to her and stare down at her bound hands, then her feet.

"Please do not make me sorry I did this," I whisper as I lock my eyes onto hers.

"I won't."

I swallow thickly, and then begin to unbind her.

She is lighter than I expect as she leans into me on the slow, unsteady journey across the room. Goosebumps arise on her mostly uncovered flesh and I have to concentrate to keep my mind on the task at hand and not the fact that she is only wearing a light tank top and undergarments.

I assist her to the toilet and hold her steady as she lowers the light, cotton garment from her hips and buttocks.

She glances up at me, shyly, and I mumble, "I will just stand here in case you need my assistance."

She nods, holding my gaze until I look away, giving her a semblance of privacy.

When she finishes I help her back to bed. She grimaces as she scoots across the bed until she is in the middle of it.

I reach for the first strap to bind her again and she pleads with me not to. I can hear voices in the corridor and am worried someone will come in and realize what I have allowed Yaz to do.

"I am so sorry," I say.

She deflates before me, sinking back onto the bed in resignation.

†

As Yaz's first day with us comes to a close, I note that she is indeed improving. She has just now walked to the toilet with minimal help from me. Other than the abdominal wound, she is doing great.

"She should be sick, based on her blood test, but shows no outward signs," Dr. Bradshaw says, just outside Yaz's room.

I feel her eyes on me. I know what she is thinking. I say it for her.

"I should be sick as well. Unlike you, I have not been in protective clothing every moment of exposure to her. And unlike Jackson and Suzanna, I am not sick."

"But you are—you. There is no way of knowing why you are not sick, and it really is not much of a surprise to me."

"Just like there was no way of knowing why my entire village died of sickness, yet I lived." *Witch hands*, the words play over and over in my mind. *Witch hands*.

The doctor tells me that Kai should arrive by first light. She also tells me that Suzanna has horrible diarrhea, and is getting very weak.

"I should go to her," I say. My fingers begin flexing and twitching, as the desire to do some energy work on Suzanna grows stronger and stronger. "The longer she waits for energy work the harder it will be to help her."

"She says not to." She nods toward Yaz's door. "I understand you will be bedding down in the pris—in the patient's room."

"Yes, that is correct."

"Do take care of yourself," she says, her voice gentle.

"I will," I promise, and then duck back into Yaz's room.

I am meant to be sleeping on the bed I have pulled in from another medical room, but instead I lie there, listening to her breathing.

"Why are you in here?" she asks, surprising me.

"I want to make sure you do not have any problems through the night."

"You are my doctor, or my prison guard?"

"Neither. I am a healer, but not an actual doctor."

"And you are my guard."

I do not mention that with her arms and legs restrained that I do not need to guard her.

CHAPTER THREE

Kai arrives at first light, I am told. It has also been said that now Jackson has diarrhea similar to Suzanna's.

When Kai comes to the medical center and requests a word with me, I leave Yaz's room reluctantly.

We stand in the corridor that leads to the bee caves but do not go all the way in. We are awkward together, standing there with a cold distance between us in our full protective clothing.

"How are you, all things considered?"

I shrug. The genuine concern in her voice has made a place in my chest clench tightly.

"You are sure you are asymptomatic?"

I nod. "I am positive."

The slight crinkling of the skin around her eyes indicates she is at least partly smiling.

"Naomi tells me you have gotten close to this pilot," Kai says.

I watch her eyes for signs of disapproval. I do not readily see any.

"Yes, I feel an affinity toward her. I believe she needs someone on her side." As soon as the word "side" is out of my mouth, I worry that I should not have said it. Will Kai not trust me with Yaz now? Will she doubt my loyalty to Karst? To her?

Kai nods but says nothing. When the expression that is visible around her eyes and forehead softens, I am convinced that she is thinking about the beginning of her relationship with Rachel. I can only hope that she will help temper the coldness so many others in Karst feel for my patient.

"Do you hear anything new about Suzanna or Jackson?" I ask, aware that I am very much out of the flow of information while I stay sequestered in Yaz's room.

"They are still sick. I understand there is no change in the last couple of hours."

I feel horrible for Kai, as she is very close to both Suzanna and Jackson.

"How long will you stay?" I ask.

"As long as I am needed."

I want to ask what that means, but do not push it with her. She will tell me her role here when and if she wants me to know.

"I will not keep you any longer from your patient. Let me know if there is anything I can do for you."

I nod. "Thank you."

†

47

Yaz dropped from the sky just over twenty-four hours ago. She has been here a mere day, but I feel like I have been in her room with her for much longer.

It is early afternoon when I learn that Thomas Grayson has arrived with his second-in-command, Aaron. Thomas was once a sergeant in the Resistance Army, but like Kai's twin siblings, Breanne and Gotham, and her oldest brother, Lewis, he joined the Peace Movement and was instrumental in the victory over the Army and the Anointed.

Thomas is the director of Tech City, the technological center of New America, and Aaron is his chief mechanic. Aaron will work on the plane.

I am told that Thomas has brought a contraption called a survey meter with him from Tech City. The sergeant is covered from head to toe in protective clothing when he comes to Yaz's room. He moves the contraption over her and his eyes narrow. The meter has shown that Yaz is contaminated with radioactive particles.

It has already been determined that her clothes, as well as the ones Suzanna, Jackson, and I wore when we pulled her from the plane, are contaminated.

Dr. Bradshaw has me swab Yaz's mouth, nose, and ears. The samples are tested and found to be contaminated.

I swab my own orifices and when scanned they prove to also be contaminated.

Next, I draw a blood sample from Yaz, and Dr. Bradshaw draws one from me, and both are read by the meter. Yaz comes up positive and I come up negative.

Yaz watches me closely. I am waiting for her to start screaming that I am obviously a witch.

Yaz is washed with a strong soap. As am I. I do not know if Suzanna and Jackson are also bathed or if they are deemed too far gone.

After Yaz is dressed in clean pants and shirt, and her bedding has been changed, Thomas comes in to test her again. The bath has greatly diminished, but not totally removed her contamination.

"I am surprised she is not showing signs of illness," Thomas says to me. Then he turns to Yaz. "Were you ever sick? In the beginning of your exposure?"

She stares at him as if he speaks a foreign language.

"Are there others like you, people who were exposed but did not get sick?" he continues.

"I—" Yaz struggles, as if she does not understand the questions.

If she has been exposed her entire life, if it is all she has ever known, she would not understand why Thomas asks the questions he asks.

"Have you ever been sick, you know, with vomiting and diarrhea?" I ask her.

"Yes, of course."

Thomas stares at her.

"When I was little, I didn't follow the rules about not swallowing the pallu." She looks at me for encouragement. I nod. "And then there was the time I ate the smooth, red berries without noting the leaves first."

"So, you were only sick when you ate something you should not have?" Thomas asks.

She nods.

He turns to Dr. Bradshaw. "Let's do blood work every twelve hours now. We need urine and fecal samples as well. Hell, do gynecological testing on her, too, while you're at it."

49

I open my mouth to disagree, but he is already leaving the room.

The doctor looks at me through her face shield.

"May I have a word?" I ask, gesturing toward the door.

"You can stay with her if you would like," she says instead of stepping out with me. "If Shelton agrees with Thomas and wants this done, I am going to do it."

"May I at least have a moment to tell her what will happen? Please, she is already scared enough." When I glance back at her, the expression I see is both angry and confounded.

"I will be back to do the examination in thirty minutes. Have her ready by the time I return," Dr. Bradshaw says. Then she adds, "I swear I will be gentle with her. I truly only want what is best for all of us, even her." With that, she leaves the room.

"What is happening?" Yaz asks as soon as we are alone.

"The meter Thomas used on us shows radiation contamination. They want to do more testing on you to determine the extent of your exposure. You understand radiation?"

"From living outside the Clean Zone," she whispers.

"What does that mean?"

She shakes her head. "What will the doctor do to me when she returns?"

"She will perform a gynecological exam on you."

"What does that mean?"

My gaze slips down to where the sheet covers her groin. "She will examine you on the inside."

"What?" her eyes grow wide with the question.

"She will take swabs of the inside of your vagina and uterus," I say, noting how heated my face has become. "She will palpate you to check for any abnormality in structure."

She stares at me but says nothing.

"I am sorry. I really am. If I had any say—"

Tears come to her eyes. I expect her to verbally assault me, but she just takes a deep breath and mutters, "I know."

Those two words warm and bewilder me in equal measure. I do not understand my reaction to them.

The exam is performed while I sit in the chair beside the bed. I keep my hand pressed against Yaz's shoulder, occasionally letting my fingers go to her forehead, careful to keep my touch ineffectual and light.

When the doctor slides her gloved fingers out of Yaz, I give my patient a light squeeze of her arm.

"Are you about done fondling me?" Yaz asks, her voice raw with anger and frustration.

"That is all," the doctor says, not rising to take the bait Yaz has thrown her way. "Misha, I will bring the sample to the lab and check back in with you later."

As soon as the doctor leaves the room, I untie Yaz's bindings.

"I will help you to the toilet, and then let you clean yourself up. If you need any help, just say so."

I wordlessly help her up and into the toilet room. I give her a clean, dampened cloth, and turn my back on her. I close my eyes, and do not allow concern over leaving myself vulnerable to her to permeate my thoughts for more than a brief second.

I help her back to bed, and when there is a tap on the door, I hurriedly rebind her.

"Yes," I finally say. "Come in."

Laura brings in a tray of food. Even though she is in full protective clothing, she only comes into the room far enough to deposit the tray on the countertop closest to the door. She nods and silently takes her leave.

I look from the tray to Yaz and she shakes her head.

"I don't want any."

When she turns her head to face away from me, I feel an almost crippling sense of sadness swell in my chest.

†

When I next speak to the doctor, she tells me Suzanna and Jackson's swabs also tested positive for radiation.

"You look tired, Misha. Are you sure you are not feeling ill?" Dr. Bradshaw asks.

"I am fine."

"Have you spent enough time under the stars?"

I am startled by her question. It is usually only Naomi, Camryn, and Suzanna who reference my need to recharge.

"Perhaps you should tonight?"

I nod. "Yes, I will go out as soon as it is fully dark."

The doctor takes her leave moments after Kai joins us in the corridor.

"Aaron reports that the plane is covered in radiation, but that it's not weaponized contamination. It's all contact, nothing on the plane is built to actually contaminate," Kai says. "Thomas has instructed Aaron and his crew to decontaminate the plane."

It won't make Suzanna and Jackson well, but I am relieved that Yaz didn't fly a plane into New America with the purpose of getting us sick.

"Thank you so much for the news."

Kai nods.

"If you will excuse me, I must step outside for an hour or so."

She bows. "Yes, of course."

I make my way to the small, high opening of the cave. This time when I approach the young guard, he steps well away from the entrance, allowing me to pass without engaging in conversation with me.

When I finally settle on the ledge, I close my eyes and ignore the way the difference in this exchange with the young man, and the previous one makes me feel particularly sensitive.

I take several deep breaths and open my hands up to the healing energy of the universe. It is an enormous relief when I feel the heat growing in my chest, followed by the low hum.

Physically, I feel better immediately. Mentally, I am still quite apprehensive.

CHAPTER FOUR

It is Yaz's third night in Karst. Right before we are to go to sleep, I am given an update from Kai. Her voice wavers slightly as she tells me that Suzanna's headache is almost unbearable now, and that she occasionally bleeds from her nose.

The thought sends tingling to my fingertips, building until it is painful.

The hardest news for Kai to deliver, though, is that teenaged Bronwyn is now sick. This causes bile to rush into my throat, assaulting me with its sharp pungency.

"I should go to them. I will do energy work on Bronwyn first, then—"

"No, Misha," Kai interrupts. "I'm sorry. At least not at this time."

"I feel so helpless," I whisper as the pain in my fingers radiates into my hands.

"I am sorry."

Surprisingly, I believe her.

"How are you physically?" Kai asks after a brief yet thorough scrutiny of me.

"I am well." I hold out my arms in a challenge for her to find any sign of illness or injury upon my body.

She holds my gaze for several moments before speaking again.

"Thomas's men have checked all of Karst with their survey meter. There was some particle transfer from when Yaz was brought in. It is believed this is how Bronwyn was exposed. Her exposure level is low," she says.

"But she is exposed, nonetheless," I respond.

"She is young and very healthy. She can fight this."

I cannot stop the churning in my gut at the thought of Bronwyn becoming sick.

"I must take my leave now. Have a restful night," Kai says.

I give her a slight bow, which she returns.

"Good night," I say.

Back inside Yaz's room, she watches me sleepily through half-closed lids.

"Is everything okay?" she asks.

I briefly think to tell her the truth, then blurt out, "Everything is fine."

Her expression tells me she wants to believe me.

"It is late. Shall we sleep now?"

She nods her response, but keeps her gaze fast upon me.

"Will you tell me something special about Karst?" Yaz asks.

I am at a loss as to what she means. "Like what?"

"Anything—something that makes it special."

My first thought is about Suzanna, about the loveliness of the dreamer, but I fear this is not my story to tell.

"Karst was built into the mountain before the war," I say instead. "It was to be a haven for its founders and their families. What was once to be limited to them, to the wealthy, soon became a haven for dreamers and artists and pacifists."

"Dreamers?" Yaz asks.

I nod but do not explain. How do you tell someone so foreign about how Suzanna dreams of past lives and sometimes of the future?

I can almost see the acceptance on her face, the moment she realizes that I will not elaborate on the subject.

She sighs softly. "You've been very kind to me."

"As I will continue to be." I smile. "Now, let us sleep, shall we?"

†

The fifth day of my care for Yaz begins for me with the news that both Suzanna and Jackson have started to lose their hair.

I have not been in to see Suzanna, upon her request, for two days. I am hoping to see Jackson later today.

Yaz's injuries are mostly healed now. The binding of her arms and legs are obviously no longer for her own safety. When she pulls against them in frustration, I look away, disgusted with the order to keep her bound to the bed.

I continue to allow her to the toilets when we are alone. I no longer go in with her—there is no need since I am

56

confident that she will not fall or become otherwise incapacitated while relieving herself. If Dr. Bradshaw or any of the others suspect I am allowing her this liberty, they do not let on.

A knock on the door startles me. I glance down at Yaz, dutifully bound to the bed, and relax for just a moment. Then I stiffen again at the sight of her bound so.

"Yes, come in," I say to the door.

It opens and Dr. Bradshaw looks in. "You can see Jackson, now, Misha. Go in with clean protective wear."

I nod to her and she closes the door.

"I will be back soon."

"I am sorry your friend is ill," Yaz says.

"I know. And I will bet that he knows that as well."

I take my leave of Yaz and change, then walk down the corridor towards Jackson's medical room. My heart pounds in my chest with dread of how I might find him.

My tap on his door is met with a grunt. I take that to mean to enter, so I slowly open the door. I fight to mask the fear I feel upon seeing him on the bed, his hair in patches, sores on his face and hands. The pale man I see is but a shell of my best friend.

"I know, I look atrocious. Scary even."

"Jackson," I say.

"Come, come closer."

I do as I am told. He reaches for my gloved hand and I do not hesitate to take his in mine, careful not to hurt him.

"I am sorry," I whisper, unsure what else to say.

"None of this is your fault."

I shrug.

"How is your pilot?" he asks.

"She is recovering from her injuries."

"Good. And I mean that." He speaks slowly, as if the effort borders on being too much.

I nod. I know sweet, kind Jackson does mean this.

"I know things look bleak right now," he says. "But always hold out hope, okay?"

I nod.

"Promise?"

I stare at him. He knows how dearly I hold promises.

"Misha," he says, his voice raw. "Promise?"

"Yes, my friend, I promise to always hold onto hope."

His smile is weak. "Thank you."

I nod. "May I do some energy work on you?"

"No, Misha." His eyes fill with tears. "There is no use to working on me now."

Now my eyes fill. "As you wish," I answer, trying to ignore the tingling in my fingers from wanting so badly to work on him.

"Good. Now go. Go to your pilot."

I cock my head at him.

"She was yours from the moment we pulled her out of the plane." His laugh is rough. "She is beautiful. If I felt better, I might fight you for her, but—" He gestures at his supine body, his already lean frame so much thinner now.

My laugh gets caught in my throat and sounds strangled.

"Go," he says. "You have been a good friend to me."

"And you to me," I respond. "I will never forget how kind you've been to me."

When I leave his room, I do not go right away back to Yaz. I do not want her to see how my time with him has upset me.

I am sitting on the floor, my back to the wall and my head in my hands when Emily, one of the first people I met at Karst five years earlier, approaches me. We are friendly, but I wouldn't call her a friend, so I am surprised when she sits beside me on the corridor floor.

"It seems like an impossible situation, doesn't it?" she says.

"Yes, it does." I look at her through the tears that plague me.

"Jackson cares for you as only a brother could."

"I have let him down."

"I do not believe that is so," Emily says.

"I cannot be strong for him. I am not strong enough to make this right."

"Do you even know what making it right would entail?" Emily asks as she leans against the wall, mere inches from me.

"I am not strong enough," I say again, much like a chant. "Never have been."

"Really? Were you not strong when you saved Camryn with your healing?"

When I don't respond she reaches for my hand but seems to change her mind. "Suzanna believes you to be the strongest person she's ever met," she says.

I quirk an eyebrow in doubt, causing Emily to hold up her hands in defeat. "She has told me as much."

The honesty I read on her face warms me.

"Really?" I ask.

"Yes, really. And are you not being strong by standing up for the pilot?"

"I guess I am."

"Yes, you are." She smiles but I see a sadness in her eyes. "I hope, when I find my true love, I am half as strong as you are."

I have heard the stories of a relationship between Emily and Kai, before Rachel, and an intimate night or two between Emily and Naomi, before Camryn, and find comfort in her resolve. I hope Emily does find her person.

She holds my gaze and we both smile.

"I should go to Yaz now."

"Yes, you should. Allow yourself to both give and receive comfort with her."

She stands and holds out a hand to help me up. I give her a second to change her mind, and when the hand remains poised to assist me, I take it, and allow her to help me to my feet.

†

The days rush by and before I know it, we are half through Yaz's second week at Karst.

I untie one of Yaz's hands and we eat breakfast in companionable silence. After I allow her to the toilets, she settles back into the bed. I do not plan to bind her hands again, but that changes when I hear voices coming from the corridor.

"I am sorry," I whisper, as I always do when it comes time to do this horrible task, "but at least I have been given permission to not bind your feet."

Her gaze stays on me long after the voices have disappeared.

"Will you remove your mask so I can see your whole face?" Yaz asks.

"I cannot," I say.

She pulls up her legs slightly, just enough to reposition herself.

"Thank you for not binding my feet," she says.

"You are welcome."

"Please remove the mask," her voice is a raspy whisper.

I am so very tempted, but falter and do not.

"Let me see you again," she whispers.

Her eyes on me are so very intense, and I feel my breaths coming faster, causing the area under the mask to sweat. It could not hurt to just take the mask away for a few moments, right?

I lean slightly closer to Yaz when I slip the mask off. The expression on her face makes me smile. Is she impressed that I break the rule, or calculating how to make me break more of them for her?

I stare at her mouth; watch the way her tongue darts out to wet her lips. I find myself leaning closer to Yaz, my lips mere inches from hers.

"Kiss me." Her voice is a strained whisper.

Coming to my senses, I pull away.

"Please don't stop—I'm—I've never wanted anything so badly in my life," she pleads.

Emotion overwhelms me, and I run from the room. I go to my quarters, where I have spent so little time since Yaz came crashing from the sky.

I pace the length of the small room and replay in my mind, over and over, how close I came to kissing Yaz.

I have never shared a romantic kiss with anyone before. I have never taken a lover. I am not a prude, not at all, but I've wanted to wait until I can be intimate with someone I really care about. I want to feel passionate toward the person I am finally with. I want love. I want what I see between Kai and Rachel, Naomi and Camryn, Heidi and Dawson.

I cannot deny the way I am drawn to this woman. I cannot deny that I want to take her as a lover. But the circumstances are all wrong.

I pace until my mind calms slightly, then I think about Yaz alone in her room, no one there to advocate for her.

I rush back to her.

When I slip into her room, she opens her eyes. Her smile is tentative.

"Hi," I say from beneath the mask.

"Hi."

I bring the cup of water to her. "Sip?"

"Yes, please."

After she drinks, I take the cup from her and place it on the counter. I approach her bed slowly.

"How is your pain level now?" I ask.

She shrugs slightly. "Not too bad."

"May I see?" What I would normally ask is if I can put my hands on her, but I have not yet told her anything about my unusual healing abilities and find myself unwilling to do so at this time. If she were to freak out, if she were to banish me from her room, I would not be able to handle that.

She nods.

I reach for the sheet to lower it but she pulls it down, away from her torso for me. I feel her eyes on me as she bends at the waist to better watch me.

"Please lie back," I say, my voice low.

She does as I instruct, and I lift her shirt and peel away the bandage. It does look good. I have not put my hands on her as much as I would like, but the early energy work I did on her made a huge difference, I am sure.

The sutures appear ready to be removed. I will talk to the doctor about that the next time I see her.

I place my fingertips on the flesh around the wound, making a steeple over it with my hands so as not to touch the sutures directly.

"Close your eyes and relax," I say in a near whisper.

She continues to stare at me, so I lightly cover her eyes with my left hand and will her to sleep. I leave my hand over her eyes even after I feel her eyelashes flutter against my palm, signaling she has closed her eyes.

I visualize the energy leaving my fingertips and soaking into her flesh. *Heal*, I say silently. *Heal now.*

The fingers of my right hand tingle where they touch her, growing warmer and warmer. The hum from deep inside me begins, intensifying slowly.

"Mmm hot," she mumbles.

"Yes, that is good. Go to sleep," I say, hoping my low voice is soothing.

I only stop when the expected chill starts to creep up my back. I replace the bandage and remove my hand from over her eyes as I pull her shirt down.

Her eyes flutter open, and then close again, and I quietly take up position in the nearby chair to watch her.

I have been watching Yaz sleep for about an hour when there is a slight tapping at the door.

"Yes," I say in response, rising and moving toward the sound.

The door opens a few inches and I can just make out Kai's face. "May I come in?"

"Yes," I say again.

Kai is in protective clothing, including a mask and gloves.

"Aaron is with me. May he come in as well?"

I glance at Yaz. She is awake now, watching. When she does not respond one way or another, I say, "Yes."

Aaron's eyes move quickly around the room, visible over the top of the mask he dons.

"Hello," he says as he steps slightly closer. "My name is Aaron."

Yaz nods.

I look from Kai to Aaron, and then back to Kai. Her dark eyes do not give away any emotion.

"Aaron is a mechanic," Kai says to Yaz. "He has been tasked with working on your airplane."

Yaz sits up as best as she can with her hands bound. "You're meant to fix it?"

He studies her for a long moment.

"Yes," Kai answers for him. "He is working on it and has a few questions for you. Would that be okay?"

Yaz nods. "Just keep in mind that I am the pilot, not the mechanic. I might not be able to tell you the more technical things."

"I would appreciate any assistance you are willing to give." Aaron moves closer, seeming to be gaining confidence with the exchange. "Let me first say that I am very glad that you survived the crash. Based on the condition of the plane, it was quite a devastating one."

He asks her something that sounds like a foreign language to me, although I am quite confident it is English.

"How are you?" Kai asks, distracting me from the technical conversation.

"I am well."

"I do not just mean whether or not you are suffering any symptoms," Kai adds.

64

"I know that." I smile at her. "I will not say any of this is particularly easy, but I am doing okay."

She nods.

"Which is so much more than what I can say for Suzanna, Jackson, and Bronwyn," I say.

"I know. But please do not let yourself get run down."

"I will be careful," I say, meaning it about so many things other than my own health.

Within a few minutes, Aaron and Kai are taking their leave of us.

"Shall I see about having a meal sent in?" I ask Yaz.

She nods.

"Are you okay?"

"I wish I could go outside and assist Aaron. That would work so much better than him coming in here and asking questions without me being able to point at things." She twists her upper body as she speaks, looking so very uncomfortable.

I vow to give her more freedoms, starting with letting her eat totally unbound at the evening meal today.

†

Yaz has just swallowed the last bit of honeyed toast when I hear voices in the corridor, causing me to hurriedly bind her hands again. When they drift away without any interruption of us, I regret having rebound her so quickly.

"Tell me about your past," I say.

"What part?" she asks.

"I do not know." Then it comes to me. "What have you eaten here that you like the most, that you didn't get in Perry?"

65

"Honey," she says. "I really like the honey on the toast."

"Are there no bees in Perry? No honey?"

"There is honey, but it is not meant for me."

I try to understand how only some in a population is allowed something as basic as honey, but cannot grasp it.

"You've always had honey, or just since you came to Karst?" she asks.

I shift uneasily in my chair.

"Tell me," she whispers. "Tell me something about yourself."

"As a child I enjoyed honey. Then I went for a period of time when it just was not available to me." I smile, thinking about the night around the fire with some of the younger people, in a village I stayed in temporarily. "I did, however, manage to imbibe in some mead once during the time of no honey."

"Mead?"

"Honey wine."

She smiles. "Oh, this story just got interesting."

"No, not really." I do not go on with any details of the time right before being taken by the Merricks, when I'd been able to indulge in the mead.

Her eyes lock onto mine. "Take off your mask again."

"I just had it off—sort of—while we were eating," I remind her.

"That doesn't count. Please take it off again," she persists.

I think about her request and before I know what I am doing, I remove the mask. I lean toward her; drawn in a way I do not totally understand.

"Come closer," she whispers.

"I am as close as I can possibly get," I reply.

She smiles. "No, you are not."

I glance down at her bound hands.

Do I dare?

Yes.

I climb over her to straddle her waist. I lean down until my face is only an inch from hers.

"Here I am. Now what?" I ask, trying to sound calmer than I am.

She lifts her head up until our mouths meet.

I gasp in surprise and pleasure.

"Untie me," she says against my lips. "I need to touch you."

I pull away slightly.

"Let me touch you," she begs.

I stare into her dark, dark eyes, and see a combination of vulnerability and confidence, then realize that is desire. That is desire and I want to feel it—really feel it.

I take the restraints from her left wrist. Her newly freed hand goes to the back of my neck and she pulls me to her, into a new, searing kiss.

Without looking, I unbind her other hand, and she cups my face with both hands, deepening the kiss.

The feel of her tongue teasing my lips apart, the way she tastes and feels, is all almost too perfect for me to bear.

I am relaxing into the sensations when Yaz's hands go to my throat, and I hover there, unable to fathom this change. Her fingers are squeezing my throat and confusion paralyzes me.

Then, just as quickly, Yaz releases the pressure on my throat and places gentle kisses where her fingers had been assaulting me mere moments earlier.

Hot tears escape my eyes.

Without moving her mouth from mine, she lifts my shirt and her hands slip under it to cup my breasts. My nipples stiffen, pebbling against the rough palms of her hands. The sensation forces a groan from me.

"You like that?" she asks against my lips.

"Yes, yes."

There is a low growl from her throat.

I struggle to speak, my lips brushing hers. "You feel— you feel—perfect—"

There is a rapid knock, and simultaneously the door opens.

"Oh," comes the shocked word from Dr. Bradshaw. "Oh, Misha."

I hurriedly climb off Yaz and straighten my clothing. I feel my heart pounding between my legs where I am swollen and drenched with desire.

When I finally force myself to look at Dr. Bradshaw, I see frustration in her eyes.

"You will need to be quarantined. We will test you now, then every twenty-four hours for the next week or so."

"I can just be restricted to this room, right?"

"I will need to discuss this with Thomas—and Shelton."

"Please, not Shelton."

"How can I not?" She shakes her head. "Please put your mask back on. The least we can do is make it look like you regret your actions."

"I do not," I say, knowing I sound like a petulant child.

"I will be back shortly."

"Who is Shelton?" Yaz asks after Dr. Bradshaw takes her leave of us.

"He is in charge here at Karst."

"I thought the deaf warrior was in charge."

"Not here," I say. I keep to myself how Shelton reports to Naomi outside of Karst, but that here he is the Director.

xxx

CHAPTER FIVE

I am sent to another room in the medical center. Shelton has decided he and Naomi will begin a more thorough interrogation of Yaz, without me present.

I can hear Shelton and Naomi clearly from where they confer in the corridor.

"She trusts Misha in a way she will never trust you or I," Naomi says.

"Unfortunately, *I* no longer trust *Misha*."

"She made a mistake."

"No, I made a mistake by allowing her uncontrolled access to the prisoner."

"Patient," I whisper from my place on the other side of the door. "She is my *patient*."

"Do not forget I am in charge here in Karst. You might be a mighty warrior out there, but I am the Director of Karst," Shelton says.

Does he even stop to think that Naomi, or any of the Peace Warriors, could so easily take him down?

I can imagine the scathing look Naomi must be giving him now. I wonder if he is signing to her or just making her read his lips.

If Suzanne had not gotten sick, she would be out there, tempering the tension between Shelton and Naomi. Of this I am certain.

I hear receding footfalls and feel so very alone now that Naomi is no longer outside my door.

I could easily sneak from this room—I am not a prisoner here. I could leave this room and go to Yaz. She is well enough for us to make a run for it. I could take her somewhere far away from others, where she would not contaminate anyone else.

I go for the door and am shocked to find it locked from the outside. Rage courses through me. How dare they? How dare they?!

My vision blurs slightly as I take in the sight of the pitcher of water on the counter. I hurl it against the locked door, and I am filled with despair when it doesn't make me feel any better to do so.

Tears cascade down my face.

Maybe five hours—or it could have been five minutes—pass before Naomi comes to me in my medical center room, wearing protective clothing.

"I've known you for over five years. I've never known you to be reckless," Naomi says.

"You have never known me to be in love," I respond, holding her gaze.

She gives me an almost indiscernible nod. "I see."

"How is she, really?"

"Yaz is not cooperating. She refuses to answer any questions and only speaks to ask where you are."

I hate that Yaz is probably scared without me, but I must admit to myself that I feel somewhat validated that she is not cooperating now.

When Naomi adds that she has quit eating and drinking as well, my smugness disintegrates into a real fear for Yaz.

"You must get me back into her room," I beg.

"It is not up to me."

"Talk to Breanne on my behalf. Please, I am begging you. Yaz needs to eat and drink. She is not well enough to be going without," I say.

"I'll see what I can do."

I hold her gaze. She is my strongest ally. It cuts me to the core to not feel like she is completely on my side with this.

"Would you not have done anything—will you still not do anything—for Camryn?"

"You cannot compare—" she starts.

"Can't I?"

Anger settles into my hands and arms. It has been a long time since the energy has manifested itself to be so negative. The heat and force are so strong that I cross my arms and tuck my hands under my arm pits to keep from touching Naomi with this destructive energy.

"Misha," Naomi begins.

"I have been waiting for Yaz my entire life," I say, interrupting her. "You will let them keep me from her? You will let me die inside—" I pound my chest for emphasis, "while she literally dies two doors down?"

"It's not safe for you."

"I do not care!" A gasp escapes me. "You might have well left me to perish at the hands of the Merrick clan. You might as well drive your sword through me right now."

Naomi flinches. Perhaps I am overreacting, but cannot stop myself. I drop to my knees and sob. My hands throb with red-hot energy.

"Misha," Naomi says as she kneels beside me.

I stop myself from using my hand to throw her arm from my shoulder and shrug her off instead. "Do not touch me."

Naomi leaves my room without another word. I curl up into fetal position and cry myself into wracking hiccups.

It is quite a while later when Dr. Bradshaw comes to me. She is in protective clothing and brings a tray of food.

She glances at the other, untouched, tray that I have ignored.

"You must eat."

I roll over on the floor to face the wall, and away from her.

"Getting weak and sick will not help anyone."

"Are you to allow me to return to Yaz, where I can help her?"

"We cannot do that, Misha."

"Then go away. Please."

I can feel her hand on my back.

"I need to check your vitals," she says.

I roll over until I am on my back and tuck my hands into my armpits. I do not make eye contact, but stare just over her shoulder, at the far wall.

"Yaz's sutures need to come out," I say.

"Okay," she says absently.

She places two fingers against the flesh at my neck and I am overcome with the memory of Yaz's hands pressed there. A tear falls, coursing down my cheek.

"Please eat, or at least drink some honey water."

I shake my head but do not speak.

As soon as she finishes checking my temperature, I roll away to once again face the wall. I listen for the click and slide of the door and its lock before I reposition back onto my other side.

†

The next time I hear Dr. Bradshaw's voice, she is outside my door with Shelton and Naomi.

Shelton says something I cannot make out. I crawl to the door to hear better.

"Misha is sick," Dr. Bradshaw says.

I force myself from the floor, lean against the door, and try to hold my weight up on weakened legs.

"So, she is not so special after all," Shelton says.

"It's not from radiation, you fool, it's from a broken heart!" Naomi yells at him.

I smile at the thought that she probably has no idea how loud she is talking.

"Do not be ridiculous," Shelton says.

"There is nothing medically wrong with Misha," Dr. Bradshaw says. "She is suffering from lack of food and sleep."

"Wonderful, now they are both trying to starve themselves to death?"

This gets my attention.

"Please be okay," I say to the ceiling, my words meant for Yaz.

†

The passage of time means nothing to me. I am hollow inside from lack of both food and Yaz. Maybe I've been curled on the floor for a couple of days, maybe it's been a week or longer.

It is Dr. Bradshaw that comes to me finally, tells me they are to let me go to Yaz as long as we both eat, and I begin to ask the pilot relevant questions.

I open the door slowly. Yaz is on her side, hands no longer tied, facing the wall. She looks smaller. The cloth of her shirt flows around her, much too big for her now.

I open my mouth to speak but only a croak comes out. Clearing my throat, I try again.

"Yaz?"

She is slow to lift her gaze to me, but when she does, her entire face glows.

"Misha," she whispers. "Oh, Misha."

The sweet sound of my name off her lips brings tears to my eyes.

She pulls me close. "I knew you'd come back."

I am desperate for her to know that being away from her was not my idea.

"They locked me away. I would never have stayed away from you otherwise."

"I know," she whispers. "It's okay."

There is a knock on the door and Laura opens it and peers inside. She is in full protective clothing and walks just a few feet into the room.

"Laura," I say.

"Misha. I have brought food."

"Thank you." I take the tray from her and set it on the table.

Laura nods at Yaz, and then hurries out.

"First we eat," I say. "Then we must talk."

I take one of her hands in mine, and then motion to the small table in the corner of the room.

"We will eat like civilized people?" I ask.

Her smile is brilliant as she joins me at the table. She does not take her eyes off me for several moments.

"You are too thin," she says.

"I am fine." I smile at her. "I hear you have not been eating so well either."

She shrugs, and then watches me closely as I eat. The scrutiny of her impassioned gaze makes me warm all over and quickens my breath. I want to reach across the small table to touch her but resist. I don't want to start something we cannot finish. Right now, I just want to get a little information from Yaz, just enough to keep the inquisitors at bay.

I push my portion of honey toast across the plate to her. I love the way she enjoys the sweetness that is so foreign to her.

She takes it and nibbles the side. When her tongue darts out of her mouth to lick a smear of honey on her upper lip, a groan escapes me. She cocks her head and smiles at me.

"I want to touch you again," she whispers.

"Soon," I say. I feel the heat rush to my belly and between my legs. "Soon."

"Promise?"

"Yes. I promise."

I glance down and am shocked that we have finished the meal.

"Tell me the story of how you have come to be here," I say.

"As I've told you, I came from Perry, to the northeast of here." She pauses and I nod. "My mission was to fly reconnaissance. I was to film the whole of the central part of the land, then return home with the plane."

"So, only you know about us—for sure anyway?"

"Not true. I videotaped the flight and all the footage was transmitted to the EOs—Elite Officers—at Perry."

"You videotaped everything? Even your crash?" I pause. "So, your people will be coming for you eventually."

"Not exactly."

"What is not exact?"

"I didn't video everything and they will not be coming for me."

I cock my head and study her face. Her expression is mostly unreadable but her mouth softens slightly almost imperceptibly.

"They will not come for me because I am a canary—I am expendable."

"Someone in Perry will believe you worth coming for."

"No, you are wrong. I did my job. I did what I've trained to do—they are now finished with me." She laughs. "I went down with a last punch, though. I quit videotaping the moment I saw you. I knew it was you, even before I made out your face. I wasn't about to share you with them, so I unplugged the camera from the console."

I do not respond to her further comment about knowing me before meeting me. That is a conversation for later. "The cord dangling from your face plate?"

She nods.

"What were you taping?"

"Everything. Water plants, farms, craters, towns, solar panels. Towers and a lot of solar panels. Fields and fields of panels."

I know she speaks of Tech City and this concerns me.

"So, your people saw everything about New America?"

"Except you and this place—" she gestures around the room. "They would not have seen the entrance to this cave city you use to hold me captive."

I wince at the word *captive*.

"I started to go back over the mountain range after seeing you, but the thought of not meeting you, not speaking to you or touching you, became unbearable. I decided to turn back to you, and shortly after, realized I would not have made it back to Perry anyway."

"You ran out of fuel?"

"Something went wrong with the engine. I wondered if it was on a remote kill switch of some sort. They didn't mean for me to go back to Perry."

"Ever?"

"Well, that might not have been true in the beginning of my mission, but most likely when they realized I unplugged the video feed on purpose."

I think about this for several moments before saying more.

"You have said before that there are two other planes?"

"My plane was equipped to spy, the others are being equipped to attack," she says. "There are also a few armored trucks. Missiles and bombs," she adds, her voice getting weaker.

"Bombs?" I cringe as I say the word.

"Yes."

I hold her gaze. She looks back at me with so much intensity that I decide to ask about the comments now. "You have said things, more than once, that make me believe you knew about me before we even met. Tell me about that."

"I've dreamed about you for so long." She shrugs, not looking as nonchalant as I believe her to be trying to appear. "At first, in my dreams you were unrecognizable. But the last couple of years, I've caught glimpses of the face of the woman in my dreams, and know it is you."

"You are a dreamer?" I ask.

"I have dreams." Her face contorts in confusion. "Don't most people have dreams—or nightmares?"

"Do you have visions? Can you see the future?"

She laughs. "No, I cannot see the future. Well, not really. I just saw you. I saw the woman I was meant to meet, and had to have faith that it would happen."

†

"I would like you to biopsy a skin sample," Thomas says to Dr. Bradshaw.

I think about earlier in the day when I removed Yaz's sutures. They stayed in longer than they should have and it was a painful procedure for her to endure.

"No," I interject.

"Yes," he snaps. "We need to be more proactive with testing."

"You can't just start carving into her!"

"Just some skin—"

"No," I say through gritted teeth. "It will start there and keep going until she is nothing but a big sample to you."

79

"Shelton agrees with me about more testing," Thomas says.

"Naomi—Kai—you understand where I am coming from, yes?" I know I sound desperate, because I am.

"I know this is upsetting to you," Naomi says to me. "Thomas, surely there is nothing more to be accomplished by continuing invasive procedures with the pris—with the patient."

I love the warrior even more after this statement.

I look now at Kai, and she holds my gaze for a very long time. I cannot read the emotion playing across her face, but feel a monumental shift in the energy between us.

I know that Thomas is the father of Kai's lover, Rachel. I wonder if Kai has any real influence over the man.

"I agree with Misha's assessment. We should not just start treating the woman as a test subject." Kai shakes away an obviously disturbing thought. "That is the type of thing to expect from the Anointed or Resistance, not Peace Warriors."

Thomas winces and I know Kai's words have hit their mark. Then he seems to shake it off as his posture becomes more rigid.

"I will speak with Shelton, and he will back me up on this," Thomas says.

I am disappointed that Kai's reference to the Anointed and Resistance hasn't stuck with him, as an example of those who would have carved up his daughter without a second thought.

"Nothing needs to be decided right away," Naomi says.

"Misha," Kai says after Thomas takes his leave of us, "will you get something to eat and look in on Suzanna?"

I move to decline, but the intense look on her face makes me decide otherwise. I nod and leave Kai and Naomi standing in the corridor.

Suzanna is sleeping when I go to her. I place my hands on her back and close my eyes. *Heal. Heal now.* My fingers tingle and grow warm. The tingle turns to pain and I have to remove my hands for a minute to refocus. Then I touch her again and refuse to give in to the coldness in my hands and arms, until I am too weak to continue.

I sit on the floor a few feet from where Suzanna still sleeps and let the tears flow. I am too weak from the energy work to do anything more than sit there and sob for a long time.

Once I am strong enough for my legs to support me, I get off the floor.

"Please do not do any more energy work on me," Suzanna says. "You will need your strength."

"I will continue to do anything I can to ease your discomfort, surely you know that."

"I'm begging you to save your energy. It is wasted on me."

I nod, not wanting to argue with her about this, but not giving in to her request either. I will return and do further energy work on her after I go to Yaz to work on making her better still.

I pause outside one of the medical supply rooms when I hear voices. I see shadows enough for three people, but cannot make out who they are.

"By next week, we begin the major phase of testing," Thomas says in a hushed voice. I have to concentrate to hear him. "If the healer hasn't gotten information from her by then, we must assume she simply will not."

81

"I agree," says a voice I do not recognize.

"Come, let us go to our quarters," Thomas says.

I rush away, down the corridor, around the corner, and am about to burst into Yaz's room when I hear voices inside.

I stand outside Yaz's room and wonder if I am only to learn things at Karst by spying through doors.

"I will always be a prisoner here."

"In time they may accept you," Kai says.

This has my attention.

"They accepted Rachel," Kai adds.

"And Misha?" Yaz asks.

There is a moment of silence.

"Your people treat Misha just slightly better than a prisoner. Is this just since I've arrived?"

"I need to take my leave now, Yaz," Kai says, her voice barely making it through the door to my ears.

I assume it is her I hear at the door handle, so I take several steps back. When Kai comes out into the corridor, I hope it appears that I have just arrived.

"Good evening, Misha," she says with a slight bow.

"Good evening to you as well."

Kai leaves me and I enter Yaz's room.

"You look pale," Yaz says.

"I'm just tired. It is nothing." I hate lying, but need time to think.

She stares at me for a very long time, and guilt causes me to look away. I will not say anything about Thomas' plan to increase testing on Yaz until I have a plan. I cringe on the inside. Me, come up with a plan?

"Your elite survived the nuclear events in Karst?" she finally speaks.

"Elite?" I ask.

"Your ruling class."

"We are all equal here. Well, now anyway."

She looks confused.

"Tell me about the Elite Officers you mentioned earlier," I ask.

"The elite had secret bunkers to hide in when the bombing started. When the war was over, they sent a few people out. When they didn't immediately die, the elite started coming out little by little."

I stare at Yaz.

"From the moment I was born, I was raised to be used by the people of Perry. I would either hunt, farm, or forage for them, or something else, something dangerous. It was meant to be an honor among the canaries, to be chosen as a pilot. I knew I wasn't meant to get out of the plane in the case of wrecking. I knew they were filming my surveillance, and that they would know if I went down. I also knew they would never come for me. I did my job and was then disposable."

"Everyone is someone's slave, except the elite?" I ask.

"The social structure is three-tiered in Perry. If you are from an elite family, you have all the comforts and power. The workers are families whose existence is at the whim of the elite, and they of course, do all the work. Below them are the canaries."

"Canaries? Like the birds? What does that mean?"

Yaz shrugs. "You just were one, there was no History of Perry for me to learn, in which I found out why I was considered disposable. I just am. Well, was." She barks a humorless laugh. "Still am," she adds.

I think about my circumstances when I was held captive. And that was exactly what it was, circumstances. I was not told from the day I was born that I was less than everyone else. How would that have manifested itself in my identity? My sense of self-worth?

"You regret helping a canary?"

"No," I answer. "Do you regret pulling the video feed? Or maybe accepting the job to begin with?"

"Accepting the job wasn't a choice. As for pulling the plug on the video—I do not regret that, not even for a moment."

I nod at her response.

"Do I wish things were different for me now? Yes. But not if it would mean excluding you from the picture," she says.

I do not fight the smile that forms on my face.

"I wouldn't mind tasting freedom with you just once," Yaz says, her voice strained.

"I would like that," I whisper in response.

"The only time I ever felt free was when I was outside the Clean Zone, hunting." She takes my hand. "I wonder what would happen if all your strong warriors were to go to Perry."

"Oh, they would definitely shake things up," I say with a smile. Then I grow serious. The Peace Warriors truly are fierce, with their swords, arrows, and guns, but could they really fight against people who mean to use explosives and airplanes against them? I shiver.

†

The following day, Suzanna requests our presence. She has asked to speak with both me and Yaz, together. At first Shelton refuses to let Yaz come with me to Suzanna, but then he relents. I am not sure why he gives in, if someone has convinced him, or if he realizes it is unkind to deny a dying woman her last wish.

We are in the corridor when I think that, if Suzanna was not so sick, I would ask her counsel on how I am to get Yaz away from Thomas and his deadline. These days, she is the only one I would trust enough to ask.

Yaz and I both wear masks, gloves, and examination gowns, the last of which is worn over our clothing. We are to go from Yaz's room to Suzanna's, no detours.

It breaks my heart to see Suzanna so weak.

"I hear Jackson is doing much better," Suzanna says, her voice raw.

"Yes, he is," I answer, a small smile playing on my lips. I am so happy that he is doing so much better, but also very saddened to see that Suzanna gets progressively worse.

Suzanna grabs my hand and motions for Yaz to move closer. When she does, Suzanna smiles at her.

"Let me testify," Suzanna says, her voice ragged. "Let me tell you a story."

"Take a drink first," I say as I lift a glass of honey water to her mouth.

She takes a miniscule sip, and then begins.

"Ash and Doc were caught in the middle when the sickness found its way to the United

States. Doc—her name was Dr. Mallory Rose, but everyone called her Doc—was tasked with inoculating the politicians and their families. Doc stole two doses, one for herself and one for her lover, Ashley Johnson. At first Ash refused to be inoculated, refused to be part of the Chosen's preferential treatment, but Doc begged her to do it with her."

"They did not get sick?"

"No, they didn't." Suzanna gives us both a weak smile. "Ash broke into the compound protecting the politicians and their precious drugs and stole half the supply of the immunization."

"Half?"

"Yes, they used it to inoculate the people who the politicians would never have considered, the dissident writers and artists, the free thinkers, the tolerant."

"It sounds a bit like the people of Karst," I say, wondering if there is something to this.

"Yes, it does, doesn't it?"

I exchange a glance with Yaz, thinking about how earlier Suzanna had called her Ash.

"It would appear," Suzanna says, her voice getting weaker, "that perhaps Doc healed their bodies and Ash healed their souls."

"It is a beautiful story," I say, at a loss for any other words.

Yaz nods her agreement.

Suzanna studies me for a long time before speaking again. "I will rejoin Karst, as another. This life is coming to a close and I must ready myself for the next."

"Please do not stop fighting this—this—" I wave my finger around, indicating the air around her, as I struggle to find my voice. "Do not give up."

"It is not giving up to acknowledge it is time to move on. The possibilities are endless." She smiles at me. "Don't be sad—be excited."

"But Suzanna—"

"I wonder if Gotham and Linet will have a boy or a girl. Have you heard anything about how Linet's pregnancy is going?"

My mind struggles to shift gears as she quickly changes the subject. Gotham is Kai's brother, and his partner, Linet, was once in the Merrick clan, but is now coupled with him. She is to give birth to Gotham's first child.

"All is well with Linet," I assure her.

"Very good," she whispers. "What an amazing life that will be."

Her voice is so low that I am not convinced I have heard her correctly.

"Yaz," she says.

"I am here," Yaz says, through the barrier of her medical mask.

"Take that damned thing off," Suzanna orders. "It is not as if we can make each other any sicker."

Yaz shyly removes her mask.

"That's better." Suzanna reaches for Yaz's hand. "You, too, Misha. Remove the mask and come closer."

I do as she instructs.

"Life is short, and precious," Suzanna says. "Always choose love and each other."

I exchange a glance with Yaz.

"Just as I will be fine away from Karst, so shall you be. If that is what you decide, that is." She takes several labored, shallow breaths.

"Suzanna—"

"I love you, sweet girl," she whispers, kissing the top of my hand. "I want you to accept love into your life. I want you to live your life—not the life others want for you, but *your* life."

"I will," I say, tears scorching a path down my face.

"Promise me."

"I promise." The tears sting my eyes.

"Go now." She looks at Yaz. "Go now and take care of one another."

I nod. "I will send Dr. Bradshaw in?"

"No, that is not necessary."

We replace the masks over our faces and step into the corridor. Shelton and an armed man I do not know await our exit from Suzanna's room.

"I know, go right back to Yaz's room," I say.

He does not look at me, but stares at Yaz in a way that makes my blood run cold.

Dr. Bradshaw is waiting at Yaz's door.

"How is she?"

"It will not be long now," I whisper.

"I will go to her."

"She asks to be alone."

"I will give her some time, and then go check on her," Dr. Bradshaw says with a nod. "Jackson continues to grow stronger."

"For that I am so grateful," I say, my voice catching. "May I see him?"

"Perhaps in a couple of days. Let him continue to rest."

"Of course," I say with a nod.

Yaz and I go into her room and immediately embrace. Thoughts of Suzanna swirl through my mind. I cannot stop crying. For a long time, Yaz holds me close, but I cannot get relief from my aching heart.

Raised voices ring out in the corridor. I know in my heart that it has been found that Suzanna has left this life. The knowledge pierces me painfully, and then I feel warmth descend upon me and know she is telling me not to take this too hard.

The voices in the corridor grow more alarming.

Yaz is pale, and I wonder if she is afraid an angry mob will break down the door and come for her.

Am *I* afraid of an angry mob?

I hear Naomi's voice over the others.

"Stop this. Go to the lounge, the prayer or meditation rooms, if you must gather. Go to your quarters if you wish to grieve alone. But you cannot stay here in this corridor."

There is some murmuring, and then it grows quiet.

I have never felt such unease in Karst. My body thrums with an energy that I do not know how to use—or control.

†

Three days later, Kai comes to me with word that Jackson has died as well. Her eyes are visible over the medical mask she wears, and they are red-rimmed and swollen.

I think about how close Kai and Jackson have been over the years, and my heart aches for his death and her loss of him.

Kai stares at Yaz with such an intensity I expect to feel my skin crawl, but it does not.

"And Bronwyn?" I ask.

"Bronwyn is doing well, expected to survive."

"We thought that of Jackson, too," I whisper.

Again, Kai is staring at Yaz and I note a slight nod from the pilot.

My stomach rumbles and I realize I have not eaten today.

"Why don't you go for some food," Kai says to me. "I am sure you and Yaz both need something to eat."

With Suzanna and Jackson both gone, I am running out of people in Karst who I would trust with both my life and

Yaz's. Naomi and Kai are the only people I feel totally safe with now. Once I would have included Dr. Bradshaw on that list, but her lack of advocacy for Yaz has dampened the esteem I once held her in. But trusting someone with my life is not the same as asking for their help in escaping with Yaz.

"Okay," I say. "I will be back shortly with some food."

"Thank you," Yaz says.

I am in a fresh gown and gloves when I go to the kitchen—thankful to find no one there—and make a large tray of food to bring back to the medical center. I do not know why I take so much, but do not hesitate to follow my instinct.

Before leaving the kitchen, I take a moment to reflect on losing Jackson. I think about the early days of our acquaintance.

When Naomi and Camryn left for Liberté, and I was left only really knowing Dr. Bradshaw and Suzanna, it was Jackson who made me feel at home.

Where Suzanna made sure I felt supported, and Dr. Bradshaw showed me I was needed, it was Jackson who stepped up to make me feel as if I belonged in Karst. He used humor and comradery to show me the more playful side of Karst.

Jackson and I made up complex games of adventure, everything from scavenger hunts to Seek, hiding ourselves and trinkets from one another, the winner our own private Chief. The talisman we most often used was a beaded bracelet Kai had left behind years earlier.

Sometimes we allowed others in—Heidi, Dawson, Emily, Laura, to name a few—but my favorite games were the ones we played without anyone else. Once he hid the talisman in the bee caves. He had tossed it in, not thinking I would go after it. The look on his face when I did and came out without a single sting—priceless!

"How did you do that?" he had asked.

I just shrugged, not telling him that I'd hummed the bees into submission. Some things I kept hidden even from Jackson, the lovely man-child whose smile lit up the entire city of Karst—as well as my heart.

I stumble out of the kitchen, heading towards my quarters, trying to see from behind a film of unshed tears. After placing the tray of food on the counter, I go to my pillow, unused for so long now, and pull out the beaded bracelet I'd hidden there before the pilot and her plane crashed into New America. I was waiting for inspiration to hit, for the perfect hiding place to present itself. And now it is too late.

I shove the bracelet into the small pocket of my loose-fitting pants. I finger it, then grab the tray of food and leave my quarters. I linger in the corridors, waiting for a new inspiration. Is there a way to leave here with Yaz? Defeat echoes through me. I am not the person to orchestrate this, yet the only one who would.

The tray of food shakes in my hands. I try to fight back the despair. I do not want to upset Yaz with the information that they will take the testing to the very end of her life. I stop long enough to compose myself before continuing toward the medical center.

From outside the door, I hear Yaz reply to something Kai has said.

"I was meant to die. I have nothing to lose."

When no response comes from Kai after several moments, I enter with the food.

91

I set the tray down on the small table, and question if I have just seen Yaz hide something behind her back, or am imagining things.

"I will leave you both to eat in peace," Kai says.

I nod, glancing between the two of them, wondering why they appear to be communicating in front of me without me understanding. *Stop it*, I tell myself.

"I'm famished," Yaz says, settling in front of the tray of food in an uncharacteristic manner. "Sit, eat with me," she says to me.

Kai leaves with just a glance back over her shoulder at Yaz.

Yaz pats the bed beside where she sits and I settle there with the tray between us. She picks up a piece of honey toast.

"This is the best thing I've ever tasted."

I pick up on a tone of sad resolve and it lodges a boulder in my throat that I must concentrate to swallow around.

Once we are finished eating our fill, Yaz brings the not-quite empty tray to the counter and comes to stand in front of me where I still sit on her bed. She takes my hand in hers.

Our eyes lock, and the warmth I see reflected back at me grows until it is hot and heavy, and I have to close my eyes.

"No," she whispers. "Look at me."

I do and my breath hitches. Her dark eyes have turned impossibly darker and there is no denying the want—the need—I see there.

"Will you sleep in my bed with me tonight?"

"Sleep?" I croak.

She laughs, pure melody. "Eventually we will sleep."

I stare at her.

"You will give yourself to me tonight?" She runs her fingertips across my cheek, down my neck, lingering on my collarbone.

"Yes," I whisper. "I would love nothing more."

She pulls me to my feet and wraps her arms around my waist. When her lips find mine, they are so soft, yet so hungry, that I gasp.

"Is this okay? Should I stop?"

"Please do not stop." I press my body against hers, and then quickly pull away. "I do not want to hurt your wound."

"It's hardly a wound any longer. Don't worry about hurting me. You've taken very good care of me and I'm as good as new."

She brings her mouth back to mine. Her tongue slips into my mouth and moves against mine, a slow, sensual dance that makes me tingle in a way that is very new to me. I do not even realize she has pulled up my shirt until we break apart, long enough for her to slip it over my head.

"I need your skin."

I gasp.

She steps back and removes her top and pants. I help her with her undergarment, then finish undressing myself.

She stands before me wearing nothing but the small bandage that now covers the almost-healed wound. I pull back the top sheet and we slip underneath, our bodies coming back together. Her mouth moves from my lips to my neck, then my chest. When her tongue makes lazy circles around my nipple I gasp, arching my back to press more fully into her.

She presses me back down and holds me there while her tongue worships first one, then the other nipple. Heat and wetness rush between my legs. Now when my hips come up off the bed, she lets them.

I grab at the sheet with both tingling hands and entangle them in the fabric.

Her hands travel down my body until one kneads the flesh of my buttock and the other mingles in the still growing wetness between my legs. I gasp and buck my hips into her touch as she finds the hard bud of my need, and smears my wetness over and around it in a frenzy of movement that drives me into sweet, sweet release.

She holds me close as I pant and writhe my way through the aftershocks of my first orgasm not brought on by my own hands.

A new need grows in me as I ache to touch her in the way that she has touched me. I slide my hand between us and when my fingers find her wetness there is no mistaking her desire. She presses against me and whispers, "Yes, Misha, yes."

I linger at her opening, concentrate on minimizing the tingling heat in my hands, swirling my fingers in her wetness.

"Go inside me," she says. "One finger at first."

I slide my index finger into her and she bucks against my hand.

"Okay?" I ask.

"Perfect."

I slide in and out of her until she says, "More."

I pull all the way out, then slide in with two fingers.

"Yes."

My mouth latches onto one nipple and I suck her as my fingers work between her legs. As her breathing increases, I go deeper and faster, marveling at how her inner muscles pull at my fingers.

She presses her face into my neck, muffling her cry slightly as she rides out her release.

"I'm coming, oh baby, I'm coming."

I do not know what the words mean, but I know what her body is doing, and I am in awe that I have caused this reaction in her.

She grabs my wrist to stop my movement. I look into her eyes and see such intensity.

"I did okay?" I ask, believing it to be so, but needing the affirmation just as well.

"Amazing, baby. That was amazing."

We have just caught our breath when Yaz goes up on one elbow to look at me.

"You must know, I had no idea I would make anyone sick. I am so very sorry," she says.

"I know this."

"And you are the most amazing person I've ever met."

"Stop."

"Stop what?"

"Stop sounding like you're saying goodbye."

Yaz looks away from me now and I know. I know.

CHAPTER SIX

I awake and the pain of loss assaults me. She is gone. Not just from the bed we went to sleep sharing last night, but from my life.

I sit up and contemplate Suzanna's words. She had said, "Just as I will be fine away from Karst, so shall you be. If that's what you decide, that is."

There are pen and paper on the counter. Neither was there last night. That is when I notice that the top sheet has a few ink marks on it. I know instinctively that Yaz meant to leave me a note. Has she never learned to write, I wonder?

Without another thought, I pick up the pen and begin leaving a note for Naomi. I do not include Kai in this correspondence, not wanting to draw attention to whatever part she played in this, because I know without a doubt that she has stepped in to help Yaz.

"Dearest Naomi," I write. "You have been amazingly charitable and compassionate toward me. I will forever hold you in my heart for this. I am sorry if I have left you feeling betrayed, but I must follow my heart now."

I slip into my clothing and pull on the boots that were recently returned to me after my initial decontamination. My fingers brush against the beaded bracelet I'd put into my pocket the day before, but I don't allow myself more than a fleeting thought about it. I stuff the leftover food from last night's meal into my medical bag and snatch it up. As an afterthought, I reach into the toilet room and grab the jar of tooth gel.

I run along the corridor, slipping into the meditation room when I hear voices coming toward me. For the first time since arriving here, I am desperate to get out of the cave city.

"Karst will never be the same," I hear Dawson say.

"The prisoner must pay," says a voice I do not recognize.

"Settle down," Dawson says. "Now is not the time for rash behavior."

When the voices grow fainter, then disappear altogether, I leave the room and continue to make my way through the maze of corridors. I strap the medical bag to my back as I move.

I slow when I see Andre at the entrance.

He steps in front of me, his face a tense mask, but he does not draw his weapon on me.

"I need to go to the meadow," I say as I hold up my hands. Anyone else making this gesture would seem docile, but I know, coming from me, it comes across as aggressive. I should feel badly about the move, but do not.

He backs away, appearing disgusted, and lets me pass.

I see Kai where she talks to some other warriors. She faces the plane that sits at the edge of the meadow, the others' backs to the machine. The others might think she is paying attention to them, but I know otherwise.

I stare at the plane and see movement. Aaron is with someone else, pointing at something at the belly of the machine. I do not need to see the other person to know it is Yaz.

There is no going back, only forward. Of this I could not be more certain. I walk, as quickly as I can without drawing attention to myself, in an arc toward Yaz and Aaron. I wait until he gives Yaz a hand up, then quicken my pace.

The engine roars to life and Aaron backs away. I sprint, running with every last ounce of energy—and hope—in me, until I am running beside the now moving plane.

I catapult myself into the cockpit and Yaz gasps.

"Out, you must get out!" she shouts over the noise of the engine.

"No," I yell back. "I am going with you."

She looks over her shoulder and her eyes grow large. I look as well and see that we are being pursued by Andre. Then I see Kai, her back to us now as she stands facing several warriors, including Andre, with her sword drawn to halt them in their pursuit of us. Kai's stance is symbolic, Andre's gun could level her, but he will not hurt Kai. Forget leadership, forget rank, Kai is the most respected person in New America, and he would not dare hurt her.

Yaz gives the plane more power and we speed up.

"I hope I can get up with the extra weight," she says. She cuts her eyes at me. "And I don't just mean you, so don't get offended."

I face forward and hold my breath as we speed up more, and gradually, miraculously, begin to lift off the ground.

"Yes!" I call out, overjoyed and exhilarated. "Yes!"

Yaz laughs, and then faces me and becomes more serious. "You should not be here."

"And yet I am," I say, my voice just loud enough for her to hear me over the engine.

Yaz focuses on the gauges in front of her for a long time, turning first one knob, then another. I study her, the way the light shines off her silky black hair. I want to run my fingers through it, but know it is best not to distract her now.

"I have nothing to use to strap you in," she says as she glances at me briefly.

"I will hold on. You do not plan to fly this thing upside down, do you?" I joke. I look down at the low, wooden box I am sitting on.

Her eyes are wide still when she looks at me. Then she turns to look straight ahead. We are quiet for several moments.

I see the charred land below and think that I can smell it. Can I really, from this height, or is it a trick my mind plays on me, drawing on memories of campfires? The plane ascends until we climb over the mountain range, and I gasp at the sight of the huge canyons that mar the earth before another mountain range grows up, almost as high as the East Mountains. It hits me that, as far as I know, I am the only living person from Karst who has seen the landscape east of the mountains that form the eastern border of New America.

"What is the plan?" I finally ask.

"The plan *was* for me to take out the other planes and the armored vehicles, and then crash into the most vulnerable part of the bunker. But, obviously, I need a new one now."

"Oh," I say. "Now what is the plan?"

She shrugs, and then says, "I have a few hours to think about it. I'll let you know once I come up with it."

"I'm not sorry," I say.

"I know. I don't expect you to be." She reaches to me and strokes softly along my jawline. "I can't believe you hijacked my mission."

"Your mission?" My eyebrows quirk up. "How many people knew of your mission?"

"I guess it doesn't matter who knows now," Yaz says. "Just Kai and Aaron."

I knew Kai was up to something, but this never crossed my mind.

"Thomas intended Aaron to be the pilot," she says.

"How would he have pulled off attacking Perry and still making it back to New America?"

"He would not have."

"Oh."

"Thomas kept sending Aaron and Kai in with specific questions about the mechanics of the plane. I figured out that they meant to rig it with explosives and guns. I simply suggested to Kai that it would work better with a pilot who knew where she was going."

"And they trusted you?"

"Not at first. Then they decided that, if I turned on them, you would be held accountable. Kai knew enough about how I felt about you, to know I would not risk you being harmed as a consequence of my actions."

"Right to the bitter end they used me against you," I say.

"Maybe Aaron, but I knew all along that Kai knew better." She glances at me. "Did you know that Thomas is Kai's partner's father?"

"Yes," I say.

"And that Kai saved Rachel from her people—twice—and always chose Rachel over any other alliance?"

I nod. I had heard the story of Kai freeing Rachel from probable incarceration and extermination under the Resistance, before she became a part of the Peace Movement with her siblings and Naomi.

"She told me she felt an affinity with our plight from the very beginning," Yaz says.

I swallow hard, noting the crackling in my ears as I do so.

"I'm sorry I went behind your back," she says.

"I will forgive you only if you promise never to do so again."

She stares at me for a long time, and then looks back out the patchwork windshield. I wonder if she is thinking how we have so little time left that it really doesn't matter.

"I promise," she finally says.

"You took the mission knowing you would die?"

"I will do anything to keep you safe, Misha. You know that, don't you?"

"I do." I nod. "So now we die together," I say, feeling oddly calm.

"No, now we adjust the plan to do our best to both survive this." She smiles. "I will figure out something by the time we are flying over Perry."

"Okay," I say, unconvinced. "Tell me about Perry."

"It's not a large area. There is the bunker, the clean zone, and the perimeter."

"And you lived where?"

"In the outer portion of the perimeter. We had rough structures built of downed trees and branches. If we built too

101

well the workers—who lived in the rest of the perimeter—would take parts of our structures and move them to use themselves."

"Tell me about your family," I say.

"We don't have family in the same way that the elite do. Or the workers, for that matter."

"I don't understand."

"The elite have known bloodlines, they take care of their young and old, regardless of that person's productivity. But as a canary, once you are no longer at peak performance, you are disposed of."

"What does that mean?" Bile creeps up my throat.

"Either you were exterminated, or you were given a dangerous job that you wouldn't survive for long." She does not look at me.

"Who cared for the young?"

"All the canaries cared for the children. Well, those children we were allowed. Only healthy children were allowed to stay with us, and only in the numbers necessary to keep the work force workable."

"That is—that is—"

She clears her throat. "Perhaps we should discuss the plan for when we arrive at Perry. We don't want to arrive unprepared."

I nod. I pull the medical bag out from where I stashed it shortly after jumping into the plane. I open it and pull out an apple and two nut bars, the leftovers from our meal the night before. I hold out the apple and she grins as she lowers her head to take a bite from it instead of taking it in her hand. I then also take a bite and this is how we eat the apple, then eat the nut bars, alternating bites.

"I don't know if the other two planes are working yet," Yaz says, wiping the back of her hand across her mouth. "If not, we should be able to use one of the explosives rigged to the plane to take them out. The other three bombs will be used to hit the weakest points of the bunker."

"If the planes are able to fly?"

"Then I'll have to wing it." She gives me a brilliant smile that makes me immediately forgive her vague answer.

"What can I do?" I ask.

"You can lift up a bit."

"Excuse me?"

"You're sitting on the gun and ammo." She inclines her head toward the box I have made my seat. "Can you lift up enough to open it? Then I'll reach in and grab it."

I do as she requested, hovering over the seat while she removes both the hand gun, and bullets tied up into a sack.

She instructs me on how to load. I concentrate hard to follow her words.

"We are meant to fight an entire town with one little gun?" I ask.

"No. We are meant to fight the town with the plane, the explosives, and the bigger gun built into my side of the plane." She glances at me, then looks straight ahead again. "The little gun was to protect me in case I survive a landing."

I stare at her profile, knowing there is something she is not telling me.

She swallows thickly. "I would take out as many of them as I could, but save a bullet for myself to keep from being taken alive."

"Whose idea was that?"

"Mine."

"So now if we survive a crash in Perry, we need to be sure to have two bullets left."

She nods, not arguing.

PART TWO—EAST

CHAPTER SEVEN

We have survived an air battle over Perry, but now we are going to crash in this strange land I know nothing about. Yes, I am in a crashing plane with the love of my life. After all we have been through, independently and together, will we be cheated out of our happy ever after? I squeeze my eyes shut for a brief moment, then reopen them.

The plane's course is now almost parallel to the ground.

We skid along the long grass that is just now coming into focus for me. The impact is jarring and wracks my entire body with pain, but I am alive. The whoop that Yaz lets out next informs me that she too is alive.

When the plane comes to a halt against some thick, lush foliage, the air rushes out of my lungs and I clasp at Yaz's hand.

"You did it," I say.

"I did something, but not *it*," she answers. "I didn't get us over the ridge, closer to New America."

"It does not matter. We are alive!" Blood courses through me, sending tingles up and down my spine. "We are alive and we are together."

She nods, slow at first, then faster.

"Yes, alive and together." She leans toward me and places a gentle kiss on the corner of my mouth. "You have no idea how much I like the amount of appreciation you feel toward a failed mission."

Now I lean to her and place a kiss on her lips.

"I do appreciate it. But there is a branch sticking in my back, and I might have lost control of my bladder during the brief moment when I did not know if we would live or die."

"Are you complaining now?" she teases.

"Oh no, love, no. I would just like to get out of this plane as soon as possible."

She unfastens the belt strapping her in and I just now realize that she has a buckle on her safety harness.

She reads me well enough to answer, "Aaron insisted on a release."

I nod.

She climbs out of the cockpit easily and comes around to my side, where the plane is flush against the brush. I secure the medical bag to my back, and then I take her hand when she offers it, and climb out. It is when I jump off of the wreckage that I roll my ankle.

"Easy, baby, I've got you." Yaz pulls me against her as she speaks.

I wrap my arms around her shoulders and hug her tightly.

"You okay?" she asks.

I nod. She steps away from me and I begin to follow her but the pain in my ankle causes me to stop short.

She turns to look at me.

"It is just my ankle," I say, trying to reassure her.

She helps me to a swath of grass beside the upturned earth in the crash path of the plane.

"Rest. I need to look over the plane, see her condition better."

I watch as my love kneels near the wreckage. As my gaze follows the long line of her lean legs, I notice the knife she has belted around her waist. The blade is wide and at least five-inches in length. Seeing it makes me feel safer. The carved wooden handle looks familiar and I think to ask her about it later.

Yaz contorts her body to look at one part, then another. She reaches under the tail end of the machine, and grunts loudly as she pulls something free from the belly of the plane.

"What have you there?" I ask as she returns to me.

She examines the seven-inch length of cylindrical metal. She shrugs.

"You do not know?"

"Other than knowing it is a pipe, I have no idea where it came from, or what its purpose on the plane was." She rolls it around in her hand, looking at its entire length closely.

Laughter bubbles out of me at the look of confusion on her face. The sound is too light for the circumstances, yet so very welcome. When she joins me in laughing, I stand, balancing on one foot, and pull her into an embrace.

When I finally get my breath, I ask into her neck, "You do not suppose it can be fixed?"

Swiping at laughter-induced tears, she shakes her head. "No, I don't believe so."

"What do we do now?" I pull away just far enough to look into her big, brown eyes. "Do we start walking westward?"

She glances down at my foot, still suspended in air, and says, "Not on that ankle, we don't."

I sit back down and stretch out my leg. I cannot believe I survived a plane crash just to hurt myself jumping out of the wreckage.

Yaz bends to kiss the top of my head. "Rest here while I look around."

"Do not leave me," I blurt, hating the desperate tone of my voice. "Please."

"I won't go far. Let me just get my bearings." She guides me into a sitting position. "I'll be only a few yards away. You—" she twirls her finger in a circle in the air, near my feet "—you do that thing you do to make your injury better."

I stare at her, my mouth agape.

"What? I heard and saw a lot during my time strapped to that damned medical center bed." The grin she gives me is sweet and shy and playful, all at once.

I ignore the poultices in my medical bag, saving those for the inevitable, and hopefully minor, injuries we will face in this new landscape. I work the energy a little while Yaz looks around. I do not do much for my ankle, though, not knowing how the stars will be and if I will get enough of a charge from them here to keep up my healing capabilities.

I look around and do not recognize any of the plants except the kudzu. We might as well be on another planet as far as my knowledge of this land goes.

†

When Yaz returns, she asks me how my ankle is doing.

"Better." It is not really a lie, I tell myself. "What should we do? Should we make a plan to go west?"

"I think we should stay here for now. The trek west will be difficult."

"We are never going back to New America, are we?" I ask.

"We will make that determination—together—but only after we've seen what this place has to offer. Is that going to work for you?"

I nod. "That works for me," I say, copying her strange phrasing.

"Are you ready to explore?" Yaz asks about an hour later.

When I stand, I still cannot put much weight on my ankle.

"Sit back down." The tone in Yaz's voice leaves me with no desire to argue with her. "Seriously, sweetheart. If you can heal a hole in my abdomen, I know you can do more for your ankle. Do not hold back. Please, our lives may just depend on your ankle being at its best."

I stare at her, then nod my head slowly. She is right. In my quest to save some healing energy for her, I could have put us both in danger.

"I will give you some time. I'll just be over there, by that tree."

She walks the ten or fifteen feet away from me and I miss her already. But I know what I must do, for her, for us.

I pull my medical bag closer and prepare a poultice, using the very minimum of the material I have brought with me. After applying it to the swollen joint, I lean forward at the waist and place both hands upon my ankle. I envision the energy running out of my fingertips and into the weakened joint.

Heal, I think. *Heal now.*

My ankle steals the heat from my hands and the flesh tingles. I continue the process until I begin to shiver. I have just steadied my breathing when a shadow falls across me.

"Better?" she asks as she returns to me.

"Yes," I say.

She offers me a hand and I take it without hesitation. When I am on my feet, just inches from her, she pulls me into a hug. "You're cold."

"It will pass," I respond. She pulls away just enough to be able to place a hand on each side of my face.

"I'm sorry if I was harsh with you," she says, her voice a raspy whisper.

"Do not be sorry. You were not harsh, and you were not wrong. I did us a disservice not taking care of myself." I smile. "I cannot promise I will never make that mistake again, but I will try."

"That's all I ask," she says.

I stare into those onyx eyes and swear I can see the whole world reflected back at me. I lean forward until my mouth brushes against hers, causing desire to rise in me. She takes a step back.

"It's getting late," she says. "We should make our shelter before nightfall."

I look around, scanning for an area where we can bed down. I'm about to point to an area that might work when Yaz stops me.

"We don't know what to expect here, as far as weather and predators, so I think we should make something more protective than just bedding down. Don't you think?"

She is right. Of course she is right. We don't know anything about the dangers of this place.

We go into the woods just far enough to find a giant, upended tree, whose roots can be used as one wall of our lean-to.

I work alongside Yaz as we gather limbs and pine straw. She shows me the types of branches we will use to construct the framework of the shelter, and what will make excellent walls and roof. I help her gather what she has shown me, but she is the one putting all the pieces together. The ease with which she constructs our shelter leaves me in awe.

I have never had to construct my own shelter. As a child, the adults did that kind of work. As a captive, my hands were saved for healing. Then at Karst, the massive cave city had been made generations earlier.

She places the metal pipe next to our bed on the right, the knife on the left. "Just in case."

We are both exhausted when night falls.

"Should we sleep in shifts?" I ask.

She seems to consider this. "How about we lie together for a while. Then I will have you sleep while I stand guard."

"Then I will take my turn."

"Yes, then you can take your turn."

We spread out on the bed of pine needles that we have assembled. When I am pulled against her body during this first night of freedom together, I am almost overrun with emotions. She is slow and gentle with her touch of me.

"May I use my mouth to love you?"

I cannot help the smile. "Yes. Please."

The wetness between my legs grows.

She kisses a trail down my throat, to my collarbone where she nips me gently with her teeth. My breath quickens and she moves lower still, running her tongue around first one, then the other of my nipples.

I gasp.

That is rewarded with a chuckle.

My hips come up off the ground as she nuzzles against my stomach. She uses my movement to insert both hands under my buttocks, pulling my sex against her face.

"Oh," I whisper, almost speechless.

When her tongue finds my wetness, I feel as if a current has run through me.

"You taste amazing," she says, her words vibrating against my heated flesh.

I groan.

Her mouth is fire-hot as her tongue dips inside me before she licks and sucks, over and over, until my body explodes in a mass of wrecked nerve endings.

"Oh, Yaz!"

I shake as I try to calm my breathing.

"You liked that?"

"Liked it?" I moan. "I loved it."

She holds me while I catch my breath. My limbs feel like jelly, but I am afraid she will let me fall asleep if I do not voice my desire.

"May I do that to you now?"

She stares deep into my eyes. "Do you want to do that to me?"

"Yes," I plead. "Yes, please."

She places a kiss on my mouth, and tasting myself on her causes the ache between my legs to grow again.

I drift down her body, stopping in all the places she had stopped on her journey down my body, until I am nuzzling between her legs.

"You are so wet," I say.

"You did that to me."

I smile, then kiss her, inhaling the scent of her.

When my tongue begins exploring her, she grabs fistfuls of my hair and holds my head between her legs while I feast. She tastes delicate, and sweet, and just feeling her body react to my mouth drives the want between my legs to new heights.

My hands grip her buttocks, holding her tighter to me. It takes several minutes of my hands growing colder for me to realize I am transferring some energy. I release her flesh and press my hands against the ground underneath her.

I quicken the strokes of my tongue and this time, when she cries out that she is coming, I know exactly what is happening.

I move up her body and rock her in my arms as she catches her breath. One of her legs has moved between mine and the pressure against my renewed wetness is divine.

I am not sure which of us increases the pressure and movement until I am sliding and slamming my sex against her thigh, but we keep up the intensifying rhythm until I scream my release into the night air.

When I awake, Yaz is holding my head in her lap as she sits and stares into the darkness.

"Shall I relieve myself and then come take over the watch?"

Yaz stifles a yawn, laughs, then agrees to that.

When I return, I sit as she had, and motion for her to put her head in my lap. She does, after gesturing with her head toward the pipe by my side.

"Don't hesitate to wake me if you think you hear anything," she says.

I nod, then whisper, "Sweet dreams."

I am surprised by how unafraid I am as I sit and keep watch over my slightly snoring lover. I cannot see her expression as she sleeps, but her stillness speaks of ease.

My eyes adjust to the night. The moon is partially obstructed and I cannot see any stars. I worry about not being able to recharge.

Slowly the sky lightens, and I can hear birds all around, as they seem to waken from their slumber. I feel Yaz's gaze on me and bow my head to look down upon her.

"What?" I ask, my voice low and soft.

"You are so very beautiful," she whispers.

My stomach growls, loudly, sending us both into a fit of giggles.

"We should probably see about eating," I finally say.

"No more food in your medical bag, huh?"

"It is not like I had a ton of time to prepare," I say, in what is meant to be a tease, but then regret my words. When she goes to speak, I hold up a hand to quiet her. "I am sorry for saying that. I did not mean any malice with my words."

She nods.

"I do have a surprise for you, though."

"Oh?" she asks.

I pull my bag closer and stick my hand inside. When I pull out the jar of tooth gel, I am rewarded with a big smile.

"Will this take the sting out of my words?" I ask.

She nods, her eyes still on the jar. "Any other surprises?"

"Maybe," I tease. Then I add, "I have a canteen for water." I pull that out and hand it to her. "And a flint and steel fire-starter as well." The last item I do not pull out, as we don't currently have need for it.

She gives me a wide, brilliant smile that I am quick to return.

After we have used the gel and I have strapped the medical bag to my back, we leave the shelter and go out into the field that spreads as far to the east as we can see.

†

The ground is spongy, giving under my feet, where we now walk. I approach a clump of very tall grass. As I reach for one of its long, narrow leaves, I hear Yaz behind me.

"Wait, that's sawgrass."

Too late, I have run my fingers along the light-green leaf, its saw-like teeth on the edges biting into my fingertips.

I pull away.

Yaz is beside me, examining my hand. "I'm so sorry, I should have warned you sooner."

I stare at the rough cuts dotted with blood on two of my fingertips.

"Are you okay?"

I nod, watching the blood form tiny droplets. I'm confused when they don't heal immediately. Little cuts and scrapes—and bee stings—usually heal quickly without any conscious effort on my part.

"I am fine," I say, not wanting to worry her over something that is probably nothing.

She gingerly takes my hand, and kisses the flesh close to the cut on first one finger, then the other. "If you are sure."

I smile. "I am sure."

She is now scanning the landscape before us. She is animated as she lists all the things we can hunt by hand—lizards, frogs, snakes; and those things we can hunt with crude tools—squirrels, rabbits, rats.

I close my eyes for a moment. In my village we farmed and gathered. There are very few times that I have eaten meat. I think about feasting on *pescado dulce* in Las Estrellas. The sweet fish was delicious. All the other times I have eaten animal protein was while I was being held by the Merricks. The feral clan hunted eyeless rodents when we were trapped deep in the cavern network. I had not wanted to eat the roasted flesh, but knew instinctively it was that or starve. I felt some guilt, but mostly was glad to have survived that time of my life. Long after we had left the deepest parts of the caves where the rodents lived, we came across Naomi and Camryn.

A cold dread washes over me as I think about rabbits and other animals she has mentioned. I am uncertain if Yaz has noticed until she speaks.

"Are you okay?" she asks.

I glance around at the expanse of tall grasses and the woods that grow thicker the farther in we travel.

"Can we not get enough sustenance from the plants?"

She watches me, and then nods. "We will do our best to."

We are harvesting sweet onion, and picking the smallest, most tender of the kudzu leaves when I ask Yaz, "Did you eat animals in Perry?"

Something flicks across her face. Uncertainty? Pain?

"The animals that were harvested in the Clean Zone—raised and slaughtered—were to be consumed by the elite.

Every now and then a worker would be rewarded with some meat or foul."

"Were you ever rewarded?" I ask.

"I am not—" She gives me a weak smile and corrects herself, "I *was* not a worker. Canaries were usually not rewarded with anything more than the right to live another day." She shakes her head violently.

"What is it?" I ask, my voice gentle.

She does not answer.

I know there is more, and I cannot help but want to hear about it. "You have never had animal protein then?"

"That's not true either." Her gaze scans the thick brush before us. She takes a deep breath. "Sometimes the elite would let us canaries go beyond the borders of the Clean Zone to hunt. We were mostly allowed to eat what we killed. There were times the prey would be scanned and the meat taken from us if it had minimum reading on the meter."

"So, if it was contaminated, you would eat it?"

Yaz shrugs. "Sometimes it was all that we had."

Well, I could certainly relate to that.

"Tell me more about the class structure, especially the difference between the workers and the canaries."

"So, as you know, the elite were protected in the bunkers during the war," she starts. "After the bombing ended, they came out of hiding with the weapons they'd amassed, and they rounded up all the survivors of the war that were healthy enough to work. They imprisoned the workers. The lowest rung of the worker class was deemed disposable—canaries."

"Who decided who the canaries were?" I ask, dread filling my chest.

"Initially, it was the workers who decided. Then it became about your birth circumstances. Once a worker, always a worker. Once a canary, always a canary. I was born to a canary, destined to always be a canary."

"Tell me about when we flew over Perry," I say.

"The canaries scattered out of the Clean Zone. We've been exposed to the toxins our entire lives, for generations now, so we can survive that. The workers will have perished in the explosions, along with the elite." She squares her shoulders, as if steeling herself against criticism from me. There will be none.

My thoughts go to her whispered "oh" while we were flying over Perry, taking fire and dropping bombs.

"When we were flying over Perry," I take a deep breath, "you recognized someone on the ground, didn't you?"

Yaz is quiet for so long, I suspect she will not answer. Then, she says, "Yes."

I wait, giving her time to elaborate on her answer. When she does not, I move on to something else.

"The oppressed, the workers, then oppressed others, the canaries. Is that just human nature?" I wonder aloud. "In New America, the surviving white Christians, known as the Anointed, persecuted everyone else. Those who did not fit the bill became either Independents, Ferals, or Resistance Soldiers. Power switched back and forth several times between the Anointed and the Resistance, before the Peace Movement Warriors conquered both and brought peace to the land."

"What were your people?" she asks.

"Independents. We were often attacked by both the Ferals and the Anointed. During the Peace Movement most Independents supported the Peace Warriors."

"You were part of the Peace Movement?"

"I was freed from Feral captivity by a Peace Warrior. Naomi."

"Oh," she says. "I made you betray your savior."

"You did not make me do anything." I swipe away a tear before it can fall. "And maybe it is me who was betrayed."

We are quiet for just a few moments.

"What about Kai?" Yaz smiles, a soft expression that calms me. "Tell me how Kai fits into all of this." After a brief pause, she adds, "I guess Kai is to me how Naomi was to you."

I smile and nod. "I guess so. Kai's family was high up in the Resistance ranks. She was a scout for them until she met Rachel."

"That is what Kai meant, when she told me that she would have given up everything she'd ever known, if that was what it took to save Rachel?" Yaz asks.

"Yes. Kai had to fight against so many different factions of people to finally be able to be with Rachel. If anyone can relate to us it would be her."

"So, now with the Peace Movement, everyone lives free?"

"All except those unwilling to live peacefully," I answer.

"Wow."

"It did not come about without a lot of blood being shed."

"But still, it did come about."

The awe in Yaz's voice makes me feel both proud of what New America has accomplished under the Peace Warriors, and dismayed that Yaz never before knew freedom.

"How can you sound so impressed when those same people meant to reduce you to a lab sample?" I ask.

"They were afraid. They just meant to protect their own."

"That does not make it any better," I say.

"Maybe not for me," she says with a laugh and shrug. "But they saved your life and kept you safe."

I take a deep breath.

"There were times before Naomi and Karst that I wished I had died with my family and villagers."

"Every moment since I first saw you from that plane, I am thankful that you did not."

"The knife you use," I gesture toward it. "That was given to you? By Kai?"

She smiles. "Yes, Kai gave it to me. She—"

A noise in the brush stops our conversation. We exchange a smile when we see that it is a doe. She is near the sawgrass that I know now thanks to Yaz, that it is not actually a grass at all. My lips part to speak, wanting to warn the doe of the serrated edges, but Yaz places a finger upon my lips to hush me.

The doe pulls up the rough, sharp sawgrass leaf and drops it to the ground before leaning down to eat the very bottom.

We smile at each other and patiently wait for the deer to eat her fill. As soon as she has moved along, we go to the clump of plants.

Yaz takes care to hold the bundle of blades in a way to ensure her hand will not run against the teeth, injuring her. We examine the bottom and see there is a white portion inside. This is smooth to the touch. When we try it, we are pleasantly surprised by the sweet taste.

"I can't believe I did not know this about sawgrass," Yaz says in wonderment.

I smile at my lover, all the more perfect for not knowing everything. Yaz knows a lot about many plants, but there are some she is not familiar with. Of course, I still only know kudzu, and well, sawgrass now. We decide it will be helpful to watch what the animals eat, and follow suit when we can.

We are foraging for the weeds Yaz knows we can eat when she stops short. Her smile is big, so big that it sends a jolt of passion through me.

I clear my throat, try to find my voice. "What is it?"

"Soap lily."

"Soap lily?" I stare at the plant with the wavy leaves and white flowers. I bend to the blossom and am surprised that it doesn't have a strong, pleasant scent.

"Yes. It is used to make soap. We can bathe with it."

"We can?" I ask, excitement making me jittery. "Can you use this plant to make us some soap now?"

She falls to her knees and begins digging near the flowering plant. She has dug down about a foot when she lets out a little whoop.

"What? What is it?"

"The bulb." She shows me a fist-sized, brown blob.

"With that you can make soap?"

My question is met with a broad, bright smile. She nods her head slowly and I rush to her to give her a hug.

Why is it that something as simple as soap makes me feel so hopeful?

Yaz shows me how she strips away the brown fibers covering the bulb. She places them in a neat pile off to the side. "I will get enough eventually to make a brush out of the fibers."

I nod, in awe of this side of Yaz, so knowledgeable, so strong.

"In time we will dig up some more, making sure we have a nice supply on hand, just in case we end up somewhere without, or the plant goes dormant and it becomes harder to find."

I nod, only half listening, happy to be so close to a bath with soap.

"The extra we dig up," she adds, "won't be as good as the fresh bulbs, but we will be glad for it if we are otherwise without."

†

I am giddy with excitement as she presents the soap to me. The layers of the plant's white, fleshy bulb have very little smell, and I cannot believe I will be able to use them to bathe. I want to wash with her, to use my soaped hands to caress every inch of her magnificent body.

"It doesn't smell nice like the soap you had at Karst," Yaz says. "But in our search for food, we can also search for something fragrant to mix it with for our next bath."

"I have some marigold in my medical bag," I say. "I've been thinking about applying some to my face and neck to help with the sun exposure."

"Save it for that, then." She runs a finger down the length of my nose. "You have sunburn here. Why don't I apply some marigold onto you when you're done bathing?"

I smile at the thought of her touching me, even if it's just my face and neck. "I would like that," I admit.

Yaz places several pieces of soap in my hand. "Start with this. If you need more, just say so. Put a little water in the palm of your hand with it, and rub both hands together."

"You could come in to show me," I say with a sly smile.

"I wish I could, love. One of us needs to stay on the bank to watch for predators."

I pout, but know she is right. Surviving an air battle and crash landing just to be eaten by an animal would be unsatisfactory, to say the very least.

"Go on, I will watch out for you," Yaz says. She absently pats the pipe she has belted around her waist.

I ease myself into the dark water until it comes up to the middle of my thighs. For a brief moment, I hold my breath while I think of Naomi in the toxic, foul-smelling river after we'd taken our leave of the Merrick clan.

I exhale slowly. This is not the Fire River. There is no strong chemical smell, no burning of my skin. I must not fear this water. I must not fear all that is unknown to me in this strange land.

I use my left hand to trickle some water onto the plant pieces in my right hand. When I rub my hands together and a thin white foam appears, I smile.

"Look," I say.

Yaz returns my smile. "Bathe, sweet girl," she reminds me.

I rub the lather over my arms, breasts, and belly. My skin tingles—not in a healing or sexual way—but with a light feeling of freshness. A bath has not felt this good since the first one I had at Karst, after weeks of living underground as a slave to the Merrick clan.

My attention is drawn back to the incredibly sexy woman on the bank of the river, looking around cautiously.

"Hey," I say as my soapy hands move between my legs. "I wish you were doing this for me."

I see her throat move as she swallows. "I do as well."

"Feels good," I add.

She shuffles her feet and I laugh.

A rustling to her left causes her head to jolt in that direction. I hold my breath until I see a deer tentatively approach the water's edge. When the animal lowers his head to drink, I can tell he keeps his eyes on me. I try to send out gentle energy even though my heart is still racing from the sudden appearance of the animal.

I slowly lower my body to rinse off the soap. The thought that it could have been a much less benign creature getting so close to us sobers me.

The deer drinks again, then backs away before turning to retreat.

I finish rinsing off, then stand guard while Yaz bathes. We are no longer playful, and stay on high alert.

After bathing, we decide to wash our clothing with the leftover soap. We are gentle with the worn fabric.

"You don't have any extra undergarments in your medical bag, do you?" Yaz teases.

"No, I do not. Perhaps we will have to do without," I tease back.

✝

My ankle is a little sore, but I keep knowledge of that from Yaz. Quickly though, I learn that I cannot hide things from her.

"Should you be doing—well *maintenance* for the lack of a better word—on your ankle? And shouldn't you be recharging?" Yaz asks on the third day we are in the east.

"It has been overcast both nights since we arrived here. In order for me to do energy work, I must be able to recharge from the stars."

She cocks her head and studies me. "You aren't still saving your energy for something, are you?"

I do not look at her. I do not want to admit that she is right. I am saving my energy in case Yaz is hurt in any way.

"If the night sky doesn't clear soon, we will need to go somewhere less cloudy," Yaz says.

"Perhaps it is just the season, or a temporary weather front." I do not want to move on yet. I like the abundance of plants here.

We continue to explore our new home, checking out the woods, the river, the sky. We have been walking for quite some time when Yaz stops abruptly and turns to face me. The look on her face leaves me breathless. I grab her, pulling her flush against me.

"I do not really understand this feeling," I admit.

"Does it feel as if you don't have me right this second, you are going to burst?" she asks.

"Yes, that, exactly." I duck my head, unsure of the thoughts swirling through my mind. "I love you, Yaz, but this does not feel like it is about love."

She places her finger beneath my chin and lifts my gaze to her. "That's called desire. It's okay if you feel strong want and need in and of itself."

"I feel desperate to make love," I say.

Her smile is brilliant. "Perhaps you are desperate to fuck?"

My breathing quickens. My entire body is on fire for her. "That is okay?"

"Yes, sweet, sweet Misha. It is more than okay."

With that we clutch at one another, yanking clothing aside, touching each other everywhere at once. Her hand disappears into my pants and her fingers brush against my wetness, then plunge inside me. She slams into me over and over and I struggle to get my hand down her pants as well.

I begin to stumble but she presses my back to a tree as she continues to slam into me. "Oh, Yaz, oh!"

My pleasure climbs higher still when my fingers slip inside of Yaz. She gasps and rocks her hips against me, movement I take as permission to go harder and deeper inside of her.

We are both gasping for air when Yaz whispers, "Your fingers—they are vibrating."

I still and try to pull away.

"No, please, don't stop touching me like that," Yaz begs, clutching at my wrist.

I peer into her eyes and see nothing but love and desire.

I resume my stroking of her, in and out, as does she, and within moments we are both climaxing together.

Yaz's voice is gentle, later, when she asks about my fingers vibrating.

"That has never happened before." I avert my eyes. "Or maybe it has. I think it happened the first night we were here. I was so preoccupied just now that if you had not mentioned it, I might not have even noticed."

"You've never noticed before when you've—you know, touched yourself?"

"Never," I say, my voice harsher than I meant it to be.

"Hey," Yaz whispers. "It's okay. It's me. You don't have to hide any part of you from me. Ever."

I look up now and lock my gaze onto hers, and I know her statement to be the truth.

†

The clouds have finally broken and I go to the clearing we have determined to be the best area to try to gather the stars' energy. It is only slightly higher in elevation from the surrounding area, but I will do what I can to make it work.

I sit down and rest my hands on my crossed legs. They are palm-side up and I take deep breaths as I concentrate on settling in to the night.

Concentration is mixed with frustration as I wait to feel the stars' energy wash upon me.

"Please," I whisper. "Suzanna? Suzanna, if you are out there, please help me."

Tears stream down my face and I am about to give up when I feel a slight tingle in the palms of my hands.

Warmth washes over me, and I know I am lifted up by Suzanna, and the entirety of the collective consciousness my grandmother taught me about.

"Thank you, Suzanna, and grandmother, and all of the healers out there working the collective energy."

The recharging is nothing like that experienced in Karst or Las Estrellas, but it is at least something, and for that I am ever so grateful.

When I return to Yaz she suggests we no longer sleep in shifts. I nod my agreement as I pull her against me and hold her tight, our bodies pressed together our entire lengths, and sleep washes over me almost instantly.

CHAPTER EIGHT

For several weeks we are at peace, gathering our food and making love under the stars as soon as I am finished recharging, or at least trying to recharge.

We work together to make two rough, but much needed, blankets out of a variety of fibers we pull from different plants. We place one over a bed of leaves to lie on, and the other we use to cover ourselves. The days are temperate here, but the nights can cool down, and it has helped to have the blankets for bedding.

I wear the wide-brimmed hat Yaz has woven for me in order to keep most of the sun off my face and neck. She has taught me how to weave with the palm fronds, and between the two of us, we have made four satchels that we use to carry the food and medicinal herbs we forage.

On a day that starts like any other, Yaz suggests we go into the grove of old orange trees that no longer produce viable fruit, to see what we can find.

We have just come out of the far side of the grove when Yaz reaches down to pull up a sweet-weed, and we hear a hiss. She withdraws her hand so quickly that her arm scrapes against a branch on the ground, drawing blood.

"What the hell was that?" she asks.

We both back away at the next hiss. She drops the woven satchel she carries and pulls the knife from her belt. My hand is on the pipe I have taken to strapping to my waist, but I do not draw it.

There is rustling in the leaves, then a large lizard, mouth opened and claws scratching the ground as it comes closer, appears from its hiding place.

Now, I do draw the pipe and hold it in front of me. The beast's teeth and claws are terrifying, and I am not certain I will find the courage to strike at it, but wield the pipe anyway. I glance at Yaz and know if she is in danger, I will not hesitate to protect her from the creature.

We back away until it retreats into its burrow, then we quickly and mindfully make our way through the grove to the other side and return to our camp.

I root around in the medical bag, then use a coneflower and witch hazel poultice on the cut marring Yaz's forearm.

"That could have been really bad. Do you think that thing is venomous?"

"I don't know, and I sure as hell don't want to find out. From now on, we stay on this side of the grove."

I nod. My heart still beats recklessly in my chest at the thought that something could have happened to my beloved.

She places a hand on each side of my face. "It's okay, sweetheart, we are safe now."

"What if it comes to our camp?" I ask.

"I kill it and we eat it," she says, only half joking. She shrugs. "We haven't seen any signs of it coming over here. Let's just assume if we stay on our side of the grove, it will stay on its side."

I hope her logic holds up, but know I will be more vigilant in the future.

I hold out my hands, gesturing for her arm.

"No, not now. You save your healing for something more important."

"Like my ankle?"

"You know what I mean. If the cut shows any signs of infection or not healing properly, then you can place your hands on it. Deal?"

I nod.

"Now, let's get back to some serious foraging. Okay?"

We are back to gathering, on our side of the grove, and with most of our attention, when Yaz grows excited.

"Look," she says, as she points to the bluish flowers standing about four inches tall.

"What is it?"

"Wild mint." She gives me a brilliant smile. "We can crush the leaves to add to the soap. You will love how fragrant it will be."

†

Later that night, I sit in the clearing some ten yards from our camp, knowing Yaz stands guard for me. The time I spend under the stars is not working as well now as it did in the beginning of our residing here. It has never been ideal here, and I do not know why, but it is getting less and less productive for me.

I do not say anything about this because we have plenty to eat here, and huge, hissing lizard aside, I feel as safe as I have ever felt.

When I go to her after, and we make love, I feel like a fraud for not telling her I am feeling weaker.

I open my eyes at the sensation of Yaz's fingers trailing up and down my arm. My gaze is met with a smile.

"Good morning, sweetheart. Will you sleep all day?" she teases.

"It is all your fault," I tease back. "You exhausted me last night."

She gives a kind smile and leans down to kiss the corner of my mouth. It hurts my heart to see doubt in her expression. I know I should tell her how tired I have become, but I cannot seem to be able to bring myself to do so.

"Shall we go to the river to bathe?" she asks.

We are walking side by side, holding hands, when we reach the edge of the field that leads to our favorite bathing spot. We pause to watch a doe feed on the multitude of flowers.

The hair on the back of my neck stands on end, causing me to turn to my left. I remove the hat that suddenly feels restrictive, clasping it in my hand tightly. There is a rustling of the tall grasses at the edge of the field, then I see an animal as big as the deer, but lower to the ground. I freeze when I see it is a large cat, an absolutely huge cat.

"Puma," Yaz whispers. "Don't run. Just stay very still."

I drop my hat and swallow my gasp as the big cat pounces on the doe. I close my eyes and concentrate on not hearing the desperate sounds of the dying deer.

Yaz gives my hand a warning squeeze, but other than that we do not move for several long moments. As the cat eviscerates the deer, Yaz takes a step backwards. I do the same, until we are back in the brush from which we had just come.

There is no doubt in my mind that we will not be bathing today, and that when we do decide the where and when, we will need to be on high alert.

I am shaking when I sit on the log next to our shelter. "I have read about the big cats. I have seen pictures. But—"

"But nothing can prepare you for actually seeing one in person."

"Yes," I whisper. "Do you think it lives around here?"

Yaz shrugs. "Hard to say. It could have come from quite a distance on its hunt. The pumas are very territorial. That appeared to be a young male."

"Young? As in not as big as it will get?" I swallow hard.

"He will probably still fill out a little." Yaz sits beside me on the log. "If he's been run out of a more dominant male's territory, he may be staying around."

"Oh, Goddess," I mutter.

"There is one thing to consider. The cat will hide the carcass after he eats his fill. We could steal a leg or some part for ourselves, get some protein into our diet."

I shake my head. "No. No way am I angering a cat that size by stealing from it."

"You're probably right. Besides, we'd have to cook it which would draw attention to us. We'd probably need to move along then."

133

I shiver and Yaz places an arm around my shoulder. "Where is your hat, I don't want you to sunburn."

"I dropped it. Near the big cat."

"Ah, I don't suppose you want to go back for it," she teases.

I shake my head. "No," I say, then decide to change the subject. "Should we gather some kudzu? There has not been any giant lizards or cats in that area."

Yaz laughs. "Yes, kudzu it is."

We are careful that day, and into the night, listening for any signs of the large cat coming our way. I have trouble concentrating while trying to recharge. This troubles me because with the addition of the big cat to our other worries, I need to keep up my strength.

†

Four nights later, we hear the far-off song of coywolves. Yaz calls them wolves. They are slightly more melodic than the coywolves I know. The song is coming from just southeast of us.

"I think we should move along now. There are too many predators here," Yaz says. "We should consider moving west or northwest, trying our luck in one of those directions."

I nod. I know she is a better judge of the animals in this strange land than I ever will be.

"Let's rest tonight. We can leave in the morning," Yaz says.

"Are we leaving with the idea that we are trying to get back to Karst, or are we just leaving to go somewhere safer?" I ask.

134

She is quiet for a long time before she holds my gaze and says, "We can do both. Let's concentrate on getting somewhere safer for now. We will keep our direction heading toward New America, until that time we decide that isn't our ultimate goal."

"I like that plan," I say.

We settle into one another's arms, too early for sleep, too apprehensive about tomorrow's journey for being amorous.

"Will you testify?" I ask.

"Testify?"

"Tell me more about the hold the elite had on the workers and canaries," I say.

"You mean how they controlled us?"

"Yes. What was the population ratio? Did they outnumber you? If you could go out into the contaminated area, and they would not go, what kept you from just running away?"

Yaz has paled and I am afraid I have pushed her too far about this.

"Every now and then a canary would decide to leave Perry. I think the elite were afraid to let anyone go, at least permanently, in case they would be gathering elsewhere and planning to take over Perry."

"What did the elite do when someone left?"

"They would send another canary after them. If they brought the runaway back, or brought back proof of their death, they would be rewarded."

I stare at her. I do not want to know what proof there could be, but let my eyes ask anyway.

"An organ, or hand, or eyes," she says, her voice low and raspy.

I am sickened at these details and that I pushed Yaz to give them to me.

"The elite would ring the bell, signaling the return of the one sent on the hunt. The canary would then be incorporated into life on the inside, allowed to serve them from the safety of the bunker."

I cannot deny the sorrow I see on her face. "I am sorry."

"Did you make me a canary?"

"No." I know this conversation; it mirrors the one we had in the cockpit the day Yaz fell out of the sky and into my life. "So, I have nothing to be sorry for."

"That's right."

"Well, I hate that life was hard for you before we met. But I am so happy to have the person you are now."

CHAPTER NINE

We leave at first light, heading north-northwest. As we walk, there is a pleasant soreness in my legs and back, a testament to our last night in our first eastern settlement turning amorous after all.

My feet register the difference in the terrain before my mind does, the earth grows firmer as we walk, becoming less spongy.

"I think we are going up in altitude," Yaz comments.

I nod my agreement, then my attention goes to a flurry of blue in the brush. The bird makes me think of Naomi, which is odd, because even if she is like many things in wildlife, a soft blue bird is not one of them. I note the vibrant blue of its head, nape, wings, and tail, all in contrast to the grayish underparts. It is a scrub jay. I am not certain how I know this, if I read about it in one of Camryn's or Karst's many books, or if I have dreamt of it.

"A bird?"

"Yes, a bird." I smile at the thoughts of Naomi it conjures for me. I hope she is doing well, and has forgiven me for leaving as I did.

As we walk, both the barren, old citrus trees, and the scraggly cypress trees, give way to pine trees that increase in girth and height as we walk, until they are towering over us.

"The kudzu is thinning. We should probably harvest as much as we can carry, just in case it dwindles further as we advance."

I agree this is the right move.

We fill the satchels we made from the pond fronds, then shove some into my medical bag.

"Look here," Yaz says. "Sweet onion. Let's take some of this with us as well."

We harvest much of this as well.

Yaz takes a deep breath. "You smell that?"

She runs ahead and I rush to keep up with her. Around the bend of trees there are smaller trees, intermittent with vines of white flowers.

"What is this?" I ask as I come to a halt beside her.

"It's suckle."

"Suckle?"

"Yes." She gives me a brilliant smile. "Watch this."

Yaz pulls the inner part out from the petals of the flower. "Stick out your tongue."

I do not hesitate in doing as she requests. I can see a drop of liquid as she brings it to my mouth and dabs it against my tongue. The sweetness of the nectar makes me smile.

"It's good, isn't it?" she asks.

She shows me again how she pulls the nectar out, then we both spend several minutes enjoying as we feed each other the sweet treat.

A few hours later, we make camp for the night. I sit under the stars and know within moments that it will not be a night of recharging.

I go back to Yaz's side and she frowns. "Did you give it enough time?"

I nod as I climb into the rough bedding beside her. "I will gain more from being in your arms this night than being under the stars."

"If you're certain."

I poke her in the side. "Do you not want to have my body tonight?"

She pulls me flush against her. Her mouth finds mine and she kisses me long and deep. A moan leaves me.

"Of course, I want your body tonight," she says into my neck.

I reach for her and when my hands vibrate, I do not pull away, but embrace the effect they have on Yaz.

†

We take our time awaking the next morning, packing up, and setting out several hours after first light. A few hours into our trek, we can make out the crumbling remnants of a road and follow it around the stands of huge pine trees.

When we round a bend in the trees, we both stop abruptly and gawk. We can see the vast wasteland of what appears to have been row after row of houses along the sides of smaller trails leading off the crumbling road.

"I wonder what town or city this once was," I say.

"I don't know. It could be any of the eastern cities from before the war."

Along one long stretch of road that is quite straight, we are amazed by the remains of concrete that lead perpendicular from the road and end in the crumbling walls of buildings positioned quite close together. Along the sides of the roads are small, flowering trees.

Yaz studies the pink blooms closely, pinching and sniffing the leaves and flowers.

"I bet these were just for show."

"You think so?" I ask.

"I wonder why people would bother with trees that didn't provide food for them or animals," she says.

"That was not unusual before the war." I remember reading one of the many books in the library at Karst, many of which were donated by Camryn, about ornamental plantings.

She shrugs. "They were odd back then, weren't they?"

I laugh. "They would probably say that about us if they were to meet us here and now."

Her laughter joins mine and we clasp hands as we walk on, following the remnants of the road, until the density and vastness of the rubble grows.

At the same time, we stop and stare. Rising from the rubble is a gold dome.

"Whoa," Yaz says. "What the heck is that?"

I shake my head, unsure what it could be. It had to have been at least seventy or eighty feet across. I see movement near my feet in my peripheral vision and step back when the largest rat I've ever seen runs within inches of my feet.

All of a sudden, the dome isn't the most interesting thing I've seen amidst all the rubble.

"A rat? It's a huge rat," I stammer as I stare at its round body and thick, hairless tail.

"That's *rats,* as in plural," Yaz says as she gestures to our left. "And a lot of them."

Skirting the edges of the gold dome, we head away from where the largest population of the huge rats appears to be. I cannot shake the feeling that hundreds of small, dark eyes are following our every move.

Soon, we realize that we need not have worried about a lack of kudzu, as this is one of the few things that appears to grow within this city.

We travel for a few hours, until the gold dome is no longer visible in the distance. Without speaking of it, our eyes have been downcast, as if watching for a return of the oversized rodents.

When we walk along the battered remains of a stone wall that runs for hundreds of yards, we find a spiraling of vines going up and down the length of it.

"Pole beans," Yaz says, her voice rising in excitement. "We can eat these raw, but if we get a fire going to cook them, you will love how they taste."

I am growing excited about the possibilities that exist in this city.

"I'm starving. Can we just eat some raw for now?" I ask as my stomach lets out a rumble.

"Of course." Yaz brushes the dust and dirt from them before tilting the canteen an inch from them to pour a little of our water over them to clean off the rest of the debris. "This will be a welcome change from kudzu."

We sit along a lower wall, one that runs for about 50 feet, perpendicular to the wall that supports the bean vines. While eating, we are aware of a bear, who is admittedly very

141

cautious and curious about us. The animal goes in a big arc around us, watching, listening. Its right ear has a large tear in it that appears to have healed, as there is no noticeable blood, just what appears to be jagged scarring.

"I think he is hungry," I whisper.

"As long as he doesn't think we are his next meal." Yaz's gaze rests upon the large, black beast. "I don't believe he would try to eat us, but he may attack if he feels threatened by us."

"Then I guess we must not make him feel threatened," I say with a smile.

"Oh, my love, if it were always as easy as that." She looks away, as if embarrassed by her sudden seriousness.

†

Yaz has used sheets of pliable metal that litter the ground to form one side and a roof that attach to the corner where the highest stretch of wall meets another. The remaining wall of our new home is created by branches that can easily be parted for us to come and go from the structure.

Our bear has created a den of sorts by piling up rubble on three sides, just on the other side of the rectangle from our home. Yaz believes that his purposeful closeness is a sign that he wishes to live peacefully with us.

Every day, we harvest from one end of the vine-wall while the bear eats from the other. After a week of living as such, the bear deposits a headless rat—one of what we now call mega-rats—quite close to our side of the shared homestead.

"I think he gives it to us as a gift," Yaz says.

"If we do not accept, do you think he will become enraged and harm us?"

Yaz shrugs.

"You want to accept, don't you?" I ask.

She slowly nods her head. "If I can get a fire started, then yes, I would like to cook and eat it. My body feels in need of some animal protein."

"Okay."

"Yes? You won't be disappointed in me for doing so?"

"I could never be disappointed in you for doing what your body needs." I kiss the corner of her mouth. "You won't be disappointed in me for not joining you?"

"Never, my love." She lightly kisses my forehead. "Help me gather some dry kindling?"

We set out to gather dried leaves, the smallest of twigs for kindling, then larger twigs, and branches.

Yaz carefully builds two tinder-nests as I place rocks in a circle around the fire site. I hand her the flint and steel set before sitting back slightly to give her some space. She strikes the flint against the piece of steel expertly until a spark hits the dry tinder.

I smile as the smoke thickens and she blows, building the spark into a flame. I hand her the twigs, the smallest first, building up to the largest, until the fire is hot and shooting up. She uses a piece of kindling to light the second tinder-nest from the first.

I bring over some pole beans for one of the fires, and she walks to retrieve the rat for the other. As she is picking up the rat, the bear stands and watches her closely.

I hold my breath the entire time she is coming back to our camp. When she is within hearing she asks, "Is he still watching?"

"Yes, but he has settled back down. He sits against the wall."

She doesn't look to the bear until she has rejoined me and sits beside me, now facing in the direction of the bear's den.

I rummage in my medical bag and retrieve some dried rosemary. "Would you like to season it?"

She gives me a brilliant smile and nods before pulling her knife from its sheath at her waist and prepping the meat. When she sets the fur to the side and places the flesh upon a spit over the fire, I must admit the cooked flesh of the animal smells good.

When she sprinkles the dried rosemary over it, the smell is amazing.

"Don't be too proud to change your mind," Yaz says.

My mouth is watering, and not from the admittedly delicious, cooked pole beans.

"Maybe I should eat just a few bites of the animal?" I say, unsure of myself.

She breaks a piece free from the side and hands it to me. I decide that I didn't kill it, I didn't ask the bear to kill it, and I would hate for the bear to think one of us was ungrateful, so I take the offering and nibble small bites from it.

My bites quicken until Yaz is giving me more and we have fully consumed the animal.

"How do we thank our furry friend?" I ask after the meal has been completed.

"I don't think we need to do more than eat the gift," she responds. She then sighs and adds, "Even though it's not cold, the fire feels nice."

I nod. "Can we keep it going?"

"I'm not sure that's smart." Yaz glances around. "We probably shouldn't risk drawing the attention of any predators that might be closer than we know."

A shiver runs through me.

"No," I say. "We should not take any chances."

†

We sit at the fire, eating the third animal to be gifted to us from the bear in as many weeks, when we hear the song of the wolves drifting to us on the evening breeze.

The bear stands and puts his nose to the air. He paces for a few minutes, looks to us, then settles back down.

"They are coming closer," Yaz says.

We finish the meal and Yaz extinguishes the fire.

"Will you recharge tonight?" she asks.

"Yes, I will try." My fingers tingle and I am not sure if that is a sign of what is to come, or if it is wishful thinking on my part.

"Let's stick to our routine—you sit upon the highest part of the wall, and I will keep watch."

The wall is just wide enough for me to sit cross-legged upon it. I place my opened hands palm-up on my lap and steady my breathing.

The hum in my chest is nothing like what I was accustomed to in New America, but it is there and I welcome it.

"Thank you," I whisper to the goddess, the collective consciousness, to Suzanna, and anyone else who may be listening and assisting on this night under the stars.

My body tingles and grows slightly warm.

"Please guide me to help and to heal," I whisper. "Make me worthy of the gift you've bestowed upon me."

I sit for a few more minutes, but when the tingling stops and I grow cool sitting on the wall, I climb down and return to my beloved.

That night, after we make love, Yaz whispers into the night air, "We should think about moving on."

"This city has been good to us, but yes, we should move on." I lie awake for a long time, wondering if we will find a home as nice as this city has been. "I will miss our pet," I say, thinking of the bear.

"I will too."

†

We have decided to bring minimum kudzu with us, to maximize the amount of pole beans we can carry. Yaz believes them to be better nutritionally and fears once we leave this location, we will not find them again.

Yaz has strapped all but one of the satchels to her back. I carry the remaining one with the medical bag. It has been growing progressively heavier with the weight of all the herbs I have found in this fertile world.

I have fallen slightly behind Yaz, and am distracted to the point of almost missing the bright red berries growing in thick brambles a short distance off of our path.

"Look," I call out. "Red—well—blackberries."

Yaz's smile brings out a big one from me.

"They are raspberries," Yaz finally says.

"We can eat them?"

"Oh, yes."

I gently pluck a small berry and place it in my mouth. It is sweet and tart and I quickly pick and shove a second one into my mouth.

I am almost speechless but finally mutter, "This is the best thing I've ever tasted. I love these raspberries."

Yaz has joined me in eating the berries. "Don't overdo it," she warns. "As with any new food, you want to be certain it agrees with you before consuming too much."

I know she is correct, so I stop my gorging.

Her smile is so playful that I cannot help but kiss her, tasting the berries on her lips as I am sure she tastes them upon mine.

We agree they are too delicate to carry with us in large quantities, so we fill the small jar in the medical bag that once housed the rosemary that we have consumed. This will be a delicacy for later, perhaps to celebrate our next homestead.

As we continue to walk, the pull of the muscles in the backs of my legs and buttocks clues me that the elevation continues to increase.

We do not know the names of the various trees, most of them as big as the pines. There are nuts high up, where Yaz climbs to reach them.

As she is climbing, I see a bear circling in a pacing manner. I am convinced, based on its size, proximity, and the rough tear of its ear, that it is the same bear from the city. Has it been following us? If so, is it meaning to stalk us, or merely also fleeing the song of the wolves?

Yaz comes down from the tree, the satchel overflowing with tree nuts.

"We have company," she says, gesturing toward the bear, which has now stopped pacing and sits under a tree, watching us.

"What should we do?" I ask.

"Give him a gift," she answers, gesturing toward the tree nuts. "I will bring some to him and we can see how he responds, and whether it is problematic."

She covers half the distance that separates us from where the bear now sits, and leaves a pile of nuts there. I watch carefully when she turns her back to the animal and starts to walk toward me.

The bear goes to the pile of nuts and stands on his hind legs over it. He nods his head up and down a few times, then goes onto all fours, and begins to crack open and then consume the nuts.

Yaz and I exchange a smile.

Yaz nods at the sack of nuts. "Do you think we can get the bear to crack these for us?" she teases.

I smile at her. "Perhaps we should just find a large rock to smash them upon."

"Perhaps," she says, giving me a quick kiss before pulling away.

"Shall we continue?" I ask.

She nods and with a quick glance back to the bear, we are once again moving.

To the south of us, the nut trees stretch as far as I can see. We decide to keep to the edge of the trees, on the path that looks like an old road, and we continue to walk to the northwest.

We have been following the edge of the trees for several days when our course veers slightly to the north. There is a large swath of land to our left that has fewer trees than the forest we skirt around, but these trees all have rusted metal frames in them.

I crane my neck to look upward, gazing from side to side, when I realize Yaz does the same.

"It's like they are car trees," Yaz says.

"Yes." Now I see they are cars, with the tires mostly rotted off. For every ten or so regular trees, there is a tree holding a car up to the sky. "It's as if all of these cars were parked together, left for years, and the trees grew up around them."

"Why would all the cars be together?" Yaz wonders aloud.

I just shrug and we continue walking, glancing every now and then at the car-forest, and occasionally stating again how bizarre it all looks.

When we come around a bend in the path, we find the oddest ruins stretched out before us, odder even then a forest full of suspended cars.

"What the hell?" Yaz says.

My mouth falls open but no words come. Like so much else that I have seen since leaving New America, I have no reference for the sprawling mass of twisted metal that rises here and there, from rubble that is also unlike anything else I've ever seen.

My eyes rest on a big, metal wheel growing up from one stand of trees. My mouth closes, finally, and I grab Yaz's hand.

"Seriously, what the hell?" Yaz says.

CHAPTER TEN

An uneven, crumbling walkway leads up to rusted gates that are adorned with poles, the tops of which have remnants of cloth that suggest flags. On either side of the large metal gate sits two huge pillars crumbling, and standing without benefit of what I assume should be a wall extending from either side.

An outline of a large "J" hangs over the gate and I wonder what the blank area to the right of it once spelled.

Although we could walk around the gate, Yaz goes to it and tugs. It doesn't budge. She tugs again and it breaks free. She jumps back to keep it from falling on her. The sound it makes when it hits the walkway bounces around and echoes relentlessly.

I look around, as if expecting people to come running at the noise.

A crow calls out beyond us.

Yaz steps over the downed gate and I follow her.

"After you, my lady," Yaz says with a crooked grin.

"Thank you, darling," I respond with some weird, made-up accent of which I cannot explain the desire to use. "Please do not forget to secure it behind us."

She laughs and I feel desire course through me at the melodious sound. My lust comes under control as soon as I think of all the dangers that could be awaiting us inside this curious place.

There is a huge structure of metal pipes or something similar looming in front of us. They crisscross each other and go hundreds of feet into the air.

Yaz cocks her head to see from different angles and the curious look on her face is adorable.

We walk closer to the strange ruins and my mouth continues to gape at the double twisting and turning tracks of metal rail. They run perfectly parallel to one another as they climb high in the air, just to twist and come back around. At places, trees grow between the tracks, while at others, vines wrap around them before reaching to the opposite side.

"What in the world?" I ask.

We exchange a look, then begin to walk along the rusted metal tracks where it dips closer to the ground. She reaches out a hand to touch it. I do the same.

I pull my fingertips away and they are brownish-red with rusty dust.

"It's almost as if the entire reason for this structure is to hold up these tracks," Yaz says, continuing to cock her head from side to side as she studies the metal network. "This must be a foundation for the tracks."

When the tracks curve up to meet the sky and treetops, we walk below them, looking up and following its path with our eyes. The tracks loop in the air, then comes back down. It is at this point, where it comes closer to the ground, that something rests on the tracks.

"A train?" I whisper as we come upon the series of connected cars, the front adorned with a faded image of some beast, all flaring nostrils, teeth, and flashing eyes.

We walk farther alongside then under the twisting tracks, craning our necks to better see. Every now and then a crow calls out, no doubt warning the others of us interlopers.

"Wow," Yaz says. "What is this?"

I can only shrug. I've seen pictures of passenger trains that went from one location to another, but I've never seen train tracks that rose and fell, banked left and right, and even looped far above the ground.

When we stop and look around again, I can better see the large metal wheel that first drew my attention. I can see now that it has things resembling swinging seats dangling every so often from its metal, spoke-like structure. It looks like a huge wheel, similar to, but so much larger than, the ones I've seen on Tech City's motorbikes.

"Look over there," Yaz says, her voice a near whisper. "That building is almost perfectly intact."

It looks old, older than anything in New America for sure. I've never seen a building that had all its walls and its roof that was from before the war and sickness. "It is from the old world, isn't it?"

"I think so," she answers.

"I would hate to run into people who aren't expecting us, nor wanting our company." Visions of the Merricks surrounding me, staring at me, laughing as they made suggestive comments, slam into my memory and I begin to shake. "We should leave."

Yaz stares at me, obviously not understanding my unease. "Why would we leave? We could have shelter and maybe supplies under that roof."

"What if someone is already partaking of its shelter and supplies?"

"Oh," Yaz says, looking around. "Should we watch it for a while first?"

"From where?"

"Behind the train?" she ventures.

"Okay." I don't think the train will offer us much cover, but I also don't think our presence will have been unnoticed if there are people here. "We could watch from there for a while."

We return to the train and study its seating on the inside. Now that we know it's there, we can easily see the building from our vantage point. The crow that has been screaming notice of our arrival has quieted and comes closer.

"Are we the only people here?" Yaz asks it. "Is it safe for us to stay?"

"If that bird answers you, I am going to have a heart attack."

Yaz chuckles. "So will I."

We have been waiting for a few hours without any sign of others when the crow grows excited and begins screaming a warning. I grab Yaz's arm and wait for her to signal if we need to run or hide.

A second crow has joined in the ruckus and we hear something or someone coming loudly through the brush between us and the building.

"Ours?" Yaz asks when a bear comes into view.

I see the scarred ear and recognize our bear's gait. "Yes," I say with a smile. "Ours."

The bear leans into a tree about fifty feet from us and uses the rough bark to scratch his back before sitting against it.

The crows carry on for only a few moments longer, then start to settle.

"Well, Bear, it's about time you caught up," Yaz says to the animal.

He grunts a response and we both laugh.

"Well, if there are unwelcoming people here, at least there are three of us now," I say.

"I would like to look closer at the building. If you'd like to wait here with the bear, that is fine," Yaz says.

"Oh no, you are not going anywhere without me." I look over to the animal. "No offense, Bear. I just want to stay with my person."

Yaz laughs, then grabs my hand to pull me along.

We slowly approach the building. I can feel Bear's gaze on us as we do. He keeps his distance but is focused on us just the same.

"The dirt around this door isn't disturbed. And see the spider webs? This door hasn't been opened in a long, long time." She releases my hand as she gestures at the webs.

"I could have done without mention of the spiders," I say.

"I'll protect you," Yaz says, taking my hand again and giving it a little squeeze.

"I know."

Yaz uses a downed limb to pry open the door at the side of the large building. She steps inside, peering around, then offers me her hand. I am in still in awe, every single day, of the way her hand feels in mine, like they were meant to go together.

It takes a few minutes for my eyes to adjust to the darkness inside. There are a few windows high up on the tall walls that let in just a little light.

The building smells moldy, but in a subdued way. Huge metal racks line the walls and create rows within the structure. Yaz turns and gives me a brilliant smile. Then she's off, walking along the rows, eyes taking it all in, still grasping my hand as I follow close behind her.

Cardboard boxes line the shelves where Yaz finally stops. They are disintegrating around their contents, showing the brightly colored fabrics inside.

Yaz pulls a piece out and holds it up. It is a long-sleeved shirt with two large front pockets, one over each side of the chest, with black words embroidered on the right breast pocket. There are buttons going up the entire length of the garment.

"Wow," Yaz says. "Look at all these shirts."

She continues to pull them out, one at a time.

I take one from her and hold it up in the dim light. "Jungle Man—Mania," I say, smiling. "Jungle Mania. I've read about jungles." I look at Yaz and she smiles.

"I love how you've read about so many things. Maybe we'll find books in here?" her voice is hopeful. "Then you can teach me to read."

I embrace her. "I would just love that!"

When I release her, I look around and am amazed by how everything inside the structure has held up so well considering the outside is all rot and rust.

She holds up a yellow shirt, pressing it against her torso. "What do you think?"

"I like it." And I do. The color perfectly complements her dark skin and black hair. I cannot wait to see it on her. And then to take it off, I muse.

She pulls out a blue one next. "This would look good on you."

I hold it up to me. I could fit three of me in it. "Is there a smaller one?"

She rummages through two boxes before finding one that will fit me better. This one is in green.

"Put it on," she says, practically dancing in front of me.

We both pull off our old, threadbare shirts. I finger the large pockets on the front of her shirt and think about how handy they would be.

"The shirt matches the green of your gorgeous eyes," Yaz says in a whisper.

I lean closer to her, kiss her slightly pointed chin, her small nose, her sharp cheek bones. For someone who is so strong and brave, her facial features are fine, delicate even.

She moves to kiss my mouth. I only let her lips graze mine. "We should keep looking around the place," I say.

We continue our search and come up with tan, pocketed pants, and dark-brown knee-high boots. Boxes and boxes of shirts, pants, and boots. We could clothe an entire village with what we've found.

It takes a while, but we both find pants and boots that fit.

After changing into my new pants, I reach into my old pants pocket and pull out the beaded bracelet. Yaz sees this and gives me an inquisitive look. I tell her the story of the bracelet, how it was made by Kai years earlier, but served as a token of my friendship with Jackson. We hold one another while we cry, then I pull away.

"We are done shedding tears for this loss," I say. When she doesn't respond, I add, "Tell me you are with me in this, that we will truly put the sadness of the past behind us."

She nods.

"I want to only remember the good times with Jackson and Suzanna," I say.

We continue to search the building, and stop short when we see five horses lined up against a wall. They are not real, of course, and are painted in strange patterns. This makes me smile, for no other reason than they are painted funny colors.

Yaz taps on the head of one and then leans closer to inspect it.

"I wonder what this is made of, it's not wood or metal."

I, too, reach out to touch it. I run my fingers along the horse's mane, as if petting it.

"I don't know, but I like this. These horses make me want to smile."

Yaz kisses the top of my head before leading me away. At my disapproving groan, she says, "We can come back to them, I promise."

There are stacks upon stacks of glossy paper folded into thirds, and encased in a plastic wrapping that has undoubtedly protected them from time. I pull one out, then look to see that they are all the same. Hundreds or thousands of these thick papers telling us all about Jungle Mania.

"It says here that the train is called a roller coaster," I say.

"Show me?" Yaz asks as she looks over my shoulder.

I point to each word and read it out loud. The smile on her face makes me continue, until I've read the entire brochure to her. We now know about the horses from the carrousel, the Ferris wheel, roller coasters, the flume, and so many other "rides."

"So, this coaster—this roller coaster—is held up by the network of metal tube things. The whole thing really is a foundation for this ride. Wow." She shakes her head as if trying to make the pieces of the puzzle of Jungle Mania fall into place.

A noise from the doorway puts us on edge.

"It's Bear," I say. "Sounds as if he's lying just outside the door."

"Well, we can rest peacefully knowing we are well guarded," Yaz adds.

We spend the night inside, on a bed of clothing, making love before falling to sleep.

†

The next morning, Bear is not at the door when we open it. Yaz sticks her head out and looks around, for what I am uncertain.

"Was there an invasion during the night?" I ask, only half teasing.

"No, and it appears Bear really likes rubbing his back against that tree."

I slip my head through the door and see Bear doing just that.

"We should have a meal, then look around."

"What do you desire today?" I ask. "We have kudzu, pole beans, more kudzu, nuts, and still more kudzu."

"How about some kudzu. Do we have kudzu?" she asks, teasingly.

I laugh. "Oh, and we have a small number of raspberries. Shall we eat them as well, before they go bad?"

"Perfect." She nods toward one of the satchels. "We won't cook yet since we don't know for sure if we are alone and don't want the fire to draw attention to us."

I nod, then pick through the kudzu to find the smallest, most tender leaves since we will be eating them raw this morning.

After we finish our simple meal, we pack our satchels onto our backs, just in case something happens and we must run for cover away from our new building. We walk around the perimeter of the large roller coaster foundation until we get to the side opposite. Here we find vines of pole beans and suckle weaving their way up the foundation and around the parallel steel tracks.

"I'm so glad to know this is here," Yaz says.

"Shall we finish our supply and harvest from here once we deplete it?" I ask.

She nods her head. "We will keep a watch to make sure no other creatures take the whole crop."

We find the remains of the carousel, barely recognizable from its photograph in the brochure, only one partial horse still attached to a pole that runs from floor to ceiling on the round platform.

Yaz studies the horse. Where the back ends there are stiff fibers sticking out haphazardly. "Interesting," she mumbles.

I nod in agreement. The outside is so smooth I never would have guessed that it was made of these hard fibers all woven together.

We have walked the perimeter of our new home and find ourselves back near the warehouse structure and the north side of the roller coaster.

Yaz starts to climb the coaster's foundation and I keep my eyes on her, hoping she is safe on the network of crisscrossing metal poles.

"Be careful, love," I call up to her.

She waves down at me and my heart soars with the joy etched on her face as she climbs higher and higher. I take my eyes off her just long enough to see that Bear is also watching her with interest.

Yaz waves more frantically at me. "Come on up!"

I place one hand on the piece at knee-level to me, but then get nervous and pull away.

"I can see everything from up here," Yaz calls to me.

I gingerly place one hand and one foot on places about twelve inches from each other and begin to climb. My feet slip slightly from the incline of each "step," but soon I learn to go with it. By the time I have gotten to the top and stand next to Yaz, my heart is pounding in exhilaration.

"I can see forever from up here," I say, breathlessly. "Wow."

I get a little dizzy when I look down, but the sensation goes away immediately, and it's just like sitting on the ledge outside the upper entrance to Karst.

"I bet you can recharge well up here," Yaz says, her voice full of hope.

"Yes, on a clear night, I bet I can do just that." I smile at my love, lean closer to kiss her cheek. "I want to try tonight if the weather is clear."

She nods at me.

"Look," I say, as I point to the east at a wetland with strange birds swimming and resting along its banks. "What are they."

"Ducks?" Yaz asks.

"Oh, yes, I see now." I remember the book of birds Camryn left with me at Karst. I think of my friend, Naomi's lover, and smile. The woman of many languages was always so kind to me.

I glance at my hands and see they are covered in a thin coating of powdery rust particles.

"Shall we get down and go look closer at the water? Perhaps we can gather a small number of duck eggs if they are nesting," Yaz says.

We scramble down, alternating between laughing and being serious when we become unsure of our footing or handholds.

Halfway down I have an image of Naomi and Radha climbing the side of a sheer cliff. Naomi is the best climber in all of New America, if you ask Camryn and their daughter, Radha. But Naomi is quick to tell everyone that Radha is even better than she was at the same age.

The image is bittersweet. In one way, it tells me they are happy and healthy, still climbing together, but in another it makes me homesick for my surrogate family.

I shake the feelings away and hit the ground mere seconds after Yaz.

"I win," she says, pulling me into an embrace.

"I didn't realize we were racing." I lean into her and kiss her lightly on the lips. When she means to pull me tighter to her, I pull away. "Oh no, you don't. Let's go explore the wetland before it gets dark."

When we make our way beyond the interior of Jungle Mania, we find that the ducks do not appear to be nesting, but hold out hope that maybe one day we can gather a few eggs to subsidize our protein intake.

"Cattails," Yaz says, her voice rising in excitement.

The ducks nearest to us half-fly and half-run on the water to put some distance between us and them.

"Cattails? Are they edible?"

"Yes, and yes," Yaz says with a chuckle.

She leads me closer to one.

"See this top part?" She points at a thin, yellow-dusted protrusion atop an almost fuzzy, brown oblong portion that looks like a small log. "This is good protein. We can mix the pollen in with our other food."

"And this part?" I point to the brown part.

"We can roast that. And we can add the leaves to our kudzu for some variety."

I am so excited that we have another source of protein. Maybe we won't need to disturb the ducks to harvest some eggs when that time comes.

"Let us take a little back with us now. We will have a small fire tonight to roast the cattail flowers. If you like the way they taste, we can come back tomorrow for some more."

I nod my head.

†

It appears that I very much like the brown flower part of the cattail. I am pleased that we will return to the wetland tomorrow to harvest some more.

When the meal is completed and the fire is extinguished, I prepare to try the new height available to me to recharge.

I climb to the top of the tracks' foundational structure and settle in. The night is clearing and, hopefully, I will get enough exposure to the stars to help my waning energy.

It takes a little time for me to get comfortable. The feeling of the metal tubes under my buttocks is still quite foreign to me. But soon I get used to the sensation, and when I concentrate on the sky, I am so very glad to have come up here to be closer to the stars.

I can feel goose flesh growing on my arms. It is much cooler up here than down below, now that the sun has set.

The stars are not as bright as what I know from New America, but they are better than I've found thus far in the strange land east of home.

I sense Suzanna is near. I wait to see if she will speak. She does not.

When my torso tingles, then grows warm, I almost miss the beginning of the process. I close my eyes and feel the surge of energy. The hum begins deep in my chest, and I know I will be at least somewhat successful recharging tonight. The vibration radiates outward, tickling down my arms as I spread them out to my side.

The corners of my mouth turn up in a smile, then my lips open in that familiar, silent scream of wonder at the regeneration every cell in my body undergoes.

Once the surge of energy through me levels off, I close my eyes again and listen. Even if the Universe doesn't choose to speak to me tonight, even if the voice of the collective consciousness is quiet tonight, this night will help me recover some of my internal strength, and for that I am oh so grateful.

I no longer feel Suzanna's presence.

The wind has picked up and, unchecked, bites into my ears. It is only a few more minutes before I am confident that I am done for the night and begin to climb down the crisscrossing pieces of the coaster's foundation.

Yaz meets me at the bottom and holds open her arms. I step into her embrace.

"The stars were of benefit tonight," I say.

She squeezes me tighter. "Very, very, good," she mumbles into my neck.

Yaz pulls back and brings her hands to my ears. "So cold," she says. "Your pretty little ears are so cold."

"It's windier and chillier up there now that the sun is gone." I sink into the warming of my ears in her hands.

We clasp hands and go to the door to the warehouse. We take turns going around to the back to relieve ourselves, then go inside.

We settle on our new bedding and the sounds outside tell us we will have another night of Bear sleeping on the other side of the door. I find his presence enormously soothing.

†

The next afternoon, when the sun comes out, I wear a large red shirt. Yaz has ripped and tied it into a sort of scarf around my head and neck to protect me from the sun, now that I no longer have the broad hat she made for me. The red shirt does a good job of keeping the sun off my face, but at times feels a bit restrictive. I know it will feel good when I once again ascend the foundation of the coaster to recharge.

It rained earlier, and the tracks are slick and coats our hands in a dark, reddish brown.

"Look at you," she teases. "Hardly had your new clothes for any time and you're already a mess."

"Me?" I ask. "What about you?"

She looks down at the front of her filthy shirt and I swipe my dirty hand across her stomach.

"Oh, you brat! That was just wrong," Yaz says.

She grabs me by the arm when I try to get out of reach of the brown hand she holds up.

"You wouldn't dare," I say, eyes narrowing and corners of my mouth twitching.

"Yes, yes I would."

She lets go of my arm and cups both of my breasts in her hands, then removes them to study the marks her rusty, dirty hands have left on the green material.

"Much better," she says.

I look down, shocked that she has dirtied my shirt so, then think of the boxes of shirts in the warehouse. I hope we can find another that fits me. I decide that later I will sort through the uniforms to pull out all that will fit us.

"I dare you to do that again," I say, forcing my face to look stern.

She cups both of my breasts again, this time squeezing slightly.

My breath catches before quickening and I watch as her eyes grow darker. Now her breaths are coming faster to match mine.

"What are you going to do about it, Misha Wyatt?"

She loosens her grip on my flesh just enough to allow her thumbs and forefingers to pinch my erect nipples.

I am panting in my desire of her. I push her hands from me long enough to rip the front of my shirt open. I hold up a hand to halt her when she reaches to touch my bare breasts.

"Not with those dirty hands," I warn her. "You should not touch my skin with those dirty hands before you put your mouth on me."

She puts her hands up in surrender before lowering her head just far enough to place her lips on my left nipple. She

165

looks up through hooded eyes and I cup the back of her head to hold her there.

†

We are foraging just outside the crumbling walls of Jungle Mania, where the largest portion of pole bean vines are located, when I work up the courage to ask Yaz the question that came to me late last night.

"If we had crashed in Perry," I begin.

"Don't go there," she interrupts.

Unexpectedly, I understand her strange phrasing. "I want *to go there*."

She takes a deep breath.

"If we had crashed in Perry and were under risk of being taken hostage, would you have made me shoot myself, or would you have done it for me?" I ask.

Yaz closes her eyes, squeezing tears from their corners. "I cannot think about that, let alone speak it."

The pain in her voice stabs at my chest and I pull her into an embrace. "I am sorry," I whisper. "I'm sorry I brought it up. We did not crash in Perry and we did not have to make that decision. I will never bring it up again."

She holds me tightly for a moment longer, then pulls away. Her face is tear-streaked but her eyes show only joy.

"You are my life, Misha, and I will always take care of you."

"And I, you," I add, believing every word we both speak.

"Let's go gather some nuts." She nods her head towards Bear. "Before that big goof takes them all."

I reposition the medical bag on my back. We never go anywhere without it because we never know what might come between us and it at any time. Except while bathing or making love, it is like an extension of me.

As we walk, I finger the beaded bracelet in my pocket. Lately it does not seem enough to have it on me as such. I pull it out. "Yaz, will you attach this around my wrist?"

She smiles. "I was wondering when you would wear it as it is meant to be worn."

She gently fastens it around my left wrist.

"I can now wear it and mostly remember the good times with Jackson. He would have adored this place." Tears sting my eyes but do not fall. I swipe at them. "I bet he would have become obsessed with getting the roller coaster running again. He was a mere boy in that big man's body."

Yaz laughs. "Yes, I can see that now."

We are at the edge of the big, nut-tree forest and our attention drifts to the task at hand. I like the feel of the slight weight of the bracelet on my wrist, knowing it was made by Kai, and was part of my joyful friendship with Jackson.

†

I have just finished under the stars, and have taken a few steps down the metal framework, when Yaz climbs up almost to my new position. One final step and her head is at the same level as my thighs.

"Do you feel energized?" she asks, moonlight reflecting off her eyes.

"Yes, I do." I hold her gaze, seeing her hunger. "And what will energize you?"

While maintaining eye contact, she unfastens my pants. I lean forward, away from the metal that was pressing against my buttocks. She slides my pants and undergarments down just enough to expose my sex.

The slightly cool night air teases my flesh, and when the contrasting hot air from her breath caresses me, a rush of wetness is created.

She holds onto the metal framework with her left hand and parts my lips with the fingers of her right one, further exposing me.

I gasp in anticipation.

She slowly licks the length of my wet slit, kisses the knot of most sensitive flesh, then runs her tongue back over me again. She does this over and over until my legs begin to quake.

"Say it, Misha. Say the words I taught you."

"I'm going to come, Yaz. You're going to make me come."

Wave after wave of sensation runs through my body as she sucks me further into her mouth.

When I stop writhing against her, she climbs up until our bodies are breast to breast, thighs to thighs.

I unfasten her pants and shove my hand inside them, inside her undergarment, into the wetness that awaits me.

"See how wet you make me?" she asks into my neck.

I love that I can do this to her.

"Go inside me," she says.

I turn my wrist just so and plunge two fingers inside her.

She gasps. "Yes, Misha, yes. Deep and hard. Fuck me deep and hard."

Her words renew the wetness between my legs, but I ignore the new need as I slide in and out of her as fast as I can until her body tenses, then shakes and quivers.

†

We are harvesting cattails when we hear it. The melodious song of the wolves drifts to us on a slight breeze. We are far from the warehouse, too far to outrun the beasts if they come upon us now.

"I am rethinking going so far from safety," Yaz says.

Bear is pacing near the crumbled wall we climbed over to leave the compound and its protection.

"I agree," I say, my voice lower than it realistically needs to be.

"Come," Yaz holds out her hand.

I shoulder the satchel I was filling over the medical bag I still carry everywhere with me. I take her hand and we walk cautiously back to the wall where Bear awaits.

Back at the warehouse, we stash our bounty inside, then walk out just a few feet from the door.

There is a flurry of activity in the trees that grow out from the coaster tracks. The crows are watching, listening, guarded, but do not call out. We will watch their reactions closely as the day passes into evening.

"Can you go without recharging tonight?" Yaz asks.

I nod. "I can, but I don't wish to. I would rather gather all the energy I can now, just in case they come closer and it becomes unsafe to do so."

"Okay, but I will go up with you."

Before I can argue, she puts up a hand to silence me. "I promise to stay out of your way. I will be just below you. I don't want for us to get separated from each other if the animals move in."

I know she is right. And I know that there shouldn't be any reason not to have her close while I recharge. Others have been close before—Naomi at Las Estrellas before I

169

settled at Karst, the guards just inside the upper opening of the cave city—but this will be the first time since my grandmother that the person nearby knows exactly what I am doing as I do it.

"Trust me," she whispers.

"Oh, there is to be no doubt in my trust of you," I say. "I've trusted you enough to open my heart to you." I smile now. "I even jumped into a moving plane to be with you. I'd say I've proven my trust in you."

"Yes, you have that. You even continue to trust me after I crashed that very plane."

"Well, you did not crash in Perry, so it was still a win."

We climb up together, Yaz just a few feet behind me. When I settle at the top, she stops and travels a small distance vertically from me.

I close my eyes, but have trouble concentrating. The moon is too bright for the best use of the stars. But I still want to try.

"I did not realize they are nocturnal," I say, in response to another chorus of wolf song.

"I didn't either."

They come closer, and I can very clearly hear the difference in their calls from the coywolves of New America.

I glance around but do not see Bear.

Yaz must know for what I look because she whispers, "He is halfway up the structure, also being very quiet."

The crows, too, are silent. It is as if the entire area holds its breath so as not to be noticed by the wolves.

I open my eyes and glance down. In the moonlight I can easily see, and when I focus on a wolf for the first time, it renders me breathless. They are so much bigger and fiercer than the coywolves I know.

There is much movement near the gate to Jungle Mania, and then the cries of an animal, a deer if I were to guess. The movement comes closer still, and I once again struggle to breathe.

We are downwind, and stay so very still, more still than the air we inhabit, and go undetected as a pair of wolves eat a newly slain doe.

We stay high in the foundational structure until much later. It isn't until Bear climbs down and the crows rustle in the trees that we come down from our great height. It is very late in the night before we are able to relax and settle into sleep.

†

The next day we are on high alert as we prepare our morning meal. We decide not to go more than a few yards from the door to the warehouse for the day. We hope the wolves will not return.

At nightfall, I do not try to recharge due to the big, dark clouds that obscure all the stars and the moon.

I rearrange and fluff up the two stacks of folded shirts that we use as pillows. These are the ones I've previously sorted so we always know where to find the ones that will fit us. Yaz smiles her approval and settles her head onto one of the stacks.

I do the same, making sure that the buttons are still facing down, so I do not wake up again with a circular imprint on my cheek.

We are not asleep for long when we are awakened by the storm. Rumbling of the thunder echoes through my chest.

The lightning is getting closer.

I can hear—or more accurately sense—Bear's agitation outside.

"Should we open the door so he can come in if he'd like?" I ask.

Before Yaz can answer the warehouse shakes from the force of a nearby lightning strike. We both jump.

"Do we want the wind whipping in here through an open door?" Yaz asks, more to herself than to me, based on her whisper and tone. She gets up and walks several paces toward the door, then stops and cocks her head as if listening.

The crash is deafening.

Lightning strikes the building and courses through me, simultaneously. Pain grips me and the cracking of wood and shattering of glass fill my senses.

I feel as if I've been struck hard on the back of the head. A shock runs through my body and every muscle tenses as I am thrown to the ground.

The impact against my back as I fall registers at the same time as the pain in my ears, the blurriness of my vision.

"Misha! Misha!" Yaz yells as she rushes toward me.

"No, don't touch me!" I fear that I will transfer pain to her, energy her body may not be able to absorb as easily as mine does.

Pain wracks my body for another couple of seconds, then… nothing.

Finally, I stop shaking and my breathing levels.

"Are you unharmed?" I ask Yaz as I stare up at her from my position on the floor.

"Me? Oh baby, you were just struck by lightning. How are you even still alive?"

It seems as if my body still buzzes with the energy of the lightning.

"Do you smell smoke?" I ask.

The ringing in my ears lessens enough for me to hear Bear clawing at the door. I pull on my clothes and boots and Yaz does the same.

"The building is on fire," Yaz says, grabbing for my hand.

"Wait," I say, pulling away from her so I can strap my medical bag to my back. This action is so second nature to me that even Yaz doesn't try to make me leave it behind for the sake of thirty or forty seconds of time saved.

At the last minute, I gather a handful of shirts from our bedding and clutch them to my chest.

"Come, now, Misha!" This time I do allow Yaz to grab my hand.

We run first in one direction, then another, as flames envelope the walls around us. When we finally make our way to the door and open it, Bear is pacing and obviously distressed.

We watch as the structure we've sought shelter in burns. In the back of my mind, I am only partially aware that we stand closer to Bear than we have ever been. I find some comfort in us staying close to each other while our sanctuary is destroyed.

CHAPTER ELEVEN

We wait until midmorning to more closely approach the ruins of our warehouse. The blackened remains are acrid.

At a time that I am meant to be helping Yaz ensure none of the embers are hot enough to reignite, I am paralyzed. Standing in front of the charred remains, I am unable to pull myself away from that time so very long ago, when the nearest of neighboring villages burned my family's village to the ground.

Everyone I knew was already dead. The sickness had swept through my village so fast that I couldn't keep up with trying to use energy to save everyone. My failure to save even one member of my family weighs heavily upon me, even to this day.

I waited until weeks after my village stopped smoldering to come out from hiding. I was young—barely nine years old—and I was terrified.

I had stayed away so long that the folks in the neighboring village did not worry that I could be carrying the illness. They knew the incubation had long passed. They knew that the act of being alive made me different.

Witch hands.

It was only that an elder came forward to remind the others that I was but a child that they let me be. She took me in, caring for me as if I were part of her family.

But she was an old woman, and within a year of taking me in, she died. She had not allowed me to put my hands upon her. She said my hands were meant for those with hope left inside them. She said she looked forward to joining her long-gone loved ones, and I should not touch her, just sit by her side and help distract her from the ravages upon her body.

After she died, the villagers cast me out. They still believed me to be a witch.

"It's okay, it's okay," I hear Yaz say into my neck. I do not realize I am in her embrace until I hear her sweet words. "I'm here now, love. Everything will be all right."

I settle myself down and pull away, staring into those dark, dark eyes.

"Thank you." I smile. "You always know how to make me calm down."

"I will always be here for you," she says, her words so earnest that my heart clenches in my chest.

"Thank you," I say in a weak voice. I shake the emotions off then. "I would like to look around now."

"I will come with you."

We walk the perimeter of the charred remains. When we get to the far side, I am shocked to find that one carousel horse has survived the fire. It is the blue and green swirled one that I loved the best.

Yaz presses against me from behind as I stroke the fake mane.

"It's so strange that this was unharmed."

She nods her agreement.

"This pretend horse and a few shirts. I can't believe that is all that is left," Yaz says.

I turn in her arms. "We are left. You and me and Bear all survived. The fire was contained to the building. We were so very blessed."

A tear runs down her face. "We were. Thank you for reminding me."

We hold one another for several moments before breaking away.

"What now?" I ask.

"Now we live among the rides."

We turn in unison to look at the structure I've been using to gain elevation for recharging.

Yaz takes my hand and leads me closer to the crisscrossing metal. We both look up, from different angles.

Yaz points upward. "I am going to drag some branches up onto the top portion of that horizontal area," Yaz says, pointing up to a place not far from where I normally recharge.

I give a tentative nod.

"I will make it comfortable. We can use branches and leaves to serve as our bedding. I can spread out the extra shirts you saved to help with the comfort—until we need to wear them. I think it's far enough away from your spot to give you space when you need to sit with the stars."

"I think it's a perfect place to call home now."

She looks at me carefully, obviously checking closer for my reaction to her suggestion.

"It will be great. I will help you with the branches," I say.

"No, love, why don't you stand guard for me while I do it?"

I study her face. I am certain she knows that I am tired these days. So very tired.

"All right," I say.

I watch Yaz as she drags branches up to our new bedroom. Bear watches her as well. When Yaz is done with ours, she drags some up to an area not quite as high as ours, but equally level. She gestures toward it and Bear just stares. She brings some pine straw that was not burned in the fire, part of what Bear brought in to use as his bedding, and places it on Bear's new bed.

"You think he understands now?" Yaz asks.

It is moments like this, when she does so much for all of us, that my heart threatens to burst with pride and love for this woman.

"Yes, my darling, I'm sure he will figure it out." I look her up and down. "Now, why don't you go clean up while I make our meal."

Yaz goes to the small metal pail we have set up and rinses her hands while I prepare a small meal of kudzu, cattails, and tree nuts. She returns and sits on the low portion of the tracks to rest until I am finished. We take our time eating.

When we are finished, Yaz suggests we go exploring. There is still a large part of Jungle Mania that we haven't thoroughly investigated yet.

I agree and we set off on our adventure.

We go around to the back side of the roller coaster, still within sight of it, but out of our normal positioning.

There are small planes bolted to a round platform with a railing around it. This is like the carousel, only smaller and less ornate. The edges of a pond encroach upon it. Since it rained last night, the water comes up to the belly of the miniature planes.

I sit in one, barely fitting. I wonder if this wasn't meant for children. Yaz, being taller than I, does not fit in any of the planes unless she hangs her longer legs outside of the confines of the plane.

We are laughing at her attempts, until finally she gives up and stands against the railing by where I sit. She leans forward and gives me a lazy kiss.

When she pulls away from me, she tugs on the railing and a grunt escapes her. The next time she tugs, it starts to move. I gasp in surprise. Her eyebrows shoot up.

A playful laugh escapes Yaz. She tugs, gets it moving steadily, and then runs alongside of it, by my side, making me go around faster and faster.

"I am flying!" I hold my arms out beside me and act as if I am one with the airplane.

Water splashes around Yaz's legs as she runs, hanging on to the railing to keep the momentum going. We are both laughing so hard that the warning does not register at first.

The crows are raising quite the ruckus, calling out, back and forth between them.

Yaz lets go, stopping her movement, and I speed away from her, out of her reach.

"Wolves," we both say at once.

Bear is at the base of the steepest part of the foundation of the coaster, the part where we should all climb since it's too vertical for the wolves to follow.

"Misha!" Yaz sloshes through the water, toward me, holding out her hand. "Misha, come, we must climb the coaster."

I try to get out of the small plane but my foot is stuck. I panic, making my movements even more clumsy.

Yaz is beside me, yanking at my arm, then my bent leg, trying to free me from the seat in the ride.

Now the call of the crows mixes with the song of the wolves. They are so close. Too close.

"Go, Yaz. Go to safety!"

"I'm not leaving you."

She tugs at me from the waist and I feel myself slip free. I climb out and we both make a run for the foundation. The wolves are at the base where Bear has climbed up. They jump and snap at him. He bares his teeth, dipping close enough that the wolves think they can get to him, then he moves up, just out of their reach. He is distracting them from us.

We try to stealthily go to the portion of the tracks that is closest, but it is also the portion closest to the ground. The tracks here run parallel to the ground, with plenty of horizontal metal beams that will help the wolves climb.

We run toward it anyway. That is our only chance of getting up and away from the wolves.

Yaz steps up onto the track first, turns to me as if to give me a hand up.

179

"Go," I chastise her. "Get yourself up to safety. I'm right behind you."

We make it past the horizontal part of the tracks before the wolves make a run at us. We are about eight feet off the ground.

The black wolf, the one we've always thought was alpha, jumps onto the lowest part of the tracks and springs forward. I feel the pressure of his contact on the back of my leg.

I cry out, mostly in shock, as I pull my leg up. I look down at him and see teeth, slobber, and flashing eyes. The image reminds me of the lead train of the roller coaster.

The wolf leaps again, this time from the ground where he landed after his first attempt at me. I feel wetness at the back of my ankle. He brushes just past my flesh, but then is gone. I look down at my leg and see where the fabric of my pants is shredded. I stare at the place the wolf could have grabbed me, snatching me off the foundation.

"Higher, Misha, climb higher!"

Yaz's voice breaks me out of my trance and I climb up farther, coming to a stop next to her.

We both breathe hard from the exertion.

Movement to my left gets my attention. Bear is climbing farther up. He is twenty yards or so away, but now even with our height.

"Thank you, friend," I say to the animal.

He looks down at the wolves, now pacing underneath us, and I swear his expression says, *That was so close!*

Yaz and I are careful as we climb up a little farther, then slide sideways along the tracks toward our new roost. It isn't until we are both settled in and calmed down that I feel as if I can steady my breathing.

180

I start to shake. Then, when I see a tear slide down Yaz's face, I lose control and start sobbing. She pulls me into an embrace and I cling to her.

"That really was too close," Yaz says.

"Yes," I agree. "Much too close."

We sit side by side, tightly gripping each other's hands, until night falls.

"I will leave you to recharge," Yaz says.

I don't want her to leave me, but I also feel like I need to be alone in my quest tonight.

"Please do not go too far," I plead.

"Twenty feet or so that way," she says, pointing. "I will be right over there."

I nod and watch as she scoots away.

Deep breaths help to ground me as I sit atop the tracks, hands up and out to my sides, absorbing what I can of the stars' energy.

I stare into the night sky at the stars dotting the blackness of the night and listen carefully. The slight murmur makes me focus harder and I concentrate. I am pretty sure there will be no connecting to the collective consciousness tonight, but I try nonetheless.

"Please, stars, bless me with your energy," I whisper. "Help me to heal the hurting, the sick, the sad."

Tiny sparks dance on the palms of my hands and I watch in awe and confusion. It does not last long and soon I am thinking about the stars again.

The glittering sky before me is glorious in its wealth of sparkling stars. I feel my body tingle and grow warm. The hum in my chest is slight and fleeting. I close my eyes tightly and try to will the night to speak to me. I open my eyes and fear the prickling of tears.

The stars are bright, full of promise, but it's not truly working.

Suzanna joins me. It is not the first time I have felt her presence while rejuvenating, but this time feels different.

I hear her voice then, as if she is sitting right next to me.

"It's time to go home," she says.

I know she is right, but we are stuck here, and even if we could return, we do not know if it would be safe for Yaz in New America.

I am finished but cannot bring myself to call my love back to me, to face the truth and Yaz. A warm breeze plays across my skin but I find no joy in it, now that I know that I need to at least suggest leaving to Yaz.

Only moments later, Yaz comes to me and wraps her arms around me from behind. Tears run down my face.

"It's the same sky, the same stars, why isn't it helping more?" I cannot stop the sob that escapes me.

Yaz turns me in her arms and looks me in the eyes. Not even the night sky can obscure the vast amount of tenderness I see in her expression. My body grows warmer under her gaze.

She takes my hands in hers.

"Maybe it's not in your hands," she says as she kisses the palm of first one, then the other. "Maybe the issue is in your heart."

"What?" I ask incredulously. "You cannot doubt my love for you."

"Oh, but I don't." She smiles. "I feel your love with every glance, every touch, and every word spoken. But I think you underestimate the love you have for your friends."

"I do not understand."

"You long to return to Karst," Yaz says.

"I long to be with you forever," I counter.

"You become less and less like you, the longer we stay here in the east."

I could pretend not to know what she's talking about, but I owe her complete honesty. I shyly nod my agreement.

"You need to go home," she says.

"You are so happy here." I am fighting for a reason not to make this decision.

"I won't be happy here, slowly watching you lose your shine."

I turn in her arms to look at her. "My shine?"

"That's what I call it in my head when you go to the stars." She smiles. "I say, look, Misha has gone for her shine."

†

The next night, I return to the top of the roller coaster to gather as much energy as I can for the next day's journey.

I sit, leaning against the tubular support beam, hands palm up. The tiny sparks on my palms are just as surprising to me as they were the previous night. They are also just as fleeting.

I quiet my mind and am shocked by how quickly I tap into the voice of the Universe, or Collective Consciousness, or just Energy, as I'm more apt to think about it at times like these.

Purpose.

I know immediately that although I do love and miss my friends in New America, even those who I feel betrayed me with their treatment of Yaz, that the real reason I am being drawn away from here is to serve a new purpose.

But what could it be?

I chuckle at myself. Of course, the universe will not let me in on the big secret until the very last moment, just like over five years ago I didn't know I would choose Karst over McNally until the energy chose for me. Just like I didn't know that *change* meant Yaz coming into my life until she dropped out of the sky.

I take several deep breaths and try to gather energy from the stars. It's almost as if now that I have come to embrace a journey to a new purpose, the stars are rewarding me with an extra bit of recharging. It is still not what I was accustomed to in New America, but I will happily embrace any little bit of energy I can absorb.

I know instinctively that I will need every ounce of physical and metaphysical energy I can acquire for the days, weeks, and months ahead.

PART THREE—QUEST FOR HOME

Chapter Twelve

The day is overcast and chilly. Hopefully the weather will hold for the beginning of our trek and we won't be traveling in a thunderstorm.

Yaz has etched a depiction of her proposed route in the dirt. The song of the wolves interrupts her explanation to me.

The crows begin their warning shrieks to let us know the wolves are indeed coming our way.

"Come," she says.

She grabs my hand and we run to the safety of the structure. Simultaneously, we begin to climb. Bear is just to the right of me, staying even with us, in his way of always watching out for us.

Below, the beasts circle the roller coaster, not looking up at us, but we know they know exactly where we are.

It is hours before the wolves take their leave. We wait until Bear and the crows have calmed down before we descend.

"It's time to go," Yaz says.

"Yes," I answer, looking at the mountain ridge we will be walking toward for the next few weeks…or months.

I quickly strap two satchels of food to my back, then place the medical bag over them so it is the most easily accessed of the supplies. I glance at Yaz and she is layering the remaining satchels onto her body.

She takes my hand, bringing it to her lips for a brief kiss. "Ready?"

"Yes," I say with a nod.

She looks behind me, then releases my hand as she goes to the map she'd drawn in the dirt. She kicks at it with her boot, erasing the markings.

I give her a questioning look and she shrugs, a rush of color to her cheeks telling me she is embarrassed. "It's not as if the wolves can read a map, but—" she says, another shrug and blush punctuating her statement.

I press a kiss to her cheek and tug at her hand. We begin our journey away from the wondrously strange and enchanting Jungle Mania.

We are not at all surprised when Bear follows us. I am quite pleased with this, to be honest.

†

The topography changes incrementally as the days of trekking away from Jungle Mania pass. The trees are bigger, the undergrowth thicker. No matter what else changes, however, the kudzu remains. There is some relief in knowing

187

that as our other provisions diminish, we can always fall back on the leafy staple.

We have stopped to take a rest in the shade of some tall hardwoods when Yaz decides to climb up a tree to harvest some nuts. Bear sees her climbing and goes up another tree two over from her, seemingly to also gather some nuts.

My gaze flickers back and forth between Yaz and Bear, and I wonder if there isn't a bit of a competition happening between the two.

Yaz is several feet higher than Bear, slowly increasing her lead, when her right foot slips and she slides down ten or so feet, stopping hard against a branch. I can hear her cursing.

Bear is frozen into place.

"I'm okay," Yaz calls down to me.

It isn't until she starts climbing again that Bear also resumes his way up his tree.

Now my eyes do not leave Yaz. I watch as she picks and places nuts from the tree into the satchel she has tied to her chest. She is harvesting for the better part of an hour when she finally begins her descent. As soon as her feet touch the ground, I glance at Bear and see he is eating his fill while perched on a large branch high in the tree.

"Yaz, love, let me see your hands."

"They are fine," she says.

I grab her by the wrist and make eye contact. "May I please see them?"

She holds both hands out in front of her, palms up, and I see the abrasions and the litter in the wounds.

"No, love, they are not fine. I am going to clean them up, then do some energy work."

When it looks like she will argue, I cut her off. "There is no negotiating this."

She rolls her eyes playfully but obediently follows me to the water canteen and my medical bag.

I clean the wounds, place some salve on both palms, then sit her against one of the large, rough-barked trees. I kneel in front of her and gently take both hands in mine. The hum builds in my belly, moves to my chest.

"Heal," I whisper. "Heal now."

The heat travels from my body to my arms, down into my hands. A slight vibration follows the heat.

Yaz's breathing hitches slightly. When I look up from her hands to her face, she is smiling.

"It's warm," she says in a low voice. "It feels nice."

I return her smile, then look back to her hands. Some of the redness seems to have disappeared, but they are obviously still injured.

Heal. Heal now. I begin to shiver and know that is all I have to give to this for now.

"They feel so much better," Yaz says. I do not know if she knows that I am disappointed in the lack of total healing. I know I should be happy about alleviating her discomfort, but I had hoped for more.

I bring her hands to my face, turn them over, and kiss the top of each knuckle on her right one. "I'm glad you have some relief," I say.

"Let's make camp here for the night. Is that okay with you?"

I look around and don't see any place good for spending time with the stars, but that is not new. "It is fine."

"Maybe tomorrow we will find a clearing suitable for you to sit under the stars?"

"Maybe." I busy myself with setting up our bedding.

I glance up at a loud noise in the tree and see that Bear is finally coming down.

"Did you get enough?" Yaz asks him when his feet are on the ground.

Bear swings his head around as if saying yes, he did.

We make our camp and snuggle together. Being close to Yaz, whether we are being intimate or not, is magical. I love how safe I feel when I'm in her arms.

†

The next morning, Yaz is all smiles when she wakes up and sees that her hands are mostly healed.

"It seems I just needed a little time for your magic to work," she says. She holds up her hands to show me the light pink lines that were scrapes just last night.

I cannot help but smile. "I am very happy to see that."

She pulls me into an embrace. My entire body tingles and it has nothing to do with the stars or energy work. I feel a tightening in my nipples, then a wetness between my legs.

She pulls out of the hug and studies my face. "Are you okay? Your face is bright red."

"I—I am—"

She cocks her head, then smiles.

"Can we—can we touch each other?"

She is tugging down my pants before my mind even registers that she is willing. Her mouth finds my sex and she begins a thorough tending to my needs. When my legs mean to give out from under me, she holds me up. When my release threatens to crash over me, she presses her face more firmly into my wetness until I come apart in pleasure.

As soon as I can breathe again, she grabs my hand and pushes it down the front of her pants. She's obviously been affected by administering to me, because she finds her release within minutes of me touching her.

She is all smiles as she helps me pull my pants back up.

"That was a very nice way to start the day," I say.

"Just nice?"

"That was an amazing way to start the day."

"Yes," she agrees.

Soon we are packed up and back on our journey.

We have not traveled but half a day when we come out of the thickness of the forest to find the remnants of a road. Since it too heads to the west, we choose to follow it.

Bear sniffs at the air and becomes agitated. Yaz and I exchange a look of concern. We are on high alert until a few hours later when he seems to have calmed substantially.

"We should stop soon," Yaz says. "It's been a long day of walking, and you should probably be able to recharge with it being so open here."

I nod. "Yes, soon."

We have just rounded a bend in the road when we stop in our tracks.

"What the hell?" Yaz says.

We stare into the entrance to a tunnel that seemingly goes right through the mountain. Since I spent five years living in a cave city, this should not surprise me. But somehow it does.

Bear inches between us and the entrance. His head is low, then he holds it up, nose in the air and ears at alert. He sticks his head into the tunnel, then pulls it out to look at us.

"It appears Bear will lead the way," Yaz says with a smirk.

"It appears so," I say, a smile overtaking my face.

"Should we make a torch?" She glances around as if looking for supplies in which to use.

"What if there is some kind of gas in there?" I ask.

Her face distorts in thought, then her attention goes to Bear as he steps farther into the tunnel.

"Bear wants us to follow him."

I take her hand in mine. "Let's go then."

As we walk behind Bear, the tunnel gets darker and darker. I am struggling to keep my breathing steady as I am inundated with memories of being stuck underground in the collapsed tunnels with the Merricks.

Yaz squeezes my hand and I am sure she can tell I am close to panic.

I walk right into the back of Bear. He doesn't react at all, just stands there as I push my fingers into his thick fur and hold on. When he begins his forward movement again, I am holding on to him with my left hand and to Yaz's hand with my right. My breathing levels out and I feel safe.

I relax even further when, about twenty minutes later, the tunnel begins to grow lighter. We are obviously nearing the other end. When I can see Bear and Yaz clearly, I remove my fingers from Bear's fur.

We step into the light, Bear a few feet in front of us, and Yaz and I side by side, and we all freeze.

CHAPTER THIRTEEN

The road is in even better shape than it was on the other side, the right side snug against a cliff wall. To the left of it, however, the land drops off hundreds of feet.

Yaz looks almost panicked. It occurs to me then that what I see as the perfect place to recharge comfortably to her looks dangerous.

"It will be fine," I tell her. "Why don't we make camp here and we can continue on the road in the morning when we are well rested."

She nods her head absently, then seems to shake herself out of the stupor.

"Yes, let's rest here for the night."

We set up camp just outside of the tunnel entrance. Bear has made his place just inside the opening. I can feel his eyes on us as we move around.

I perch on the edge of the road, to a few warnings from Yaz to be careful, and settle myself in to recharge. I am pleasantly surprised with the ease at which the energy comes to me. I am much more surprised when I hear Suzanna's voice say, "Teach her."

Teach who?

"Teach her," she repeats, then she is gone as quickly as she came.

Once I finish under the stars, I go to Yaz and settle down beside her for the night.

†

The next morning, we pack up at first light. Bear hangs back, waiting for one of us to lead the way on the road that grips the side of the cliff.

I take the lead, as I am the most comfortable with this terrain.

It takes us several hours to slowly travel the length of the dangerous road. When we round a bend and the road goes toward a thinly treed forest, I can hear Yaz's sigh of relief.

Bear is on high alert. His actions are curious. He is hyperaware, but doesn't seem as agitated as he normally would when acting so tuned in.

We have just stopped to enjoy a light meal before returning to our journey, when we hear a loud rustling ahead and to the right of the road.

Yaz's hand goes to her belt and rests on her knife. I pull the pipe from the side of my medical bag. Bear stands stock-still.

My heart pounds in my chest when I see another bear. This one is slightly smaller than Bear. The new animal slaps the ground with its front paw as it huffs air out of its mouth.

Bear raises his head and sniffs the air, not responding to what looks to me like aggressive behavior from the other bear.

The new bear raises up on its hind legs, its nose sniffing the air just as Bear's does. Bear mirrors the standing position.

After the bear returns to all fours, Bear does the same, and they seem to start a game of follow the leader in the woods several yards away from us.

When the bear nears us, Bear puts himself between it and us.

"What should we do?" I ask Yaz.

"It's not acting too bothered by us. Maybe we should just start walking again and see what it does."

"Okay. I am hoping that if it gets aggressive with us, Bear will step in."

"I hope so, but know his behavior might change now that there is another bear around."

"Do you think it's a female?" I ask.

"I don't know. I sure as hell won't be the one to try to check its sex," she says, laughing.

"I guess we just won't know then," I tease. "Let's start walking slowly."

We begin our trek again, with both bears behind us, keeping our pace steady and listening intently for any quick movements behind us.

"I'm tired and we should find a place to sleep for the night," I say.

"Will you be able to sleep with the addition to our party?" Yaz asks with a slight gesture of her head behind us.

"I suppose settling down for the night is one way to figure out if we have anything to fear from the bear. If it doesn't try to take our food or make us its food, we should be okay."

Yaz nods. "Maybe we should sleep in shifts tonight, just in case."

And that is what we do, taking turns sleeping a few hours at a time. Both bears sleep, Bear between us and the other one, throughout the night.

In the morning, we pack up and decide to keep moving as planned, as long as the bear doesn't start acting aggressively with us.

We've traveled several hours when the bears begin to jostle one another as we walk. When we stop for a break, Bear starts grooming the new bear.

"Is Bear courting her?" I ask.

"It appears so." Yaz smiles. "You don't think they will— you know—with us right here?"

I laugh at the innocence in Yaz's voice. "It's not like we haven't done that—and more—in front of Bear."

"Oh no, what if we've messed him up and he doesn't know how to do it like a bear now?" Yaz teases.

We laugh together, then decide it's time to resume our trek. We start to leave and hear noises behind us. Bear is making short grunting sounds as he walks back and forth in front of the bear while looking at us.

"What do we do?" Yaz asks.

"We keep going and let him be a bear?"

We start walking and when I glance back, Bear is still pacing but is also paying more attention to what appears to be his new mate.

Yaz takes my hand. "Just keep walking. We have to let him go."

I squeeze her hand. "I know. It's just going to be strange without him."

"It's best for him. How would your people feel about him waltzing into New America with us?" Yaz says.

Since I cannot say how they will be with us, I surely do not know how they would handle a bear.

"You're right. He needs to go and live like he's supposed to."

"I'm happy he's found someone," Yaz says.

I smile at how genuinely pleased she seems to be for him.

We walk the rest of the day without seeing or hearing Bear. I feel a little uneasy when we settle in for the night. Bear has been with us for so long, I have gotten so accustomed to feeling the security that comes with having such a large protector nearby.

"I am going to recharge," I say, once we finish our evening meal.

"I'll keep guard," Yaz says, pulling me to her for a quick hug. "Go get your shine."

I have just gotten comfortable when the vibration starts building inside me. I haven't felt this strength in the stars since the night right after being struck by lightning.

I am about to summon the stars further when I have a vision of Naomi. She is traveling with two other people, all on horseback, when I see an ambush in the making. Four feral people hide behind a stand of trees.

I do not doubt that Naomi can take all four, but only if she becomes aware of them before they jump her and the two others.

Naomi's two companions are joking with one another behind her. I know she would not put up with such behavior, but obviously doesn't hear them, doesn't know they are not paying attention.

My mind's voice calls out to her. When her head jerks around, as if looking for the source of the sound, I know I have connected with her. Somewhat.

I try to warn her against going forward, but she does not understand my message.

I grow angry, so very angry. Why are there still people who only wish to do harm, to take from others and hurt or kill them?

The sparks are back, dancing upon my palm.

A jolt of pain pierces my hand. I concentrate on the four ferals about to attack Naomi. Just as they pounce, before they make physical contact with her and the others, a bolt of lightning flies from my hand and strikes the ferals.

I cry out with the pain.

Yaz is there, by my side, immediately, drawing my attention away from the scene that was playing out in my mind. I pull away from her, try to recapture the image, but to no avail.

I don't know if this was a vision of what is to come, or if I did indeed interact with Naomi in real time in New America. The not knowing unsettles me. I gently rub my palms together, wondering about the over-heated sensation on them.

I am too tired and too weak to make it back to our bedding. I am barely aware that Yaz carries me the ten or so yards to where we have set up our camp for the night. I feel safe in her arms, but also so unsure of what we are going into.

†

We have been traveling seven days without Bear accompanying us when the road begins to crumble under our feet.

Yaz takes my hand. "Something feels different."

I do not tell her that I have felt that ever since my lightning vision of Naomi. "It does," I say. "Stay close to me?"

She pulls me against her side. "Of course."

We walk closely for a few hours when she stops abruptly.

"You heard that too?" I ask.

"Yes. It almost sounds like—like voices."

Just as the words are out of her mouth, we are surrounded by people. Some hold weapons—guns, sticks, swords—and some are unarmed. There are about fifteen in all, all staring at us with disbelief on their faces.

A woman steps forward, the leader, I presume. She looks me up and down before her gaze goes to Yaz. Her smile confuses me.

"Yazmine," the woman says. "It is you." She pulls Yaz into an embrace.

"Arla," Yaz says, wonderment obvious in her voice.

I fight back a feeling of jealousy.

"And you," the woman says, staring intently into my eyes. "You are the teacher."

My heart hammers in my chest.

She turns back to Yaz. "Come, come into our town and we will catch up with each other."

We follow Arla through the woods, the rest of the people behind us, until it opens up into a neat village. The number of people behind us has grown to fifty or more.

Arla stops in front of a small building and looks at me.

"Isabella told us that someone named Suzanna was sending a teacher for young Sachi."

Arla turns and faces a woman sitting just outside the doorway to a small building. The elder sits, eyes unfocused, rocking back and forth. Yaz and I exchange a look.

"She had a lucid moment—the first in many years—then started talking about the beautiful woman with the long, silver hair."

"Suzanna," I whisper.

I watch her for several more beats before going to her, placing a hand on her head. I hear Suzanna whisper, "Leave her be," just as clear as if she were standing beside me. I remove my hand and give a slight bow.

"Find the student," Suzanna whispers into my ear.

"You have a youngster here who—who thrives under the stars."

"Sachi," Arla whispers. "Her grandmother, Isabella, was meant to teach her the power of the stars, but lost touch with reality before Sachi was old enough to learn."

"I am Burke." An older man joins us. He is slight and tall, and very dark. I glance at Yaz and she appears to be trying to remember the man. Her brow is furrowed but she doesn't react to him in any other way.

"The child is prone to outbursts, brought on by frustration, no doubt," Burke says.

"May I see her?" I ask.

"Yes," Arla says to me. Then she turns to Yaz. "But first we need to know how you have come to be here."

Yaz looks from me to Arla.

"We won't keep you long," Arla says. "Give us the condensed version."

"I was sent on a mission to the west."

"Recon or attack?" Arla asks, bitterness dripping from her words.

"Recon, to be followed up with someone else attacking," Yaz responds. "My plane malfunctioned, and crashed. Misha was the healer who helped me with my many wounds."

Arla stares at me for a long time. "I guess I owe you a debt of gratitude."

I nod acceptance, but do not say anything. I just keep my eyes trained on Yaz.

"And this place in the west?" Arla asks.

"They call it New America." Yaz glances at me, then continues. "It is a strange land with very little in resources, but a lot of strife. There tends to be a lot of violence there."

I am not disturbed by the vision she paints of my home country. I know why she does so, that she wants it to sound as unappealing to them as possible.

"So, you crashed—" Arla prompts Yaz.

"I crashed, and Misha nursed me back to health. When I was well enough, I volunteered for a mission to take out Perry."

"With the plane you crashed?"

"Yes, it was fixed and armed." Yaz takes a deep breath. "The plane itself was meant to be a weapon."

"They sent two of you on a suicide mission?" Arla looks perplexed.

"Not exactly. I was meant to go alone, but someone hijacked my mission," she looks at me and smiles as she says this part. "And, well, here we are."

I am amazed by how each word she speaks is true, yet the overall picture she presents to them is so very different from the harsh reality of her time in New America.

"Why did they want Perry eliminated?" Burke asks.

"Because they knew my presence there was just the beginning of their issues with Perry. I knew the elite would not be happy until New America was conquered."

"Yes, they are that brutal and that greedy," Arla says, distain in her voice. "And did you destroy Perry?"

Yaz nods her head. "Yes."

"I can't wait to hear all about that," Arla says.

"In good time. If it's all the same," Yaz says. "Can we please go to the child now?"

Arla stares at her for a long moment before nodding her head.

Arla and Burke take us to a small hut and I am shown the door. At first, they mean to stop Yaz from coming in as well, but I say, "Please, I would like Yaz to accompany me." I do not know why I insist on this.

We go in to the small back room together where we are met with a guttural, unwelcoming, noise.

It takes several moments for my eyes to adjust to the dim light. A child of eight or nine years sits in the middle on a pile of cushions. Her hands are tucked into her armpits when she looks up at me from under black, unruly curls. Her eyes are big, blue-green, and shining.

The girl's gaze flits between me and Yaz.

"Is it okay that we have come to visit with you today?" Yaz asks.

The girl nods her head, then settles her attention fully onto me.

"You are here to teach me?" Sachi asks in a whisper.

I hold her gaze and try to keep my thoughts laser-focused. There is no way for me to know what the child is capable of. If she can hear my thoughts, I don't want her to know how much the thought of teaching her overwhelms me.

"I will come for you when the stars shine their brightest," I say.

She nods her head. I take Yaz by the hand and we exit the hut.

A tall, lean woman with long brown hair awaits us outside the hut. She looks Yaz up and down as a slow smile forms on her face. "Yaz-ma-taz."

Yaz's eyes get big. "Tegan?"

The woman's stern face twitches before she bursts into a wide grin. "I was the only one allowed to call you that, as I recall."

"Tegan—"

"Yaz, how have you been?"

"You—you are alive!" Yaz takes several steps closer, hesitates, and then closes the distance between them just as Tegan opens her arms. The hug is short and I notice it only involves the area around their neck and shoulders. This is a very different embrace than the one Arla pulled Yaz into upon their meeting.

"But you ran," Yaz says. "You ran and Clair brought back your—" she swallows hard, then continues. "You ran and Clair killed you. Then she returned to live inside as a reward."

"I am alive and well," Tegan says as they pull apart. "And you—look at you."

"Tell me everything," Yaz says, her voice growing hoarse in wonder. "Tell me how you weren't hunted down after you made your run for it."

"First you tell me how you got your claws into this beautiful woman," Tegan says as she turns to face me.

Yaz seems to come back to the present.

"Tegan, this is Misha. Misha, meet Tegan, a dear childhood friend of mine from Perry."

Tegan reaches out her hand to me and I hesitate only a moment before mirroring the action. Then she takes hold of my hand and brings my fingers to her lips. She touches them briefly in a light kiss then lowers my hand and releases it.

"It is a pleasure to meet the one who has obviously stolen my friend's heart," Tegan says.

"Thank you. It is indeed a pleasure to meet you," I say, feeling a blush on my cheeks.

"Indeed?" she asks, her voice lilting in humor. She turns to Yaz. "And so proper."

Yaz gives her head a slight shake, and Tegan throws her hands up in what appears to be mock surrender.

"I will show you to where you will sleep. I was told it should be only one bed. That's how I knew you were fuc— sorry, that's how I knew you were intimate with your travel companion."

Yaz gives her a stern look, but then melts into a smile.

"Sleep tight," Tegan says. "Tomorrow I will tell you of how I escaped the hunt for me all those years ago."

Yaz nods. "Thank you."

Tegan turns to me. "Welcome to Mt. Falcon."

Her words are serious, but her smile is playful, and I wonder about this strange woman.

"Thank you for your hospitality," I say.

Yaz and I enter our quarters, a modest hut that is clean, with big windows to allow in the sun and starlight. I find it small, but very charming.

"So, this Tegan woman—"

Yaz smiles but shakes her head. "That is a story for later."

"Oh?" I ask, keeping my tone light and teasing.

"Yes. First, do you think Arla speaks of your Suzanna?" Yaz asks, her face unreadable.

"Yes, I know it is she." When Yaz's expression remains unchanged, I continue, "Suzanna spoke to me when I approached the semi-comatose elder."

Yaz stares deep into my eyes, then nods. "You will teach the child how to harness the star's energy, yes?"

I pull Yaz to me and hold her tightly.

"This is a great responsibility, but you don't have to—"

"Yes," I interrupt her. "I do have to. But how can I possibly teach the child what she needs to know in the short time we plan to be here? It took my grandmother years to teach me how to control the energy and be a good steward of it."

"Do you think we are meant to stay here?" Yaz asks.

"I truly do not know."

"What will you do?"

"I will ask the stars for guidance tonight. Before I go for the girl."

Yaz nods her agreement.

"In the meantime, I would like to take a rest. With you."

We stretch out onto the lush bedding and hold one another close.

It is several hours later when Arla wakens us.

"I am to take you and Sachi to the perch," Arla says.

"The perch?"

"That is what we call the highest point in Mt. Falcon. It is the location to which Sachi is drawn."

"I would like to go without the girl first," I say.

Arla looks from me to Yaz, and back again.

"Let's allow Misha to get her footing in this land that is so new to her, before she begins with the girl's lessons." Yaz holds Arla's gaze as she speaks.

The path Arla takes us on weaves behind the barn where llamas and goats are housed, to the other side of the vegetable garden, then up a rocky path. I feel so many eyes follow our progress. Several people near the perimeter are heavily armed. I wonder if it is the norm for this place, or if Yaz's and my presence here influences this.

I think to ask how many people live at Mt. Falcon but do not. The view of the valley and the mountain range is beautiful, but from here the range seems even more insurmountable.

"We will leave you to it," Arla says.

I'm not particularly fond of the familiar way Arla takes Yaz's arm, but it is best that I do not harbor any negative energy before recharging under the stars, so I shake it off and sit with my legs crossed.

I shut my eyes and open my hands up to the healing energy of the universe. Immediately, the heat grows in my chest, followed by the low hum that vibrates through me. I am anticipating the sparks to dance across my palms but they do not. This is a relief.

The energy is much stronger here than anywhere I've been outside of New America. I breathe deeply and let it ground me, let it build up my strength, let it settle my mind and ease the weariness in my body.

"Help me find my purpose," I whisper. "Help me know what to do."

I open my eyes and watch as the stars glow brighter and seem to swirl around my head. *Teach the child*, the energy tells me. *Teach her the lessons that will help her to help others*.

"How do I know when I've taught her enough?"

You will know. You will teach her, then you will leave.

The stars settle back into their usual brightness and I know I will not be told anything else tonight. Before I can stand to go tell the others I am ready for Sachi, she appears at my side.

"Sit," I whisper.

She does as I instruct, then mirrors my position with her legs crossed and hands out, palm-side up.

"Quiet your mind, dear," I say. "Close your eyes and think about conversing with the stars' energy, or the universe, or collective consciousness, or even a god or goddess."

The hum begins again in my chest. It is steady, and invigorating. It increases, rises higher and louder, until I am aware that it is not just in me, but also coming from Sachi.

"How do you feel?" I ask.

"I feel warm and tingly. And like a million bees flutter their wings against my flesh."

"Yes," I murmur, liking her description. "Deep breaths."

I can hear her breathing growing deeper, sense her energy building.

"The first lesson," I say, "is to only do good with your energy."

"Even if someone is going to harm me?"

I think about this. After all that has transpired, would I change how I handled my gift in the past? Could I have fought against the Merricks and the ferals that came before them? If I had fought, and was successful, leaving the Merricks before meeting Naomi and Camryn could have kept me from being able to help Naomi when she fell into the fire-water, or Camryn when she almost lost her baby. So no, I would not do any of that differently if given the opportunity.

But what if someone was going to harm me or Yaz? Would I do so then? And did I not do that when I intervened on Naomi's behalf in my vision?

I decide the vision does not count since I do not know if it actually happened or not. I force that from my mind, not wanting that negativity hanging over me and Sachi during our time under the stars.

"Whether or not to use your gift to protect yourself or others, is a very personal decision. Just know that it should not be made lightly." I reach over and place a finger under Sachi's chin, guiding her face until she makes eye contact with me. "Just know that sometimes the harm against you is putting you in a place to be able to help someone else."

Sachi slowly nods her head.

"You understand? Truly?" I ask.

"Yes, I understand." She holds my gaze for several seconds before continuing. "Who taught you about your power?"

I hesitate for a moment at her use of the word "power." I do not see it like that. It is a gift, perhaps even a talent, but not power. It is my energy work—it is what I do—it is how I make a difference in this crazy world. I decide not to address the semantics with her at this time.

"My grandmother taught me." I feel the smile grow with the thoughts of her. "My grandmother shared the energy of the stars with me. She taught me right from wrong. She told me how using the energy from the stars to harm others will drain the life right out of me."

I recall the way I felt after harming the ferals with lightning in the vision, how I could not even walk the few feet to our bedding. I shudder at how just a vision had that effect on me, so how would acting out in the present be?

Sachi seems to tense beside me. I push all negative thoughts from my mind and take several long, deep breaths. This helps to clear my head, but not to settle me down.

I wonder if I should continue on with a second lesson, but my heart is racing and I fear I am spending too much time under the stars tonight.

"How do you feel now?" I ask her.

"I am a bit queasy. It's never been this intense, for so long under the stars," Sachi admits.

"We will end the lesson here then. Go, rest, and tomorrow evening we will sit together again."

Sachi stands up, but I wait a few seconds. I'm surprised when she bends down and throws her arms around my neck.

"Thank you, Misha. Just knowing someone else out there understands and can guide me makes me feel so much better."

"It is my pleasure," I say, meaning it. I like this girl, and really want to help her to reach her potential.

When I return to Yaz her smile is tentative. "Everything go well?"

"Yes," I say as I step into her embrace. "I am just so very tired."

"Tired after recharging?" She presses a hand to my forehead, as if checking me for fever.

"Yes," I whisper. "After recharging with someone else."

It occurs to me then that I spent a lot of energy trying to keep the child from seeing too much of my thoughts.

"I'm sorry." I pull away from her slightly, then place a small kiss on the corner of her mouth. "I think I would like to go to bed now."

"I will come with you. I can hold you until you fall to sleep?" Yaz asks, a little nervousness in her voice.

"I would like nothing more."

This gets a smile from my love.

†

I settle in, sitting side by side, close to but not touching, Sachi. We sit quietly for several minutes before I speak. My hands rest in my lap and Sachi mirrors the position.

"How are you today, Sachi? Anything about last night you need to talk about?"

She clears her throat. "I went right to sleep. Why did the stars make me so tired?"

"I am not certain, but I felt and did the same."

I try to remember if sitting with my grandmother during our lessons had a similar effect on me, but I come up with nothing. Memory is a complex thing, I muse. It could be that the energy here is different from that in New America. It could also be that my grandmother was older, wiser, and better at teaching than I am.

"But do not worry. We will stop the lessons each night before we are too drained," I say.

Sachi nods her head.

"We will charge for a short while, then we will return to the lesson," I say as I turn my hands palm-side up.

She does as I do, and we sit there, the humming from each of our chests seeming to join together, the heat in me rising. When the tingling in my hands gets to be more than I need, I bring a stop to our recharging.

"Let's begin the lesson," I say as bring my hands back to my lap.

She also places her hands in her lap. She turns halfway so she is almost facing me.

"If Arla, or Burke, or Tegan were to be injured, what would you do?"

"I would place my hands on them and imagine the injury healing."

"You have done this before?"

"Yes, I have." She glances down at her hands, then looks back up at me.

If she knows the mechanics of energy work already, then I am only needed to teach her the nuances, the proper stewardship of her gift. This comes as a relief.

"At what point do you stop?" I ask.

"When they are healed or I become cold and weak."

"And how do you know if you *should* use your energy on someone?"

"If they are sick or injured," Sachi says, her voice betraying her confusion.

"Today's lesson will be about asking permission before you touch someone, and respecting them when they resist." I feel a response about to come from Sachi and know what it will be. "If they are not conscious, and you cannot ask, then you are to only move forward if you truly believe that is what they would want."

Show her, the energy tells me. I am startled at first, as I am not trying to connect with the energy, or anyone else except the child next to me. I give a nod, a gesture that is not at all necessary, I muse.

Taking a deep, but steady breath, I concentrate to pull up the memory of Suzanna. I recall the times that she only wanted me to use the bare minimum of my energy to keep her comfortable, not to try to stop the ravages of age.

"I see you," Sachi says, awe lacing her voice. "I see you and the woman with the long silver hair. Is that your grandmother?"

"No, that is Suzanna."

"She doesn't want to be cured."

"Before Suzanna became gravely ill, she only allowed me to use a little energy to keep her comfortable. She told me that I needed to take care of myself as well, and to be ready if someone else needed my help."

"So, don't waste all of my power on one person?"

"Not if they do not need it to live. And even then, you need to also protect yourself. Do not let others take so much of you that you do not have something left for yourself."

"I understand."

"You will need to protect yourself by preserving your energy when you can." I want to say the words *protect yourself* enough times that she will remember the need to do so, even when under a lot of pressure, or the need is thrust upon her quickly and strongly.

I wipe my sweaty palms against the fabric of my pants. I breathe deeply for a few beats before concentrating on the memory of my grandmother getting sick.

"No, Misha," my grandmother tells me. "It is my time to go."

"But, Grandmother—" I argue.

"Part of mastering your gift will be knowing when not to use it. Now is one of those times."

I watch with Sachi as a young Misha is taken off to bed, only to awake to news that her beloved grandmother and teacher had died during the night.

As I sit now, beside the child, I don't fight the tear that draws its hot trail down my cheek.

She closes her eyes and breathes deeply. She opens them and turns to me, and I know she is learning the additional lesson when she says, "That is enough for tonight?"

"Yes, it is enough. We will meet here again tomorrow."

I return to Yaz in our quarters. She seems agitated.

"What is wrong, love?"

"Nothing is wrong. Well, something feels off." She won't hold eye contact and this disturbs me.

"Did something happen while we were apart?"

"No," she says, too quickly.

"Are we not to share everything with one another?" I ask.

"Yes, we are."

"Is this about how Arla looks at you?"

Yaz's head snaps up. Now she does hold my gaze.

"Nothing will ever happen between us," Yaz says.

"Again." At her look of confusion, I add, "Nothing will happen between you two again."

She sighs.

"You two were once intimate."

She nods confirmation. "A long time ago. It was only physical, there was never any real intimacy."

"I see."

"I swear you are the only one for me now. It is only you."

I smile and take her into my arms. "I believe you."

"Thank you."

"So, tell me," I tease. "Were there others? Tegan maybe?"

She pulls back. "Yes, there were others. We were very open with sex. When life is otherwise so bleak, you find comfort wherever and whenever you can. But, no, never Tegan. We were like sisters."

I brush my lips against Yaz's. "Do I need to remind Arla that you are spoken for?"

"No, sweet girl, you do not. I have made that perfectly clear already."

"Good. I would much rather put my energy to better use." This time when I pull her to me, it is a long time before I am ready to let her go.

†

I sit beside Yaz, enjoying a light meal of berries and bread when Arla comes to us.

"Tell me about taking out Perry," she said as she sits.

Yaz glances at me, then looks back to Arla.

"A lot of it was pure luck," Yaz says. "My plane took out the other two planes just in time, and then those planes helped to blow up the bunker. I don't know that I could do it again if my life depended on it, to be honest."

"And you?" Arla asks me. "What did you do in this epic, *lucky* battle?"

I look to Yaz, and my lover starts to speak on my behalf.

"Wait," Arla says, raising a hand. "I want to hear this from the teacher's mouth." She turns and faces me more fully. "What part did you play in the battle against Perry?"

214

My face is flooded with heat as I recall doing harm to others. I might not have harmed them with my gift, but I still harmed them nevertheless.

"I—" I falter and Yaz squeezes my hand.

"Just tell Arla what happened," Yaz prods me.

"I had a hand gun. I shot at anyone who was shooting at us." My mouth goes dry and I almost expect lightning to crash down upon me for my part in taking those lives. When I finally am able to look at Arla, she is smiling at me.

Now Arla turns to Yaz. "She is a sweet one, isn't she?"

Yaz does not answer, just keeps hold of my now sweating hand.

"Yazmine, did you kill canaries?"

Yaz sits up taller, stiffens.

"Only when it was unavoidable." She holds Arla's gaze for a very long time. "Things have not been the same the last couple of years. After so many runners were supposedly brought back by other canaries, no one trusted anyone else anymore. Things were becoming more and more brutal among the canaries, and between the canaries and workers."

"So, it wasn't such a big deal to kill your own?"

"They were not my own. These people took to the hunt to be rewarded with life on the inside for bringing back proof of death of the runners."

"Yet here we are, us runners, thriving outside of Perry after all."

"Those who were left behind had no way of knowing it was all a lie." Yaz lets out a sigh, deflating as if she just cannot think any more about it. "And I must say I felt safer out there," she gestures over her shoulder, in the direction we had traveled from, "just knowing Perry and everyone there is either gone or incapable of pursuing me. Or pursuing you."

Arla gives a slow nod. "Very well." She sits back and throws a berry into her mouth.

I know it is almost time for me to go, but I don't want to leave Yaz right now. I do not know what to expect from these people and want to be here for my love.

"It's getting late," Yaz says, her voice gentle.

I glance up at the starry sky and excuse myself to go meet with Sachi. I am generous in the placement of a kiss on Yaz's lips before I take my leave. I know jealousy is an ugly thing, but I cannot help feeling as if Arla would be happy to replace me in Yaz's bed.

I go to the clearing and find Sachi waiting, hands palm-side up.

"Good evening, Sachi."

"Good evening." She turns to me but waits until I am also sitting before speaking further. "I believe tonight will be our last lesson."

I smile at the wisdom I see in her young eyes. "It may very well be."

I wait until the warmth grows in my belly and chest before I begin.

"The last lesson my grandmother taught me was knowing when not to use my energy, even if someone requests it. Sometimes not using your energy is more merciful than using it. And this, too, can be about the person not wanting to have their life prolonged." Like with Grandmother, I reflect.

She is silent beside me.

"I have said it already, and here I say it again. Protect yourself, dear Sachi."

Not being able to save my grandmother was devastating enough, but when a short time later the sickness came to my village, things were very different.

I concentrate on going back to the most painful time of my life, back when I was so very young. Sachi's sharp intake of breath tells me she sees.

"Bring the healer!"

"Come to us next!"

"Why is she not getting any better? Stay with her longer!"

If it had not been for the words p*rotect yourself* that had been told to me over and over by Grandmother, told to me until I wanted to put my hands over my ears to block them out, the villagers would have killed me with their need. I almost killed myself trying to save my mother. If I hadn't collapsed from exhaustion, I would have died from the effort of trying to save my mother and the others.

When I feel the pain of losing my family crash through me, wave upon hard wave of grief, I shut down.

"Shouldn't I see everything?" Sachi asks.

"You will undoubtedly have your own pain to deal with in life, you don't need the burden of mine as well." I look into her eyes. "You saw enough to understand the lesson, yes?"

"Sometimes it is better not to intervene."

"Yes," I agree. "And?"

"Protect myself," she says with a nod. "I do understand."

"Do you have any questions about today's lesson?"

"No," she answers.

"Anything else you would like to ask about?"

She is crying now.

Without asking, I know she is sad that it is time for me and Yaz to move on. We both know that it truly is time.

"No other questions right now," she says, her voice small and brittle.

CHAPTER FOURTEEN

We sit at a large table with Arla, Burke, Tegan, and two women whose names I cannot recall.

"You should stay here," Arla says.

"We must get to the other side of the mountain ridge," Yaz responds.

"What is there?"

We are quiet. I have been dreading this conversation.

"Is it a rich land, full of wealth?" Burke teases. "If not, you have no worry that we will follow you."

The others laugh.

"No, it is a poor land with way too many social issues," Yaz says.

"Then why go back?" Arla asks.

My gaze goes back to Yaz.

"Because Misha has some unfinished business to attend to. She would like to make peace with one of her friends."

I love her for making our mission sound small. I love her for not mentioning my purpose in a way that would tempt them to go to New America. I take her hand in mine and she gently squeezes my fingers.

"Take the teacher to the edge of New America and then return," Arla says. "Tegan can accompany you."

Tegan raises an eyebrow at this suggestion.

"You belong here with us, Yazmine," Arla says in a firm tone.

"No," Yaz says. "I belong with my love."

Arla stares first at Yaz, then at me. When she curtly stands and takes her leave, the other Falcons follow, all except Tegan.

"She means nothing with her abruptness," Tegan says.

"She means everything with it," Yaz counters.

Tegan smiles, then her lips turn down into a frown. "I will miss you, my friend."

I wonder if that means Tegan does not think Arla will force us to stay. The sheer number of Falcons could easily make us stay here with them. I shiver at the thought.

"I should see to Arla," Yaz says as she stands. She turns to me and says, "I won't be long."

I sit quietly for a long time with Tegan. She is getting restless and I know she only stays with me out of respect for Yaz.

"I believe I will take a short walk," I say to Tegan. "I'd like a closer look at the gardens," I say, not really a lie.

"Sure. Look around all you'd like." Tegan stands when I do, then nods her head. "Let me know if you need anything. I will be in the community room."

I watch as she makes her way toward the large building in the center of the village.

When my meandering brings me to the llamas, I am delighted to watch them for several moments. They are unique, they are only slightly aware of me, and they do not hold my attention for too long. I feel an uncontrollable need to be near Yaz.

As I approach the large, currently unlit, fire pit, I see Yaz standing near Arla. They speak softly to one another.

I go to them, not out of jealousy but out of solidarity with Yaz. I want to know any and every pressure this woman and these people place on Yaz.

It is obvious to me that Arla registers my approach, but she does not acknowledge me.

Yaz takes my hand and I let out a deep breath in relief at the welcoming gesture.

"We will never crest the mountain ridge," Arla says. "Of this we promise. But you must promise that you will never speak of us."

Yaz looks at me. I think about Dr. Bradshaw, Naomi, and so many others. Loyalty is a funny thing. If it is not shown to you, it makes it hard to give in return. Yaz has been loyal to me throughout our time together.

I nod my acceptance.

"Because if your people," she glares at me, "ever come to conquer us, we will kill each and every one of them."

I have seen the large number of firearms and I believe her words wholeheartedly.

"That is understood. We will tell them that the land here is uninhabitable," I say.

†

The next morning, Tegan brings a sled loaded down with food.

"Overkill?" Yaz says to her.

Tegan laughs. "Maybe. You never know when your journey may take longer than you think."

"I am so very glad to know that you are alive and well," Yaz says to Tegan.

"I am so very glad to know that you are happy." Tegan looks at me, then adds, "Both of you."

"It was nice to meet you," I say, feeling totally inadequate with my words.

"Yaz," Tegan says, her voice much lower. "Please do not trust any promises Arla may have made to you. Stay aware at all times."

"You think she will try to lead an invasion against New America?" Yaz asks.

I feel my eyes widening and my palms grow hot.

"I think it strange that she takes you at your word and lets the two of you just walk away. That is not Falcon behavior." Tegan looks from Yaz to me and back to Yaz. "Just be careful."

Yaz nods and I see her eyes dart from side to side.

"And what about you, Tegan?" Yaz asks. "Will you follow if she rides upon New America? Will you follow if she attacks me and Misha and the others in New America?"

"I am still the same Tegan. I would never betray you. But Arla—Arla has changed. So many here have changed. Unease has taken over the last several years. They distrust everything and everyone who is not as they are."

Yaz holds her gaze for a long time. Then she nods.

"Now, enough of the heavy talk," Tegan says. "You two have a good life and take care of each other."

"Thank you," Yaz says to Tegan before pulling her into an embrace.

"Get off me, you lug," Tegan teases. Then she turns to me. "Take care of my friend, will you?"

I smile. I do like this woman. "Yes, I certainly will."

Tegan embraces me briefly, then steps back.

Sachi has come up from behind me, and I turn away from Yaz and Tegan to say goodbye to the child.

"I would like to travel with you," Sachi says.

"Your purpose is here." Of this I could not be more certain.

"And your purpose?" she asks.

"To return to New America. To be of service there." And, I think, to give the people who were not welcoming to Yaz, or supportive of me, the chance to redeem themselves. I did not expressly know this until now. I understand now that our return to New America is a test for how the people in my old life will act, when given a second chance. If they cannot pass a simple test of compassion after all that has happened, then peace does not stand a chance under the Peace Movement.

"There's more to what you are saying," Sachi says. "Are you worried about how you will be received?"

I glance at Yaz, who is still talking with Tegan, and I look into Sachi's blue-green eyes. I am certain that withholding the truth will not do her any good. "Yes," I say. "I am."

"If things don't go well?"

"Then I guess Yaz and I pay with our lives—or at least with our freedom."

"I can't imagine ever worrying about something like that with the Falcons."

I smile. "Be thankful for that."

"Do you think our connection will remain when you get far away?" Sachi asks.

"It is possible." I cock my head. "Would you like that?"

"Very much," she says, looking down at her feet. "I like you."

"I like you as well." A thought comes to me. "You should go to your perch at sundown," I tell Sachi.

She nods.

"We will travel one half day to the west," I say.

"Then you and I will communicate via the stars," Sachi adds.

"Yes, we will attempt that."

Yaz comes to my side and puts her hand on my lower back. "What are you two whispering about over here?"

Sachi gives me a questioning look and I nod.

"We are going to try to communicate through the stars tonight."

"You are?" Yaz asks.

"Yes." Sachi is all puffed up and smiling. "Because we are connected now."

We bid our farewells to the Falcons and continue our journey, the sled secured by a rope around Yaz's waist, dragging behind her.

"Do you really think you will be able to talk to Sachi?" Yaz asks.

"I don't know. It will be a good experiment."

"And you'll try to maintain that connection, even as we get farther and farther away?"

"If that is what the stars tell me to do."

Yaz nods, and we walk in silence for a long time before she suggests we take a rest.

A large bird flies overhead before perching on a low branch.

"That is not a crow, is it?" I ask.

Yaz shakes her head slowly. "No, that is a falcon," she responds.

We both watch as it flies away. Goose bumps rise on my skin and the hair on the back of my neck stands on end.

Yaz physically shakes off whatever she is feeling, then fakes a casual shrugging of her shoulders.

I, too, shake off the strange feeling that tickles at the back of my mind.

"Let's walk a little farther," Yaz says.

I do not argue. I would like to put some real distance between us and the unease that grows within me here. I find myself looking skyward, looking for additional raptors. I half expect another one, or ten, or a hundred to appear in the blue, cloudless sky.

When a time goes by with no additional birds flying in sight, I begin to settle a little.

"I never did hear why they call themselves Falcons," I say as we continue to make our way. "Did you find that out while you were without me?"

She slows but does not stop our forward movement.

"Canaries," she says. "When a canary molts and morphs into a falcon, they become much stronger. The first people to escape the elite vowed that they would no longer be meek canaries, but become the larger, stronger birds. Falcons can be brutal in their place on the food chain. Those who'd run wanted to be reminded of their new position in their world."

I think again of the large bird we'd seen when we began our journey. I do not respond, and Yaz says nothing else of the matter.

When we stop much later, I look around.

"That outcropping is a good place for me to try to connect with the stars."

"I will prepare our evening meal while you do that," Yaz says.

"Thank you."

I settle in and deepen my breathing. The stars are bright on this night, which is encouraging. I feel the heat in my chest growing and realize I am humming.

I feel Sachi almost immediately.

She is wishing me a safe journey and thanking me for her lessons.

I wish her well and can hear her small voice say, "Peace to you."

†

We resume our trek to the west at first light, planning to take the most direct route through the cratered stretch of land that was obviously bombed over and over during the war. We believe this will take us to the last mountain ridge separating us from New America.

As we stand near the edge of the first in the string of craters, Yaz seems to read my mind.

"Maybe we shouldn't go through the bombed area. Maybe it is poisoned with radiation."

"It will add a few days to the journey to go around it," I say. "But if it is contaminated—"

"Let's go around. I don't want to bring more sickness to New America."

I nod my head, my heart breaking at the pain I see in Yaz's eyes as she says this.

She grabs the rope attached to the sled of food to reposition it around her waist, and we begin walking again.

I cannot shake my doubt about the Falcons' intent but can't really articulate what is bothering me. I continue to find myself scanning the sky as we walk, half expecting to see another falcon flying overhead. If Yaz notices this, she says nothing of it.

It is five days later when we stop at the foot of the mountain range. We will make camp for the night here. We sit beside each other on a log as we finish up our evening meal.

"We should talk about what happens when we finally get to New America," Yaz says.

I nod. "Yes, we should. But we really do not have any way of knowing the type of reception we will receive."

"They will probably take me into custody."

"Then they will take us both into custody," I say.

"You don't have to—"

"Yes," I interrupt her. "I do. I must."

I get up from the log we sit on and step to face her, standing between her knees. I straddle her, then sit on her lap facing her, looking into her eyes. I grasp the collar of her shirt to hold her still.

"We do this together, every step of the way," I say.

She is silent, but nods. Her dark eyes hold so much love, so much passion, that it nearly steals my breath. But there will be time for that soon enough.

"I've made a lot of promises to a lot of people, it seems. I've kept most of them. The most important promise, though, is the one that I make to myself."

She stares at me with wide eyes. "And what promise is that?"

"I will do whatever it takes to be happy. And I can only be so with you."

She smiles. "Misha, you are an amazing woman."

"As are you," I respond, then lean in for a kiss.

Yaz's hands cup my face as she deepens the kiss. When she pulls away, she says, "Shouldn't you be recharging under the stars?"

"No, I will recharge here with you."

My fingers nimbly unbutton her shirt, then my hands move to cover her bare breasts. She draws in a sharp breath.

She swats at my bottom with both hands. "Up," she demands.

I stand and she quickly removes my clothing.

"Yours too," I say.

She undresses, then pulls me back onto her lap. Her lips go to my left breast and I hiss when she draws the nipple into her mouth.

"That feels so good," I murmur.

She places a hand in the center of my back to support me, then moves the other between my legs, all the while not stopping with the exquisite action of her lips and tongue on my nipple.

When her fingers stroke through my abundant wetness, I let out a long moan and drop my face to her neck. She matches my moan when I nibble at the sensitive flesh just below her ear.

She slips a finger inside of me and my muscles clench around it.

"Is this okay?" she asks.

"It's perfect."

227

She begins slowly pumping her finger in and out of me. My breathing hitches when I feel the addition of a second finger.

I grip her shoulders. When her thumb begins rubbing against my most sensitive place, I throw my head back and call out my desire.

"Come for me, baby," Yaz urges, even as I am beginning my release. Her words intensify the feelings and I come hard, quaking in her lap.

She stills as the twitching of my thighs lessens.

"You're so beautiful," she says, over and over.

I laugh. "You are as well, my love."

Slowly, she slides her fingers out of me and pulls me in for a tight embrace.

"Let me taste you," I whisper into her ear.

She shudders.

"Yes?" I ask.

"Yes. Please."

I stand, staring down into the most beautiful, loving expression I have ever seen. I give her a deep, but short, kiss, then drop to my knees before her.

My fingers part the swollen folds between her legs and I cannot help the visceral response of my body to the wetness I find. She is so ready to be loved.

I place a gentle kiss on the soft curls over her sex and her hands go to my head, lightly holding on.

When my tongue strokes through her wetness, she tightens her grip on my head, wrapping her fingers in my hair.

"Yes, Misha," she says.

I smile against her, then let my tongue circle and lick. When I stiffen my tongue and penetrate her with it, she comes undone.

"I'm coming," she pants.

I press my face deeper into her folds and continue my strokes and sucking until she finishes her release.

That night I sleep soundly in my love's arms, knowing that together we can face anything.

CHAPTER FIFTEEN

We stop, the sled coasting to a halt behind Yaz. I can smell the charred land. New America is just over the next ridge. We can be home in a few days, or next week at the most. Excitement drums through me. And then I remember that we don't know what fate awaits us.

We have decided we are best off trying to get to Naomi. There are fewer people in Liberté then at Karst, and we are uneasy about Karst's leadership. Will we be able to get to Naomi and Liberté before anyone else sees us? Will Naomi be there, and if she is, will she be willing to help us?

These thoughts are interrupted as a group of men approaches us. We are surrounded. Five men in total. I see the jeer in their expressions and my stomach roils.

"Hey, look here. This one has strange eyes," one says. They all turn to look at me. "You will be bedding down with me tonight."

The awkwardness of the ensuing chuckles sends ice into my veins.

"We will be heading out now," Yaz says, her voice tight with barely achieved restraint. "Good evening to you."

I take a step in her direction and the man grabs me by the arm. "Not so fast."

"I'll take the dark one," a wiry man with a scraggly beard says. "I bet she's wild."

"Fine, you can all share her, but I get the green-eyed one."

Yaz moves like the puma upon the deer, fast and without hesitation, as she grabs a sword from the waist of one of the men. She takes out two of the men before any of them even react.

She grabs me and whips me behind her, whirling around until she is standing between me and the three remaining men, including the one who has claimed me as his own.

They rush at Yaz until she is no longer in front at me. Her back to a large boulder, she has nowhere to go. The determination—and fear—on her face makes my own anger rise. It bubbles up inside me until the humming in my chest is accompanied by a roar in my head.

In my mind, I see Naomi taking on the ferals who killed Nain. Then it is her as she fights alongside Kai and Rachel, Breanne and the others, against the remaining Merrick clan. The thought of all the battles that needed to be fought sickens me, these men sicken me. The way they are taunting Yaz now, outnumbered, backed up in a manner of no escape, infuriates me.

What I do next will determine whether we live or die today, of this I cannot be more certain.

I block out the thought of Grandmother's lessons about never using the energy to harm. She said it would probably kill me to do so. I would rather die protecting Yaz right now than to live even a moment with the knowledge of her pain or death.

To Yaz's right is the man who had claimed me. Instinctively, I believe Yaz will go after him first since she probably feels more anger towards him, and he's more easily accessed on her right since she is right-handed.

Heat radiates down my arms to my hands, painful in its intensity. I stare into Yaz's eyes for a moment and hope she reacts how I believe she will.

"Fight!" I scream.

She lunges forward, to the one I predicted, striking a blow against his sword.

I hold my hands up in front of me, palms out, fingers splayed. My ears ache, my head pounds, but I force the anger out of my body, through my hands.

My fingers glow the instant before lightning flies out of my hands. I hold two men in the bolt of electricity as they stiffen, convulse, then one after the other their eyes roll back into their heads.

Their arms go limp at their sides and the clank of their swords falling to the ground rings in my ears.

I believe I see—or sense—blood dripping down the side of Yaz's face. The rage builds stronger. In my peripheral vision I think I see Yaz take down the man she's been engaging, but I am not certain.

I push my outstretched hands further in the men's direction. I have never felt a rage like this before. I have never felt the pain of energy running out of my hands like this.

"Misha, Misha!"

I am crying. Yaz is holding me as I sob.

The two men I struck in rage are at our feet, skulls crushed and bodies smoldering.

"Oh, Goddess."

"Don't look, sweetheart, don't look," Yaz says.

I sob. "I had to do it. I had to. They would have killed us."

"I know. It's all right. Shhh."

I cry into her shoulder for a long time. I am cold, barely standing on my own.

"We must go. We must leave in case there are more of them."

I nod my head but my legs do not move.

"Are you harmed?"

I crumble to the ground. I see Grandmother, her face unreadable. I knew the consequences, yet still did harm to others. In all the times I've been abused, or enslaved, I've never used the energy in my hands to harm anyone. Until now.

"Do no harm."

"Hush," Yaz whispers.

"I would do it again, love," I say, my voice hoarse, raw.

"Shhh. It's okay."

"Leave me here and go back to Mt. Falcon where you will be embraced."

"No. Wherever I go, I am taking you with me. Karst is closer now. We will go there."

I feel myself being lifted and do not fight against it.

I am so cold. So very cold.

When I open my eyes again, I am in a meadow, one slightly familiar but not really known to me. The sunshine warms me and I am surrounded by women in long red robes. I look down at my arms and see I too am cloaked in red.

Grandmother is there. And Suzanna. I cannot identify anyone else but feel my connection to them. We are either related by blood or by the collective consciousness, of this I am certain.

"What have you done, child?" Grandmother asks me. Her voice is disjointed, not quite accusatory, but not loving either.

Suzanna comes to me.

"Suzanna!" I cry out as I reach for her.

She takes a step away from me. "No child. You must go back. Return to life."

The red-robed women all disappear and I am once again cold, shivering.

†

The smooth gliding I've been trying to identify has turned into a series of jerks and jolts.

"What's happening?" I croak out.

"The terrain is getting rougher. I don't know if we can continue with the sled."

I look down and see that I am tied to the supply sled the Falcons gave us. It all comes rushing back to me, the assault on us, the way I used my energy to kill two men. I wait for the regret and it doesn't come. Only relief for Yaz's safety surges up inside me. Is this the bigger infraction? Is the not caring about killing two men the larger sin than actually causing their deaths?

I don't realize we've stopped until Yaz has a cup of water at my lips, begging me to drink of it. I do as I am told.

"Where are we?" I ask.

"I'm not sure, exactly. We are taking the easier, long route down the range instead of going straight down the northwest face."

"Because I've become a burden."

"Because you saved my life, again, and I will do whatever it takes to get you the medical or spiritual healing you so badly need."

I stare at her but cannot respond for a long time. When the boulder in my throat dissipates enough for words to sneak past it, I whisper, "I love you."

"I love you, too."

"What is next?"

"I think it's time to leave the sled behind. I will strap you to me and we will descend the range here."

"You can leave me—"

"I will strap you to me and we will descend the range here," she repeats, her face both hard and soft at once, beautiful and fierce.

It registers as she unties me from the sled that I am strapped to it in fetal position since I am a good two feet taller than it is long. My resourceful lover thought of everything. Except, of course, what the people of New America will think when I am brought back to them in this state, a half-dead traitor carried in by an escaped invader.

†

The jolting and jarring of my body in her arms conveys to me how tired she is. I want to tell her to put me down, to rest, to give in to fate with me, but I cannot form the words. Besides, I know her well enough not to insult her by verbalizing such a thing.

"I love you," I whisper.

She gives no indication that she's heard me. I am unsure if I've thought the words or actually spoke them.

I can no longer smell the charred earth. Is it because we've left it behind, or are my faculties failing me?

I am still cold. So very cold.

She stumbles, jarring my body painfully. I want to tell her again to leave me behind, to turn around and return to her people at Mt. Falcon.

The rocking gait of her carrying me lulls me eventually into a state of near-rest until the movement stops abruptly.

I am aware that I am touched in too many places at once for it to be only Yaz's hands on me. Now it is not her soft, warm body I rest against, but the hard, cool ground. I am still for several moments.

I shake my head until it is clear enough for me to glance to my right to see Yaz—strong, beautiful, magnificent Yaz— on her knees with the tip of a sword mere inches from her neck.

"Noooo!" the word blasts through my head but I am unsure if it has come out of my mouth. "Leave her be!" My lips are cracked, my throat dry. I try again. "Please. Don't hurt her!"

"Misha, Misha," a loud voice says.

I struggle to focus and the face of my savior comes into view. "Naomi."

"Oh, thank the goddess."

I lift my hand to sign to her but it is limp, cold, and clumsy.

"Don't let them hurt my love," I say, hoping she can read my lips since my voice is barely over a whisper.

"Gotham," Naomi says over her shoulder. "Get those men away from the pilot. Now."

"Yes, Counselor."

I am confused by the title.

"There have been some much-needed changes around here," she says. Her smile then is brilliant. "Thanks to you and Yaz."

Yaz appears next to Naomi and I smile. "Hi, love."

"Hi, yourself."

"We made it," I say in a whisper.

"Yes, we did make it."

"Let's get her onto a horse with you now, shall we?" Naomi asks.

I am lifted from the ground by many hands, and gently placed into Yaz's arms atop a horse.

"Stay with me," I say to Yaz.

"Always."

I watch as Naomi mounts her beloved gray mare, Cinders. Then I let my eyes drift shut.

It is but a blur as I am taken into Liberté and placed on a mound of bedding. I catch glimpses of both Yaz and Naomi as I feel hands on me.

"Misha, it is Loretta. You remember me? From Las Estrellas?"

"Yes, I remember." My eyes go from her face to Yaz's. I met the healer the first time I went to Las Estrellas, with Naomi.

"I am going to remove your clothing and put you in an herbal bath. Is that acceptable?" Loretta asks.

I nod, or at least I believe I nod.

The water feels—magical. Is it that Loretta, the very science-based healer from Las Estrellas, has embraced even more of the mythical side of healing than even I expected of her?

"Thank you," I whisper.

"Will she be all right?" I hear Yaz's voice from several feet away.

"I don't know." That voice belongs to Naomi. "Do you think we should get her under the stars? At Karst, or Las Estrellas, where it has always been best for her?"

"Yes. But only if it is safe to move her." Yaz sounds exhausted, weary.

"It is probably even less safe not to," Naomi says.

In a blur of activity, I am lifted from the tub, wrapped in a blanket, and placed once again in Yaz's arms on a horse. Sometime later I am finally settled, still in my blanket, upon a plush parcel of grass.

"What happened?" I think I hear Naomi finally ask Yaz.

"It is her story to tell," is the response.

"Has she been injured, or is this an energy thing?"

"Mostly this is energy. Please, let her tell you the specifics."

"Where did this happen?" Naomi's voice sounds harder.

"Just north of where you found us, just into New America."

"Did it involve another person? One of our own?"

"Ferals. All of the guilty are dead," Yaz says, her voice louder now.

I close my eyes and a vision comes to me. I struggle to focus as the images fade in and out, swirl in my vision, then assault my mind with a sudden viciousness. A hundred or more well armed Falcons rush down the side of the mountain and attack my fellow New Americans. They are brutal and laugh at me when I complain that they promised to stay away as long as our warriors did the same.

My eyes flutter open and I look up into Yaz's brown eyes. "You must tell them everything," I plead.

Then I hear Sachi's voice in my head. Her words are unmistakable.

"The Falcons are coming," I say to Yaz. "You must warn our warriors."

CHAPTER SIXTEEN

Two days later, I leave the comfort and safety of Las Estrellas to join our warriors as they prepare to go off to battle. Kai has expressed her wish to have me stay behind, and Naomi has supported her in that, but I will not stay here while my friends and lover face such a daunting task.

I watch as Breanne talks to Yaz, explaining the workings of the bow she holds in one hand. Yaz takes the offered weapon and straps it to her back. She also carries a rifle given to her by Aaron. Only two other people appear to have firearms, the rest of the warriors carry swords or bows.

Kai's horse shifts beside Rachel, and I see Kai carries a sword and Rachel a bow. I have seen Rachel's skill with the bow, as well as Kai in action with her sword. They are equally talented fighters, even if very different in method.

There are twenty-five or thirty warriors, many whom are our best, bustling about the area near the entrance to Karst. I look around and wish Suzanna was here to bless them. I also wish we had more time for the rest of the warriors to join us here.

After nearly six years of mostly peace, our warriors are spread throughout New America, many simply too far away to make it on time to assist, I am sure.

I have traded the loose fitting and flowing clothing that I've been wearing while recuperating for a pair of pants and a light jacket. My medical bag is strapped to my back. It is loaded down with herbs for calming, lavender and rosemary oil for use as analgesics, and much gauze. A few tourniquets have been placed inside as well.

Protect yourself. I hear my grandmother's words and am not certain I will be able to. Not at the cost of my friends' lives. I know I will do whatever I need to do to protect the people that I love.

Yaz has finally finished speaking with Breanne and comes to my side.

"I know nothing I say will make you agree to stay behind," Yaz says.

"That is true," I say. "You do not have to fight, you know."

"Yes," she interrupts. "Yes, I do."

I nod. "Please be safe."

We embrace, and after a short, sweet kiss, she leaves my side to go to her place amongst the warriors. I mount my borrowed horse and retreat to the back of the pack, where I can better watch for when my services will be needed.

The air around us fills with a loud screech, and my mouth falls open as Falcons seem to come from everywhere on the mountainside, all at once. At first things seem to move in slow motion, but quickly they speed up to dizzying movements.

I ride the mare closer to the sounds of metal upon metal. Gunshots ring out and several of our warriors fall, unresponsive. As if in tune with everyone, all at once, I know who not to try to assist, who are beyond my help.

Yaz is always in my peripheral vision, even as I apply a dressing to the leg of a New American warrior I have never seen before. *Heal, heal now.* I only stay by his side long enough to know he will do as I say and keep pressure on the bandage over the wound.

There are easily eighty more Falcons descending upon us. And above them there are wave upon wave of others, ready to pillage our warriors. I know—I truly know—that as good as our warriors are, they will not survive this attack.

I rush to Breanne when I see she is bleeding profusely from a wound to her thigh.

After I tend to her, she tightens the wrapping holding her bandage in place and says, "I am fine."

She stands, unsteadily, and my gaze goes to where Kai and Yaz fight side by side. They are sorely outnumbered and appear to be tiring.

For every one Falcon that Kai, Naomi, and Yaz take down, there are three more in their place.

"Please forgive me," I say to no one, yet everyone, as I ride hard to the base of the mountain.

I jump off my horse and onto a ledge. Although it is only a few feet off the ground, from where I stand, I see the entire atrocity taking place before me.

I scream when Yaz falls to the ground and is about to have an enemy sword pushed into her flesh. Kai takes down

242

that Falcon before they can kill Yaz, but then several are upon her as well.

"Forgive me," I repeat as I call out to the universe. I feel the heat burning inside me, the pain almost unbearable as I pull together every ounce of energy I have.

Thunder clashes all around. At that moment my gaze goes to the side of the mountain where I see Arla, dressed for battle, firing a gun at one of my people.

I give myself into my anger as a bolt of lightning strikes my outstretched hand, and with a gut-wrenching scream I hurl the lightning at the Falcons on the mountain.

I gasp, unable to breath as I watch the lightning flow from my hands to Arla, then another Falcon, and another. They fall, writhing on the ground, sounds of agony filling my head, the pain of a hundred deaths filling my chest.

My last thought is that my people, my Yaz, are all going to be okay.

†

I stand in the middle of a circle of elders. They wear the red robes that now feel familiar to me. Suzanna steps forward and opens her arms to me.

The familiar fragrance of the meadow outside of Karst surrounds me, but I do not know where I am, exactly.

I can hear the buzzing of bees, smell honey, feel the warmth of the sun on my face.

"Come now," a woman says. "It is time to join us."

It is at this moment that I realize that again, I too wear a red robe. I know the color bears some significance, but I am losing my battle with staying aware, of keeping my thoughts lucid.

When I walk to Suzanna and step into her arms, I am aware only of no longer feeling any connection to Karst, or New America, or horribly, Yaz.

"She will be fine," Suzanna says, as if reading my mind. "Yaz will be fine. Now come with me, dear one. It is time for you to come with me."

Epilogue

The sun is bright on this clear day. Still, I pull my eye shades from my face and stuff them into the pocket of my cargo pants. In the distance the playful yips of a family of coywolves echoes off the sides of the mountains I stand amidst.

I dismount and stand at the edge of the ridge, leaving young Sachi sitting atop my horse.

"Kai!"

I turn at the sound of my name.

"Is something wrong?" Breanne asks me as she rides closer to where I stand.

"No," I answer. But yes, something is very wrong. I should not still have to mourn the loss of loved ones, not like this.

My sister holds my gaze for a long moment, then nods.

"Take your time, Kai," she says as she rides back to the others.

I take a deep breath and think of how far we have come, and hope that with Misha's ultimate sacrifice that maybe, just maybe, the fighting and dying has finally come to an end. My eyes go to the large burn area, the area on the side of the mountain that was scorched by lightning. I have found myself hoping that the area remains charred and barren as a tribute to Misha.

I become aware again of Sachi on my horse behind me. When my band of warriors went to Mt. Falcon to scour for enemy survivors, all we found was the young girl, sitting upon a mound of bedding in the middle of the village.

"I am so glad you've finally come for me," she'd said. She walked up to my horse then, one bag clutched in her hand. "Misha promised you would come."

I shake free of the recent memory.

From my position on the ridge I can see the meadow just outside the entrance to Karst. People are bustling about. They prepare for our ceremony to honor Misha.

I can make out Naomi and my cousin, Camryn. They stand on either side of their daughter, Radha. When Naomi squats in front of the child and starts to sign to her, I look away. Even though I doubt I could read her hands from this distance, I want to afford her some privacy.

Bronwyn plays a game of rock-scotch with some of the children from Las Estrellas and Liberté. Their voices do not carry as I would expect carefree children's calls should, and I am pretty sure they have been warned by the adults to respectfully keep their voices down.

My gaze goes to Rachel and, as if she knows I am here, she looks up at the mountain. I press my fingers to my lips and whisper, "I love you."

Dawson and Heidi join my beloved, and she looks away from the mountain, from me. She embraces each of them, then follows them toward Karst and out of my field of vision.

I turn to watch as a lone figure walks into the meadow, head bowed, hands in her pockets. From her gait I know it is Yaz. I smell the flowers even though I know the scent does not reach my position on the ridge.

Yellow, orange, red, and green blanket the wide-open space. The colors run together as tears blur my vision.

Through the stinging in my eyes, I swear Yaz approaches someone standing in the meadow with her arms wide open. I see a flash of auburn hair and hear laughter.

A bee buzzes near my head and I gently swat it away. When I look back down to the meadow, there is no one there. I glance around and do not see Yaz or the person she was approaching in the meadow.

My horse scuffs his hoof and I turn to look in his direction.

Sachi sits up straighter and smiles at me. "Misha and Yaz are together," she says.

"You saw them?" I ask.

She smiles and her blue-green eyes light up. She says no more.

I place my eyeshades back on my face and remount the horse. Sachi holds on tight and we begin our descent home, to New America.

The End

THE LAST FALCON

A KARST SERIES SHORT STORY BY RENEE MACKENZIE

After days of watching the meadow, I finally see her. Just as I am about to move on to another town to look for her, there she is, standing with her arms out, gazing up at the sky. It is only dusk, so I am a little confused as to why the healer looks for stars now, but I don't plan on wasting too much time worrying about that.

Other than the healer, who was also Sachi's teacher, the meadow is empty. I am surprised not to see Yaz, but know I will in good time.

After one last glance around, I move in. My fingers curl until they look like talons, and my movement is as smooth

248

and silent as a falcon in flight. I am at her back—I can already taste the sweet revenge—and my hand slips in front of her to cover her mouth before she even knows I am there.

She fights against me, not nearly as hard as I expected her to, but I wrap my arm around her from behind and within seconds she is neutralized.

I have her gagged, hooded, and over my shoulder when she stops resisting all together. I must admit, I expected so much more fight out of Yaz's lover. She seemed so spirited when I met her at Mt. Falcon and I thought she'd be even stronger after making it all the way from Mt. Falcon to New America.

My prize isn't heavy by any means, but after struggling to get her to the mouth of the cave I have chosen as my base, I find myself wishing I'd decided on something not so far up the side of the mountain.

I set her down in a seated position near the back wall of the cave, gently, as I am not a monster, after all. I don't really want to hurt her.

Yanking off the hood, I stare down into a face I have never before seen.

I am met with wide, panic-stricken eyes. Her body is racked by deep, erratic breathing. I pull the gag from her mouth and she starts gasping, almost hyperventilating. I stand there, shocked silent, scared to say anything that might make her panic worsen.

As her breathing steadies, she scoots backward, away from me, until her back is against the wall.

I stand there for several moments, letting her catch her breath. I'm not quite sure what to do or say, and when the words do finally make it out of my mouth, I cringe at the ridiculousness of them.

"You aren't the teacher," I say.

Her eyes flash, with disbelief or anger, I am unsure.

"Of course, I am not," she says, the words rolling off her tongue in a chastising tone.

I am stopped short for a moment, first by the realization that she is spirited after all, and second with the unmistakable pull of desire at the appearance of this very attractive woman.

"Where is she?" I ask, the sting of her tone *finally* causing anger to grow inside me.

"To whom are you referring?"

I look her over closer. "Misha."

"You thought I was a ghost?"

"Ghost?" I ask, confusion replacing my anger.

"You thought I was Misha's ghost?" Her eyes travel over me now and it's infuriating. "Who are you?"

I yank the gag back into place over her mouth as I try to recalculate my plan.

First, however, I must better secure the woman who is not who she is supposed to be. When I pick up the cuff attached to the chain I have previously secured into the floor of the cave, she scrambles away as if to make for the exit.

"Oh no, you don't." I grab her by the arm and use my body to pin her against the wall, pressing perhaps harder against her than I need to, as I bend slightly to secure the cuff to her ankle.

When I straighten and stand over her, she stares first at the chain she is now attached to, then at me, as her face reddens with obvious rage.

This woman who is not Yaz's Misha makes so much noise against the gag that I know I will need to either knock her out or let her talk. I must eventually have some peace and quiet in order to think.

I pull down the gag again. "What?"

"Who are you and why have you kidnapped me?"

I cannot let her go now, not if I want time to try to correct my mistake. I will need to keep her as well as snatch up Misha. But what was that about Misha's ghost?

"What do you want from me?" she asks.

"Tell me why you referred to Misha's ghost."

She swallows hard. "You don't know?"

"Know what?" I am losing patience. "Out with it! Now!"

"Misha is dead."

"And Yaz?"

"She is gone."

"Gone?" I ask.

"Yes, gone. She disappeared the day of Misha's memorial service. Many believe her to be dead as well."

"This can't be. No, no, no."

"Please tell me who you are and what you plan to do to me."

I decide it can't hurt to tell her. There is no plan now, after all, if what she says is true.

"I am Tegan of Mt. Falcon," I say.

At the last word, the woman's eyes grow wide in recognition. Her eyes flit over me, causing me discomfort.

"Are you—are you contaminated with radiation like Yaz was when she first came here?"

At first I am unsure of what she means. Then it dawns on me.

"I have not been to Perry for years. Mt. Falcon is clean from radiation."

I give my head a little shake, wondering why I care if she knows any of this.

"What is your name?" I ask her.

"Emily," she whispers, the single word resonating with defeat.

"Emily," I repeat, looking at her, really looking at her, and seeing how incredibly beautiful she is.

"What do you want with me?"

"You were supposed to be Misha."

"Yet obviously, I am not." She squares her shoulders in a strange, vulnerable defiance. "Why Misha?"

"To lure out Yaz." I clench my teeth and add, "To make them both pay for what they did to my people."

"Your people attacked us. Your people got what they deserved."

I raise my hand, but before striking her, I lower it and roughly pull the gag back into her mouth. I storm out of the cave, but do not go far, just putting a little distance between me and this woman for a few moments.

†

An hour later when I return to the cave, Emily makes those goddess-awful noises against the gag again. I pull the cloth down. "What?"

"I need to relieve myself." She holds my gaze now in a way that surprises me.

"Oh."

I look toward the far-right side of the cave and decide it will have to do. I take her by her shoulders and easily pull the slight woman to her feet. I have one hand in the center of her chest, holding her against the wall, when I bend at the waist and with the other hand, I unlock the cuff. Her gaze follows my hand when it places the key back into the pocket of my cargo pants.

"Relieve yourself over there," I say as I point to the far side of the cave. "Make it fast."

"Surely you don't think—"

"*Surely* I do. Now go if you must."

She looks uncertain at first, then holds up her hands for me to unbind her.

"Do not make me regret this," I say as I untie the rope binding her wrists.

She looks up at me and smirks. "You have several inches on me and you are obviously strong, so no, I won't try to get away."

I stand up taller to emphasize the height difference.

"Will you turn away, at least?"

I shake my head. "No, just do what you have to do."

She goes to the far side and remains facing me. I suppose having her back to me while incapacitated in that manner would make her feel even more vulnerable. Her gaze appears to be fixed just over my shoulder and I stand very still so as not to draw more attention to my likely menacing presence.

When she is finished, I bind her wrists, gag her, and chain her to the cave floor. She has sat back down, leaning against the cave wall, when I leave.

I perch on the outcropping just east of the cave where I have the best view of the meadow and farmland. I expect to see the warriors gathering to come for my prisoner, but see no one and nothing.

I am surprised and unsettled.

When I return to the cave, I remove the gag from Emily.

"Did you find what you were looking for?" Emily spits out.

I do not answer.

"Did you find out that you have kidnapped the only person in Karst who won't be missed?" she asks.

"Karst?"

Emily's eyes widen slightly but she doesn't say anything else.

"I thought you called your country New America?"

"We do. Karst is but a village, just like Las Estrellas, Liberté, or Grover."

I stare at Emily; at the defiant lift of her chin I have come to expect.

"There is no one special in your life who will see you are gone?" I ask.

"No, there is no one."

"Why don't you have a partner?" I know it's a rude question, but ask anyway.

"Why do you care?"

My gaze goes from Emily's eyes to her mouth, then her delicate neck. Indeed, why do I care? I shake away the distraction, then say, "Because if you had a partner, they would be searching for you."

She shrugs but says nothing.

"Your friends will notice you are gone."

"Maybe, but it might take days, or weeks."

"I cannot believe—" The look of challenge on her face stops me. I shake my head, dismissing the conversation.

"Did you bring back some food or do you plan to let me starve to death?" Emily asks.

I roll my eyes exaggeratedly, then let my gaze roll over the length of her body. I would hate for her to become thinner, as I quite like the way she looks.

I retrieve the pack from near the entrance and remove the smallest, most tender, leaves of kudzu that I have. I untie her wrists and hand her a plate of kudzu.

I sit against the same wall, several feet away, as I eat my own plate of leaves. I notice she is not eating. "What?"

"You couldn't find any herbs for seasoning? You couldn't even cook them?"

The questions rile me more than they should. I jump up, snatch the plate from her hands, and dump the contents into the dirt on the far side, where she earlier relieved herself.

"No fucking wonder no one is looking for you!"

I ignore the startled look on her face and storm from the cave. I let the warm breeze outside wash over me. Taking deep breaths, I settle myself down. I cannot let her rile me up. I must always remember I am in charge, and that even if she doesn't physically fight me, she is still resisting, and obviously doing a fine job of it.

Yes, I think, I need a new plan and I need it immediately.

For now, though, I need to go back in, ignore her, and reestablish a calm demeanor. I am going to pretend that she isn't gorgeous, and isn't driving me crazy.

I return to the cave and prepare another plate of kudzu leaves. I hold it out to her and she shakes her head. Without a word, I set the plate within her reach. She will either eat it, or not, and I don't care which.

After a long stretch of silence, I clear my throat and say, "Karst is so big that they will not notice right away that you are gone?"

255

She reaches for the kudzu and places a small leaf in the mouth, chewing slowly before taking two more leaves. I wonder if she eats now to distract from the question I have asked, or if she is indeed hungry. Either way, it makes me strangely giddy to watch her eat the food I have given her.

Without looking at me, she responds, "And I left a note for a friend that I was going to Las Estrellas for a few days. She will cover for me at first if anyone asks of me."

"Why did you do that?" I don't really expect her to confide in me, but still ask.

"Because with so many of the people I am used to having around me gone, it was just so—*I* was just so—empty." She glances up at me briefly, then looks away again.

I swallow hard. "Every single person I know and love is gone."

She takes in a deep breath. I hold her gaze.

"I am so sorry for your circumstances." She hesitates a moment, then says in a lower voice, "I don't know what you expected the warriors to do. The Falcons outnumbered, out-gunned them."

"I expected your warriors to fight, yes. But I did not expect Yaz to fight alongside them, and I didn't expect Misha to indiscriminately kill every single one of them."

"Why were you not killed?" she asks.

"Because I didn't go to battle."

Because I wasn't allowed, I muse. Because Arla didn't trust me? Because she knew I would not go to battle against people who most likely posed us no harm, especially with Yaz there?

She'd told me to stay behind to bury Isabella, Sachi's shell of a grandmother who had just died, and to look after Sachi and the livestock.

"Why not?"

"Because Arla—our leader—made a promise to Yaz and Misha that the Falcons would never invade New America, and she was breaking her promise. I, on the other hand, promised Yaz that I would never raise a weapon against her, and I keep my promises."

"And yet here you are," Emily says, her voice soft, softer than I would have ever expected under the circumstances.

"Here I am."

I was returning from burying Isabella when, from a high ridge, I'd seen the warriors come into Mt. Falcon. I stood there, unable to move, as I watched Sachi embrace them, go willingly with them.

I don't know how to explain exactly what I expected to gain from snatching Misha. I am not certain I could have ever hurt her or Yaz. I was just crazy with grief, both with the death of almost my entire people, and the taking of the only other survivor, the child.

"What can you tell me of the fate of the child named Sachi?" I ask.

"The young healer."

"Yes, the healer. What can you tell me of her?"

"She is well. She is not kept captive, you know. She is happy to be in—"

"I know. Do not worry, I have no plans to disrupt her life there. She wanted to be brought to New America, to be reunited with Misha."

"The latter did not happen."

"Misha died before Sachi got to her?"

"Yes." She swallows and clears her throat. "And Yaz was gone as well."

"Tell me about that," I request.

"She just disappeared into thin air."

"That's impossible."

Emily's laughter is loud and not at all humorous. "Misha killed your entire army with lightning and you are hung up on the impossibility of Yaz disappearing?"

She has a point. And I find that fact both infuriating and sexy as hell.

"I need to relieve myself."

I nod. "Okay."

"But this time in private." When I shake my head, she continues. "I will not defecate in this cave with you watching."

I hold her gaze for several moments, and know she will win this argument in the end, so I might as well just give in now without further resistance.

We exit the cave and walk several yards to some brush. She is totally free of restraints except for the rope I tie around her waist before I allow her out of my sight, so she can do what she needs to do in private. She returns to me without issue and we are in the cave, me about to bind her again, when she comes at me with a rock she pulls from the front of her pants.

Pain is fleeting as I move out of range of her strike, a second too late, and the rock grazes my head. Within seconds I have her disarmed and pressed against the wall.

I am furious at her, but even more so at myself for letting my guard down.

When I pin her right arm against the rough cave wall, she pounds on my chest with her left fist. I grab that hand and pin it too against the wall.

"Do not forget for even a moment who is in charge here," I say between gritted teeth.

"As if I could," Emily sneers. "Just do whatever it is you plan on doing."

My grip on her wrists tightens.

"What is your end game?" she asks. "What? Kill me? Send pieces of me back to Karst to taunt them?"

I am disgusted by her words but try not to show that.

"What?" she continues. "Will you rape me? Will that make you feel like a strong, competent warrior?"

I clench my teeth and feel my nostrils flare.

"Well, just do it already! Just do it and let's be done with this!" she yells.

I release her wrists and slap my flattened hand against the wall, just to the left of her head.

She flinches.

I cringe, and then storm out.

I pace in front of the opening of the cave, expecting her to come out, yet not really expecting that either.

What is my end game? I don't have one. I have nothing, especially not control of the situation with Emily.

I know I should have released Emily the moment I realized she wasn't Misha. I let my anger over the deaths of my people get the best of me. And I must also admit that I wanted to keep the sexy woman close to me for a little while.

But now what? I raised my hand to a woman who presented no further threat to me. I may not have struck her, but I raised my hand to her nonetheless.

The sun is setting, creating an orange and pink sky that mocks me with its beauty. I settle against a rock where I can watch the entrance to the cave, wanting to make sure no predators get to Emily in the night.

My eyes sting and I want so badly to close them, but I will not leave Emily alone and vulnerable without at least watching out for her. If she tries to steal away in the night, I will follow a respectful distance until she is in safe reach of where I grabbed her.

At first light I return to the cave. Emily is curled in a fetal position with her head resting on the bag of kudzu.

I am watching her, breathless at the sheer beauty of her while she sleeps, when she opens her eyes and quickly sits up.

I reach for the bag of leaves and she draws away from me, as if afraid I will touch her. I put both hands up in a gesture of surrender and she seems to relax. I yank the stake attached to the chain out of the ground and throw it to the side where I'd forced Emily to empty her bladder the day before. Next, I add to the pile the ropes I've used to secure Emily, and the cloth that was once her gag. As I stare at the tools I've used against her, my stomach roils and I feel the sting of bile in my throat.

"Up," I instruct.

"Where are we going?" she asks.

"You are returning to Karst," I answer.

"And you?"

"You don't need to know that."

She is on her feet now and her hands go to her waist. "Just like that?"

"Yes. Just like that." I offer her the bag of kudzu but she just stares at it. "Now go."

Emily stands there, glaring at me.

"You'll waste time gawking at me? You'll risk me changing my mind?"

She squares her shoulders and takes a step into my personal space.

"I will go home and tell the warriors all about you. They will hunt you down."

"Then so be it." I try to keep my face unreadable but doubt I'm accomplishing that. "Please go."

I ignore the pounding of my heart against my chest wall. I silently plead with her to hurry up, to leave me alone, so I can crumple onto the ground and let out the anguish that is about to overtake me. I am defeated, as subconsciously I knew I would be. My game plan, apparently, was to hurt Yaz before dying myself at the hands of her or the warriors of New America. All along, I was on my own suicide mission.

But no, now I can just walk away. I can return to Mt. Falcon and live my life out as the last Falcon, or I can stay here and raid gardens and stockyards, stealthily live off the people who have taken everything else from me.

She swallows hard. "I am not sure I can find my way back. I had a hood over my head coming here, don't forget."

"Oh," is all I can get out of my mouth.

"Yes, well, I am so sorry to ruin your grand gesture, but I have never been anywhere but Karst and the neighboring meadow and farmland."

I raise an eyebrow.

"I am not a scout, or a warrior. I cannot read the terrain or fight off unwelcomed advances from marauding bands of men."

"There are marauding bands of men?" I ask, aware that my eyes have widened in surprise.

She shrugs. "There could be."

"So, what do you propose? An escort back?"

She smiles. "Yes. Thank you!"

†

A few hours later and halfway down the mountain, I still cannot believe I have let her talk me into escorting her back to Karst.

"Can we stop to rest for a few minutes?" she asks.

I nod and look around for a good place to take this break. I gesture toward a boulder and she sits on it. I hold out the bag of kudzu and she shakes her head.

"I'm sorry," she says, "but I cannot eat any more of that stuff. I will save my appetite for some boiled egg and cheese."

I think about the animals that the New American warriors freed from their pens at Mt. Falcon. I wonder if any of them have returned to the perceived safety of what they know. If I do return home, will I be able to gather them so I, too, can eat something other than kudzu?

"Where did your mind just go?" Emily asks me in a soft voice.

I shake my head, unwilling to answer.

"Will you go back east after I have returned to Karst, or will you stay in New America?"

I stare at her for a long moment. I don't sense any reason other than curiosity for her question. "I will go back east." I only now know this is my plan.

"What will you be going back to?" Emily asks.

"There are plentiful resources just southeast of Mt. Falcon. I will be fine there." I wonder if I'm trying to convince her, or myself, of this.

"Resources?" she asks. "But what about companionship? What about love?"

I bark out in laughter. "Companionship? Love? Those are luxuries that are no longer in my grasp. I will concentrate on survival."

She grows quiet.

I only wait a few moments, then break the silence. "What do you think? Do you think that Yaz is dead?"

Emily stares at me for a long time. "I don't know what to think. If she's not dead, then she is out there, somewhere, feeling very lost and alone."

I feel the sting of tears threatening.

"And right now, at this moment, I regret that more than just a handful of people didn't go looking for her when she disappeared." Emily swipes at a tear. "The grief—oh if she's alive, the grief she must be feeling," she says, her voice catching.

My tears are no longer containable, and spill down my face.

"Tell me about you and Yaz," she says. "You grew up together, yes?"

"Yes." I nod. "Me and Yaz-ma-taz were born only a few months apart." I tap my chest. "I was older and wiser."

She rolls her eyes at my statement.

"We both lived in the perimeter of Perry." I don't use the word canary, because I will never say that word again.

I look skyward, then continue. "I left Perry just under two years ago."

"You left and she stayed?"

"Yes. We—well, when you leave Perry, you don't know what you will find. I left without knowing anything about Mt. Falcon." I shrug. "I took the chance, and she did not."

"You must have been scared," Emily whispers.

"Yes, but staying was even scarier."

After a moment, just as I am about to suggest we start walking again, Emily says, "I hope Yaz is alive." She reaches out as if to take my hand, but stops and pulls away before touching me.

I swallow back my disappointment that she didn't touch me after all.

"Was Yaz welcome to stay in—" I struggle over the difference between New America and Karst.

"In Karst? Yes, she could have stayed there, or gone to Las Estrellas, or Liberté. I would have guessed that she would join Kai and Rachel in McNally. She would have been welcome in any of those places."

"Who are Kai and Rachel?" I ask.

"Kai is a Peace Warrior. She and Rachel are coupled. Kai had a soft spot for Yaz."

"Well," I say. "Maybe by now Yaz has showed up at one of those places."

"It is possible." She sighs. "Indeed, it is."

"Indeed? You talk like Misha."

"Well, you talk like Yaz," she teases back.

We share a smile.

"So," Emily says. "Tell me more about—"

I hold up a hand to quiet her.

Her eyebrows shoot up when she hears the voices drifting up to us on a warm breeze.

I place my finger to my lips to ask for quiet, then almost laugh out loud at the absurdity of expecting any such thing from this woman I've kept chained in a cave.

When she does stay silent, I stand and creep around the boulder to my left. I look down and see that some warriors have gathered at the foot of the mountain.

I return to her and whisper, "It appears they have missed you after all."

"Maybe," she responds absently.

I close my eyes to settle myself. When I open them again, Emily is staring at me.

I clear my throat, then say, "Go to your people. You should be able to make it down to them from here without any assistance."

"We can go down together. We will just walk right up to them as if nothing is amiss. We'll tell them you are from an independent clan—"

"Shh."

She looks at me, her head cocked to the side.

"We can't do any of that. Now, you go down to your people."

"I promise I won't tell them anything. Just come down with me. You don't even have to stay with me. Just go and blend in with the others in one of the more remote villages," she says, her words rushing out.

"No, I can't go with you. Sachi will recognize me. Even if she means no harm in doing so, she will tell her new people who I am."

She pulls me into an embrace and I am shocked to feel tears coursing down my cheeks. After a long moment, I pull back from the embrace and place my hands on her shoulders. I use gentle but firm pressure to turn her into the direction of home.

"Go now," I say.

I don't wait for her to begin walking away before I turn and start back in the direction of the cave. Only once do I turn to see her making her way down the trail toward the warriors.

†

I sit cross-legged in the middle of the cave, waiting for the warriors to come for me. Only fleetingly do I wonder if they will kill me here in this cave or take me back to one of their villages as a prisoner before killing me.

My legs grow stiff after several hours of sitting there. It has grown dark outside, and I find it curious that they wait so long to come after me.

I close my eyes and see Emily's face—her beautiful face. I don't understand her sudden affinity for me, but am convinced it has to be the result of her traumatic experience of being held captive by me. Prisoners do sometimes grow attached to their captors, but she will get over it soon enough.

At full dark I relent and stretch out on the hard cave floor to allow my eyes to rest. Maybe sleeping would be the best way, maybe they will be humane and kill me in my slumber.

Sometime later I jerk awake at the sound of my name.

"Tegan," the voice says. "Tegan are you in here?"

I sit up and see Emily standing just outside the cave entrance, the morning light making her fair skin all but glow.

"Emily?" I get to my feet.

I hear the sharp intake of breath before her whispered, "Tegan."

I am almost breathless at the way my name sounds from her mouth. Only now am I aware that she has never before addressed me by my name.

"What are you doing here?" I ask, my voice ragged to my own ears.

She comes into the cave slowly at first, then picks up the pace until she stands before me. "I—I—"

"Are you all right?" I close the distance between us. "No one harmed you, did they?" I feel my muscles tense with the thought.

"No one harmed me." She stares at me, her face so open, so vulnerable. "I wanted to see you."

I am stunned by this turn of events, so I simply hold my arms out to the sides and smile. "See me?"

She tentatively reaches out, her fingers very gently tracing the side of my face.

My heart pounds in my chest. "I don't understand." But I am pretty sure that I do.

"I—I don't understand it either, yet here I am. I missed you."

"What did you tell your people?" I truly can't believe that is the question I ask as this beautiful woman stands before me, telling me she missed me.

"That I'd just needed some time away, and that I would be going off on my own more."

I want to ask what exactly that means, what we are doing here, now, but instead I lift my fingers to her face and follow a similar pattern to the one she'd made on mine.

"I want to kiss you," I say.

She says nothing, just leans in farther and gently brushes her lips against mine.

My breath catches and I close my eyes to fully embrace the feel of her lips. When her tongue teases my mouth, I part my lips to allow her inside.

She presses more firmly against me as we deepen the kiss. Her tongue is warm and silky in my mouth and I want her—no, I need her—so badly that it hurts.

Now her hands are hugging at my shirt, clawing at the snaps that hold it closed. I pull my body an inch away from her, keeping our mouths together, and rip open the remaining snaps. She laughs against my mouth.

"May I remove your clothes?" I ask.

She nods her head. I quickly finish removing my shirt and pants, then my undergarments. She runs her fingers along my neck and clavicle, then stills when I reach for the bottom of the light shirt she wears. I pull it over her head and let it fall to the floor beside us, then I slip her pants down her legs. She wears no undergarments and smells of citrus and fresh-grown grasses.

She steps back into me and when her body is against mine, I grow slightly faint with the enormity of it all. She gently kisses my mouth, then looks me in the eyes.

"Yes?" she asks me.

I am so touched by the look of concern in her eyes, yet so confused since I feel as if I should be the one asking for consent here.

"Yes. But are you sure—"

She interrupts my question with a searing kiss. It takes me a moment to realize that she is pushing down on my shoulders.

"I want you on your back," she says, her voice raspy.

I do as she requests, laying on the clothing we've just shed.

She straddles me, poised over my lower belly, an almost dazed look on her face. Her eyes are dark and her lips are redder than normal, plump with desire.

My breath hitches. I run my hands up and down her sides, let my thumbs graze the outside of each gorgeous breast as I do so.

She gives a slight shake of her head and a wicked smile. When she grabs my hands and holds them against the ground above my head, I am momentarily stunned, then relax under her.

"Who is in charge?" she asks.

"You. Oh, Emily, you are in charge." My words sound desperate to me, but then again, with the throbbing between my legs now, they are desperate.

She bends over me and kisses me deeply. I can feel her hands adjusting, and without pulling her mouth away, she rearranges her hold on me to free up one of her hands.

I could easily get away, but have absolutely no desire to.

Her free hand is now tracing a trail between my breasts, down my abdomen, to my drenched sex, and—oh, goddess, that feels incredible. I gasp. Her hand stills momentarily but continues when I respond by bucking my hips up to regain the friction.

She smears my wetness over my sex and just when I think I will explode in pleasure, she slips a finger inside of me. My hips buck harder and she sucks on my mouth until I come apart.

She releases my hands and I wrap my fingers into her hair, holding her mouth to mine until I finally stop quivering.

"Wow," I whisper.

"Everything all right?" she asks, playfully.

"Wow," I repeat, slightly louder this time.

She is looking down on me with the most adorable expression I have ever seen. She's obviously quite proud to have reduced me to a single word response.

I slip my hands from her head to her neck, letting them linger on the delicate structure, the soft skin. I move down to her chest and cup each breast, my thumbs brushing the very responsive nipples.

"I won't break," she says.

I smile at her. "I am well aware of how strong you are."

"Yeah?"

"Yeah." I squeeze her breast a little harder, watching the expression on her face shift slightly. I lift off the ground to kiss first one, then the other of those stiff, wanting nipples.

Her expression is growing more and more dazed. I am in awe of the mixture of sweet and sexy that I see on her face.

"Inside me," she says. "I must have you inside me."

I leave my left hand cupping her breast while I trace the other down her body until it is between her legs. She is soaking wet and the fact that this reaction is to my touch sends a bolt of heat through my entire body.

I slip inside her with one finger and slowly move it in and out. When she whispers, "More," I go in with a second.

My hand leaves her breast now and goes to her lower back. Her body is gripping the fingers inside her tightly, and I can feel her sex swelling against my hand.

She rides my hand, wetness pouring from her, until she grows rigid and comes hard. I sit up beneath her to wrap my free hand around her waist and hold her against me.

"You are so beautiful," I whisper into her ear.

She pushes me onto my back and smiles.

"Am I?"

"Yes."

"And what else?"

I am confused. Does she want me to list off all of the emotions she elicits from me? I mean, I will, obviously, but—

She smiles. "And I own you."

I laugh. "And you own me."

She bends to nip at my abdomen.

"And now, sweet Tegan, I want your mouth on me."

†

"Good morning," I say into the side of Emily's head. Her hair smells sweet and fresh and I want to stay here with her, this close to her, forever, despite the stiffness in my back and limbs from lying so long on the hard cave floor.

"Hello," she whispers, her voice sex-drunk and raspy.

I straddle her, playfully holding her hands over her head as she had done to mine the night before. "Hello." I bend down to kiss her neck, her clavicle, her shoulder.

"You didn't get enough last night?" she teases.

"I don't think I will ever get enough of you."

She smiles and my heart pounds in my chest. How has this woman gotten me to this point in just a matter of days? Now I smile, knowing she'd had me here after only moments.

"What are you smiling about?" she asks.

"I don't know. What are *you* smiling about?"

"I've never been this happy," Emily answers.

The statement is so powerful in its simplicity that for a moment I can hardly breathe, let alone speak.

"I'm sorry," she whispers. "Should I have not said that?"

I clear my throat, willing my voice to work. "You should always say what is on your mind with me."

"Good."

"I want to make love to you again, but I also think we should discuss what it is exactly that we are doing here."

She puffs out her lower lip in a mock pout. "Talk?" She sighs. "You have me under you—naked—and you want to talk?"

"Just tell me if this is us spending one night or making a life together."

"I want to be with you. I want to make a life with you," she says.

271

"So, we must decide where to do it."

"Come with me to the southern part of New America. We will just assimilate in and no one will have to know where you are from. Sachi is in Karst. We will just steer clear of there."

"Okay."

"Okay?" She laughs. "And here I thought I'd have to really sell you on the idea."

"So, I'll make you work for it?" I tease. "How about if you can make me scream out your name in passion again, I will go anywhere with you that you'd like?"

She giggles. "Give me one of my hands back and I will do just that."

Wetness rushes between my legs. I know this won't take long. I let go of one of her hands and use my own to trace the outline of her lips. She moans.

Just as I feel her fingers in my wetness, there is a flurry of activity behind me and I feel hands on my shoulders.

Emily's scream pierces my fear and I strike out, trying to get free so I can protect my love.

My back hits the wall so hard that it knocks the breath out of me. I stare into fierce brown eyes as I struggle to move air in or out.

I see Emily get to her feet in my peripheral vision, and she is pulling at the warrior's arms.

"Get off her!" she yells. "Kai! Leave her be!"

The warrior's face is clouded with confusion and her hold on me lessens just enough for me to shove her off. I bend at the waist and struggle to breathe.

Emily is at my side then, rubbing my back, making soothing sounds. Slowly, I am able to take a deep breath, and the near panic I was experiencing starts to leave me. I stand up straight and Emily places a hand on the side of my face.

"Tegan, are you okay?"

I nod. My gaze goes from Emily to the warrior behind her who looks utterly shocked. Emily's gaze follows mine.

"I guess," Emily swallows thickly. "I guess I should introduce you. Tegan, this is Kai Brodie, a New American Peace Warrior and longtime friend. Kai, meet Tegan, my lover."

Heat floods my face and my stomach does a little lurch-thing at the sound of the word "lover." I know instantly that I want her to call me that for the rest of my life.

The warrior stands there, indecision written all over her face.

Emily takes my hand and intertwines our fingers. I know she is challenging Kai over whether or not she will accept this explanation.

Kai averts her eyes and I wonder if she has just now realized that she is the only one in the cave wearing clothing. Emily must have the same thought because she lets go of my hand and leans down to pick up my shirt and pants. She hands them to me before gathering her own clothing.

We dress in silence.

Kai clears her throat. "Tell me, Tegan, where are your people from?"

I want to stand taller and tell her the truth, but also know that Emily needs to be in agreement with me before I do that.

"When you brought Rachel to Karst, I had my doubts about your coupling, but accepted her as your choice of lover without questioning her, did I not?" Emily asks.

Kai bows slightly to Emily and I see a tenderness in her expression. "So, you did." Then she turns to me and repeats the bow. "Tegan, it is a pleasure to meet you."

I mirror her bow. "But?"

Kai's head cocks with her lack of understanding.

"You will now tell me 'But if you hurt her, I will make you suffer.'"

"Well, yes," Kai says with a smile. "Exactly that."

"I will not knowingly hurt her—ever."

"Can I ask where it is that you live?" Kai's voice is a forced casual.

"Wherever Emily tells me she wants me to live," I say, hoping my voice sounds playful.

Kai turns to Emily. "Where shall I tell your friends you will be residing?"

Emily hesitates just a moment. "We will be doing some traveling, south or west, probably. We will know home when we get there."

Kai nods. "You will not be staying here—" She glances around the cave. "You will not be in the 'Falcon's nest' as Sachi so eloquently calls this place?"

I stiffen. So, Kai has known all along who I am.

Emily squeezes my fingers briefly, then turns to Kai. "Will any of this be a problem? If so, we could just as easily head east."

"Go wherever you would like, dear Emily, but only because that is what you want. You are both safe here in New America, as long as you choose to live peacefully by our rules." She turns to me now. "Be good to Emily, whether as lovers or not, and you will be welcome here."

I nod, then clear my throat. "And Sachi? Is she well?"

"Yes, she is well. She just might need a lesson in being more direct." Kai laughs. "I see now that I misinterpreted her words when she told me to 'tread carefully in the Falcon's nest.' I thought the danger was to mine and Emily's safety, not to my extremely inappropriate welcoming of a guest."

Emily laughs, music to my ears.

I look at Kai. She is a good two inches shorter than myself, slighter, but I do not doubt for even a second her ability as a warrior. The shaved sides of her head give her a fierce look, but her gaze is now open. I am instantly grateful that Emily has her in her life, has her as a protector.

But I am also ready to step into the role as Emily's primary protector and her life partner.

"Would you like to stop at Karst before you begin your journey? Maybe say hello to Sachi?" Kai asks.

Emily holds Kai's gaze. "In time. Right now, we just want to be on our own."

"As you wish," Kai says with a slight bow. "I have infringed long enough on your time. I will take my leave." She turns and bows more fully at me. "Welcome, Tegan. Please consider me a friend and ally."

"As long as I don't harm Emily," I add for her.

"Yes, that." Kai gives me a brilliant smile, and I cannot believe how much I like this woman already.

She takes her leave and Emily immediately pulls me into an embrace. When she pulls away, her eyes become darker and her breathing heavy. "So, where were we?"

I laugh as she lifts my shirt up and bends to lightly bite the flesh on my abdomen.

The End

ABOUT THE AUTHOR

RENEE MACKENZIE

As a Navy brat, Renee MacKenzie lived on three continents before her family settled in Virginia. She currently resides in Naples, Florida, with her partner and their poodle. Renee works for the National Park Service at Big Cypress National Preserve and enjoys pickleball, wildlife photography, reading, and hiking. Even though Renee has been paid to do all sorts of jobs, ranging from dental assistant to bartender, field sampler to pet sitter, and maintenance worker to property officer, she insists she's only had one job—writer. All the rest has just been research.

OTHER AFFINITY BOOKS

Heart Strings Attached by Ali Spooner & Annette Mori
Socialite Remy has her world shaken. Bartender Chancy has
her orderly life turned around. When a mutually beneficial
business agreement between Remy and Chancy turns into
undeniable attraction. Will the two ignore culture norms to
explore their intense desire for each other?

The Panty Thief by Annette Mori Someone is stealing
panties, but who? And why? Joey Hartford is a fourth-year
medical student who insists she doesn't have time for a
relationship. A new tenant in her apartment building is
proving too tempting to ignore. Sabrina is in her final year of
her doctoral program focused on completing her dissertation.
Meeting Joey is dangerous for so many reasons. Add a

suicidal ex-girlfriend who suddenly reappears in Sabrina's life and Joey's jealous friend-with-benefits, and things get complicated quickly.

Country Living by Jen Silver
Peri Sanderson achieves her dream of moving from London to a cottage in the English countryside with her wife, Karla. Peri sees their future as pastoral while chatting with the locals in a quaint village pub. Sexy urbanite, Karla, has other ideas. Secrets are everywhere. Peri quickly senses something not quite right among her rural neighbours and Karla. Temptation, betrayal and intrigue combine to change the lives of both women beyond anything they could have imagined.

Before the Light by Samantha Hicks
One year after, her long-time partner Meredith's abduction, and their subsequent break-up, Kathleen Bowden-Scott's life is spiralling out of control. She meets Bethany Jones and despite an instant attraction Kathleen shies away. In this fast-paced, romantic suspense, lies are exposed and hearts unite as Kathleen and Beth fight for their future.

Wanted for Christmas by JM Dragon
Belle Farrow knew what she wanted for Christmas—work. She had little to offer but a minor degree in cookery and household management. Certainly not enough for a decent chef or housekeeper position. Then she saw an advert in the local newspaper. Wanted: Housekeeper/cook/nanny for the period of Christmas until the New Year. This is Christmas. Perhaps Santa reads the ad column too and pushes a little spirit of the season to that request.

Dreams in a Jar by JM Dragon
When you believe your life is a never-ending spiral of despair and the only personal joy you have is inside of a novel, would you grab a chance to hide away in the local bookstore and dream of adventures? Thea's life is about to embark on a journey she never envisioned when local bookstore owner, Marion, is taken ill. Her niece, Sheryl Appleby, takes over the reins and her presence provides Thea the courage to take a leap of faith. Can she embrace the butterfly effect, or are Thea's dreams bottled in a jar forever?

Pleasure Workers by Annette Mori
Alex Cortez is accomplished at two things, fixing broken equipment and pleasuring women. She is happily doing both at the Ranch in Nevada. Danna Nichols, newly widowed, feels lost and alone. When her good friend Lindy invites her to check out the newly established Trophy Wives Club, it awakens dormant feelings and desires. An instant attraction happens and the two form a bond under unlikely circumstances. Will the challenges of their social status tear them apart before they can enjoy the pleasures of their new love?

The Trophy Wives Club by Ali Spooner
What happens when under-appreciated professional women are offered their dream jobs? When one of Atlanta's elite businesswomen and wife of a prominent judge sets her sights on a goal, life begins to change for these women. Friendships and romance bloom in a unique fitness club on the outskirts of Atlanta, where more than a workout is offered.

<u>Unknown Forces</u> by Samantha Hicks
Jennifer Wilson spent the last seventeen years raising her younger sister Kelsey after a boating accident killed their parents. Riley hasn't had an easy life either and her friendship with Kelsey is the only thing steadfast in her life. When tragedy and secrets emerge, Jennifer and Riley must learn to lean on each other. The growing attraction between them only complicates matters. When events conspire to keep them apart, will they trust the unknown forces that keep pushing them together, or hide from their feelings forever?

<u>A Window to Love</u> by Annette Mori
Two life events, two paths colliding, two souls destined to meet. Mandie Carter lives an uninspired life. No passion, no romance, and just when she thought things couldn't get worse, life throws her a curve. Gail Forrester is barely hanging on. Buried under mountains of debt, only her much in demand architectural designs keep her afloat. Now, they must find a way forward together through what life and destiny has in store for them. Only then can they hope to step into that window to love.

<u>Free Spirit</u> by Erica Lawson
Priory McAllister has fought off boardroom sharks, handled high-pressure jobs, and thought she'd seen it all. She found her dream home and couldn't wait to move in. Unknown to Priory, two ghosts...Rhee and a mischievous Dylan...have inhabited the house since 1935. They have no intention of leaving. Jacey Ryder, Priory's long-suffering secretary, gets to play referee between her boss and a bossy ghost, as each side try to lay claim to the house. What can she do when an unstoppable force, (her boss) meets an immovable object,

(the ghost) besides hope for a peaceful solution? They are like two peas in a pod—two *angry, stubborn* peas in a pod.

Addicted to You by Erin O'Reilly
Elin Prescot's dream to be a top fashion designer is finally within her reach—then Marissa Banks enters her life. Snared by her first taste of passion, Elin is consumed by desire for more. Her life spirals out of control until she meets Doctor Aimee Sullivan, who understands all too well what Elin is going through. Can Elin let Aimee into her heart? Or will her addiction keep her enthralled with Marissa? This story explores first love, intense passion, manipulation of emotions, and the gentleness of real love and true romance.

At Last by JM Dragon
A perfume company in trouble, leading to a town in peril. Old Loves. Unrequited Loves. New passions. Can the reclusive Gene Desrosiers save her family company and the people she cares for, even though some are not aware of it yet? Will an ultimate sacrifice win the day, or will Grady end up a ghost town of unfulfilled lives? This love story will warm your heart.

After Dark by Samantha Hicks
Can a love that starts out in terror be real or last? Meredith Ashcroft disappears on her way to a client meeting. Five months later, art gallery manager Stephanie Edwards is also held and tortured by the same sadistic man. Thrown together trying to overcome their shared ordeal, they find themselves falling in love. Is it true love or just an attachment to each other born out of fear for their lives?

Affinity
Rainbow Publications

eBooks, Print, Free eBooks

Visit our website for more publications available online.

www.affinityrainbowpublications.com

Published by Affinity Rainbow Publications
A Division of Affinity eBook Press NZ LTD
Canterbury, New Zealand

Registered Company 2517228